PATRICIA COUGHLIN

JOYRIDE

Silhouette®

SPECIAL EDITION®

Published by Silhouette Books
America's Publisher of Contemporary Romance

For my niece, Kristen O'Connor,
with congratulations and best wishes
for her new career.

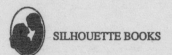 SILHOUETTE BOOKS

ISBN 0-373-09982-7

JOYRIDE

Copyright © 1995 by Patricia Madden Coughlin

This edition published by arrangement with Harlequin Books S.A.

® and TM are trademarks of Harlequin Books S.A., used under license. Trademarks indicated with ® are registered in the United States Patent and Trademark Office, the Canadian Trade Marks Office and in other countries.

Printed in U.S.A.

Books by Patricia Coughlin

Silhouette Special Edition

Shady Lady #438
The Bargain #485
Some Like It Hot #523
The Spirit Is Willing #602
Her Brother's Keeper #726
Gypsy Summer #786
The Awakening #804
My Sweet Baby #837
When Stars Collide #867
Mail Order Cowboy #919
Joyride #982

Silhouette Summer Sizzlers 1990

"Easy Come..."

Silhouette Books

Love Child

Silhouette Intimate Moments

Love in the First Degree #632

PATRICIA COUGHLIN

is also known to romance fans as Liz Grady, and lives in Rhode Island with her husband and two sons. A former schoolteacher, she started writing to fill her hours at home, after her second son was born. Having always read romances, she decided to try penning her own. Though she was duly astounded by the difficulty of her new hobby, her hard work paid off, and she accomplished the rare feat of having her very first manuscript published. For now, writing has replaced quilting, embroidery and other pastimes, and with more than a dozen published novels under her belt, the author hopes to be happily writing romances for a long time to come.

Congratulations!

Dear Readers,

Starting a first job is an exciting, stressful, unpredictable time in anyone's life. It is even more so for Cat Bandini, who must juggle a job she needs, the job she really wants, and a man she really doesn't. On her own at last, Cat is eager to unleash the free spirit inside her to pursue the dreams of travel, success and passion that sustained her through a lonely childhood.

Those dreams definitely do not include a man whose own tragic past has left him with little faith in either dreams or himself...a man like Bolt Hunter. Cat's honest faith in true love and happy endings is in direct opposition to Bolt's beliefs and experience.

Luckily for Cat, starry-eyed optimism is contagious and she soon has Bolt believing in the magic of true love and trusting in things he'd once sworn didn't exist...things like fresh starts and happy endings. Though Cat must eventually lose her rose-colored glasses, she can still see that there's room in every woman's dreams for a man like that, a man willing to change his mind, admit he was wrong and risk everything to prove to the woman he loves that fairy tales can come true.

Patricia Coughlin

Chapter One

Cat felt like hugging someone. Wrapping her arms around someone and squeezing as hard as she could. She was that happy.

If her friend Gator Simms had stopped by to tell her the good news in person rather than phoning, she would have hugged him. As it was she had to settle for gripping the telephone receiver and doing a little dance that left her entangled in the yards of spiraled phone cord that enabled her to indulge her penchant for roaming as she chatted.

"Cat? Cat? Are you still there?" Gator asked.

"Yes," Cat shouted as she dropped the receiver and hurriedly went about unwinding the cord from around her legs. "I'm here. I'm just...sort of...Oh, drat...under, over, back...there," she said triumphantly as she reclaimed the receiver and brought it to her ear. "All set."

"What on earth are you doing?" Gator asked. He sounded exasperated.

"I was..." Cat hesitated. Gator was a friend, it was true, but she still probably ought to make an effort to put her best foot forward, to show him that she was responsible and in control, the right woman for the job and all that. "I dropped the phone. Sorry."

"Well, try and hold on to it, will you? This is important."

"You're telling me? This job has saved my life, Gator. I still can't believe your friend picked me to do it."

"Well, he did. If you're still interested."

"Interested?" she echoed. "Interested in getting paid two thousand dollars, plus expenses, to fly to Montreal, fetch a vintage Chevy convertible and drive it back here? Trust me, I'm not just interested... I'm thrilled, I'm ecstatic, I'm dancing on air." This time she caught herself with the cord twisted around one leg and froze. "Figuratively speaking, of course. Seriously, Gator, I can't thank you enough."

"Just don't mess up."

"Please. Driving a car from Montreal to Florida is hardly brain surgery."

"So don't try and turn it into that, okay?"

Cat pressed her splayed fingers to her chest as if he could see her. *"Moi?"*

"Yeah, you. I know you, remember, Cat? Just keep it simple. Like you said, it ain't brain surgery."

"Relax, Gator, I'm an excellent driver."

"I know, I know, but you're also a little..."

"Do go on."

"Eccentric. Just a little," he added hastily, as if to smooth her ruffled feathers. As if being called eccentric was the sort of thing likely to ruffle her feathers. He really didn't know her that well after all, Cat decided.

"I wear my eccentricity like a badge of honor," she muttered.

"What did you say?" he asked.

Cat rolled her eyes. "I said I'm honored that you trust me enough to recommend me to your friend. I won't let you down."

"Good. You're still planning on making the drive alone, right?"

"I really don't have a choice. All my friends who graduated with me in June already have real, honest-to-goodness jobs. I'm the only one delivering newspapers and watering other people's houseplants to pay the bills."

"If you wanted an honest-to-goodness job you should have majored in accounting or some other real honest-to-goodness profession."

"Photojournalism is a real profession," she corrected with a touch of irritation. "There just aren't many openings in this area."

"Well, don't even think about moving anywhere else until you finish this job, okay? I have this sudden vision of you ditching the car somewhere in Pennsylvania to take a job with the *Rocky Mountain Gazette*."

"Gator, honey, the Rocky Mountains are not in Pennsylvania," Cat pointed out, "but I get the message. And it's probably just as well I'll be traveling alone. It will mean fewer distractions, and I'm hoping to take some shots here and there for a project I have in mind."

"Just don't carried away."

"Not a chance. It is okay if I make a few stops along the way, isn't it?"

"As long as they are along the way. No side trips, no detours."

"Of course they're on the way," she assured him, not nearly as certain of that fact as she was that the Rockies weren't in Pennsylvania. She shrugged. How far off the planned route could Wilmington, Vermont, be? "Stick to the straight and narrow, that's my motto."

"Since when?"

"Since I got this job."

He groaned.

"Heavens, Gator, you sound positively stressed. Since when have you been so obsessive?"

"Since I'm the one who brought you and Tony LaCompte's very expensive car together. I mean it, Cat, this guy is a fanatic. If you so much as put a scratch on the chrome, he'll—"

"I won't," she interrupted. "Relax. Make a cup of chamomile tea, why don't you? It's great for the nerves."

"My nerves will be just fine as long as you promise me you understand the ground rules, stick to the route outlined on the map I'll be giving you, when in doubt play it safe and above all do not speed and do not have any accidents."

"Stick to the route, play it safe, no speeding, no accidents. Got it," Cat assured him before promising to stop by his antique shop the next morning to pick up the map and a check to cover her traveling expenses.

Without the hindrance of the telephone cord, she was free to dance around the living room of her small apartment. She made her own music by singing, turning Gator's warning into a fitting version of an old hit from the sixties.

"No speeding, no accidents," she crooned exuberantly, "just fun, fun, fun in my '57 Chevrolet."

She closed her eyes and pictured the coming weeks. She could see herself behind the wheel of one of America's great classic cars, the open road before her, the wind in her hair. All she had to do was pack and pick up the paperwork from Gator and she was on her way.

Her dance ended abruptly. Well, almost on her way. She still had to call and tell her uncle Hank that she would be out of town for a while. She approached the task with the same blend of annoyance and sense of duty that other twenty-two-year-olds probably felt reporting in to their parents. And with good reason. For all intents and purposes, Uncle Hank was both mother and father to her and had been since her parents were killed in an auto accident seventeen years ago.

Her mother's older brother, Henry L. Hollister, had been a confirmed bachelor and a devoted Army general and utterly ill-suited to raise a five-year-old girl . . . especially one as free-spirited and stubborn as Catrina Amelia Bandini. But he had never stopped trying, and in spite of the fact that he was rigid and overbearing and maddeningly overprotective, Cat loved the old bear dearly.

That's why she had to call and tell him about her plans, even though she knew it would mean a lecture about the dangers awaiting a woman traveling alone and more warnings on top of those Gator had already issued.

Steeling herself for the inevitable, she dialed the number of her uncle's house in Tampa, which was over an hour's drive from where she had purposefully chosen to live. Cat half hoped he would be out for the evening and she could get away with breaking the news to his housekeeper, Marietta, or, better yet, his answering machine.

No such luck. He answered on the seventh ring. The fact that he answered told Cat it was Marietta's night off. The telephone was high on the general's list of necessary evils of the modern world. Growing up, Cat had thought more than once that he would be very much at home in a world where communication took the form of drumbeats and smoke signals.

"Hi, Uncle Hank," she said.

As always, the gruffness in his tone faded instantly as he recognized his niece's voice. "Catrina, what a nice surprise. How are you, honey?" Without giving her a chance to reply, he asked sharply, "Is everything all right?"

She laughed and shook her head at his predictability. "Everything's fine here. How about with you?"

"Fine, fine. I still have that box of books I cleaned out of your old room anytime you want to come and pick them up."

"I will, Uncle Hank, soon, I promise."

"I could drive them down to you if you're too busy."

"No, no, I'll come for them. Maybe in a few weeks. I'll plan on spending the weekend, if you like."

"I'd love it and you know it. I miss you, Cat."

"I miss you too, Uncle Hank." She wandered across the room and perched on the rolled arm of the overstuffed chintz sofa she'd bartered off Gator the very first time she'd wandered into his shop. "I hope I'm not calling at a bad time," she said to her uncle. "It took you a while to answer."

"There's never a bad time for you to call," he assured her. "I'm playing chess. This will give my opponent a chance to plot strategy."

"Your opponent?" she echoed on a note of gentle teasing. "Anyone I know?"

"I don't think so. A young man who served under me a few years back. His name's Hunter."

"Doesn't ring a bell," she said, slightly disappointed. "I was hoping maybe you had a date."

Her uncle chuckled. "I'm afraid not, but not for lack of encouragement on your part."

"Well, at least you're getting to play. I know how much you love chess. Why don't you teach Marietta to play?" she suggested, as if the idea had just popped into her head. "Then you'd have an opponent on hand six days a week."

"Nice try, Cupcake, but that would be—"

"Mixing business with pleasure," Cat grumbled, finishing his thought for him. "Personally, I've never understood that taboo. It seems to me that a healthy dose of pleasure would make any business more tolerable."

"Interesting theory. Might it have something to do with your current state of employment, do you suppose?"

The tables had turned. Now he was teasing her. Cat grinned into the phone.

"As a matter of fact, my main reason for calling is to tell you that I have a job."

"Cat, that's terrific news. Congratulations. Is it with that magazine you told me about?"

Cat winced, realizing that in her haste to trump his teasing remark, she'd overplayed her hand a bit. "No. Actually, to tell you the truth, it's not that kind of job. Not a real one, I mean. But it is a step up from walking Mrs. Swenson's poodles at five every morning."

"Tell me about it," her uncle invited with a laugh.

Cat told him about her plan to drive from Montreal to Florida, keeping her tone upbeat in the hope that he might catch her enthusiasm and not think too deeply about the particulars. For that reason she also refrained from mentioning any details other than to emphasize how much she would be earning for a couple of weeks' work at the most.

When she finished, she heard her uncle sigh. Not usually a good sign, but definitely better than having him ask outright if she had utterly lost her mind, his reaction to her short-lived plan to spend a year on a shrimp farm in Ecuador.

"Cat, you know you don't have to take on these crazy odd jobs just to make ends meet while you're looking for a real job. I'd be happy to give—"

"I know you would," she interrupted in a quiet, resolute tone. She'd had years of practice. "But I wouldn't be happy taking money from you instead of making it on my own."

"Making it? You call driving some old clunker hundreds of miles making it? My God, Cat..."

"It's not some old clunker. It happens to be a very valuable classic automobile in perfect condition."

"All the more reason you shouldn't be driving it all alone. Don't you realize what could happen to you on the highway all by yourself day after day? Anything could happen, that's what."

"Uncle Hank, anything could happen to me right here in my own apartment. That's life."

"It's also a good argument in favor of you moving back here to live."

"Oh, no," she said with a small laugh. "I'm not going to get dragged into that one again. I like living on my own and I'm perfectly capable of looking after myself...at home and on the road. I know how much you worry about me, Uncle Hank, and I love you for it, but you have to accept the fact that I'm twenty-two, not five."

"It's not easy," he said, his tone rueful. "To me it seems like only yesterday you were five years old, running through the door with your knees skinned and your eyes on fire because the little boy down the street had pushed you off the swing."

"Are you forgetting that I pushed him back before I ran home to you?"

Hank Hollister chuckled heartily. "No, I'm not forgetting."

"And I'd do the same today."

His laughter faded. "Today I'm not worried about you getting pushed off a swing."

"You don't have to worry about anything, Uncle Hank. Truly. I promise you that I'll be exceptionally careful and not take any chances. I'll keep my doors locked and my emergency money tucked in my shoe. What more could you ask?"

"Let me come along with you."

Cat wasn't entirely sure he was joking. "Sorry, this is a solo mission, General. But if I was going to have a copilot, you'd be my guy."

"Don't try to charm me, young lady."

"All right, I won't," she said, laughing. "Now go back to your chess match...and promise me you won't worry too much."

He ignored her request and pressed her for more details about her new job than she wanted to provide.

"Enough," she said at last. "You practically have a moment-by-moment schedule of the whole trip. Now will you promise me you won't worry?"

"I promise you."

"Because I'm going to be fine. Really I am."

"I know you are, honey. You're going to be just fine."

The general hung up the phone and stared at it in silence for a few minutes before returning to his study and his waiting guest. Cat was right. She was going to be just fine. He was as certain of that as he'd been of any mission he'd ever undertaken.

He had a very important mission in mind now, already formulated down to the smallest detail, but it was nearly an hour after resuming his chess match that he gave voice to his plan and sensed his opponent staring across the chessboard at him in disbelief.

"You want me to do what?" Bolton Hunter demanded.

General Hollister took time to move his knight before looking up.

Damn his black heart, Bolt fumed silently as he realized that the brilliant move he had spent the past five minutes plotting had just been masterfully blocked. Of course, the old fox could afford to look up now. He'd no doubt settled upon his strategy for the endgame before he tossed this little bombshell of a request Bolt's way.

The general shook his head ruefully at Bolt's disgruntled frown. "Land's sake, man, you look as if I ordered you to kidnap a foreign diplomat."

"You once did," Bolt reminded him.

Hollister laughed quietly and clamped his pipe between his teeth. "I did, at that, didn't I?"

"Actually, I think I'd prefer that to what you're asking me to do now. At least it's more in my line."

"You don't say?" Hollister responded, sitting back contentedly in his leather armchair. "I was under the distinct impression you'd lost your taste for that sort of thing."

Bolt was grateful the general had chosen to use the word "taste" rather than "stomach" or "guts," either of which would have come closer to describing his take on his situation.

"I have," he said tersely. "That doesn't mean I've developed a taste for doing busywork."

"Who said anything about busywork?"

Bolt made an impatient gesture. "Busywork, running errands, what clsc would you call being asked to drive someone else's car from Canada to Florida?"

"I'd call it a favor," Hollister replied with his usual calm. "A big one. You know how much my niece means to me and you know how impulsive and...headstrong she can be on occasion."

"Actually, since I've never had the pleasure of meeting your niece, I don't know a thing about her."

The general gave a small snort. "Don't be hasty. You might not deem it such a pleasure to meet her if you had the chance. I'm afraid living with me for all those years has left the girl with an aversion to all things military. And uniform or no uniform, my boy,'' he concluded with a small chuckle, "you still look like a soldier."

"So I've been told," Bolt muttered, meeting Hollister's grin with a sardonic look as he unconsciously ran his hand over his closely cropped dark brown hair.

For a while after leaving the military he'd worn a full beard and let his hair grow until it touched his shoulders. He wasn't sure if it had been a natural reaction to ten years of following orders right down to the length of his whiskers or simply a way of trying to become a new man. A different man from the one he'd once believed himself to be. Whatever the reason, he'd eventually tired of the maintenance involved in all that hair. He spent a lot of time on his boat and in the water, and short was simpler. Bolt liked to keep things simple.

That was why the general's request made him wary. It sounded so simple, and he had learned that things that sounded too simple seldom were.

Bolt dropped his hand to his side. "I guess old habits die hard."

"That's what I'm hoping," Hollister replied.

Bolt tensed. "Meaning?"

"Meaning that several of your old habits make you the perfect man to handle this little matter for me."

"I disagree. I hate to drive."

"Ah, but this isn't driving like you've always known it. This is a '57 Chevy, a convertible, the sort of car every red-blooded American man dreams of taking out on the open road."

"Not me."

"You will, trust me. It will be Route 66 revisited, the wind on your face, just you and highway, only you'll be driving north to south instead of east to west."

"Sir, with all due respect," Bolt began, picking his words as carefully as he had once learned to pick his way across a mine field, "driving in any direction is not what Hollister Associates hired me to do."

"That's why I didn't wait to call you into my office to discuss this," the older man countered placidly. "I'm talking to you about this on a personal basis, man to man."

"I understand that, General, but there are other things to consider here...the firm's liability, for starters. I'm sure this car we're talking about is extremely valuable, perhaps even irreplaceable. That means there are insurance considerations involved. And the time factor. Right now I have other obligations..."

"I'll handle all that," Hollister promised with an impatient wave of his hand. "This will take top priority."

"There's also the matter of our agreement that my assignments would be limited to consulting. No active involvement."

"Hell's bells, man, I'm not asking you to pull off anything fancy, simply to do a little favor for a kid just out of college and still wet behind the ears."

Bolt stared at the board in frustration and impulsively moved his knight forward. Hollister immediately countered by sliding his king to the right.

"Check," he said. "Now, is that all that's bothering you about this? The question of liability?"

"Damn," Bolt muttered. He looked up. "No, that's not all. It's probably a standard shift, as well. Do you know how long it's been since I drove a standard? And the gas problem. Where the hell am I supposed to find leaded gas on the interstate? Not to mention—"

"Cut the bull," Hollister broke in. "Are you saying no to the job?"

"I'm saying it's out of my line. If you like, I'm sure I could find someone reliable who—"

"I don't want someone reliable, damn it," he snapped. "I want you."

Bolt slanted his former commanding officer a wry look. "Thank you, sir."

"You know what I mean. Damn it, Bolt, you're the only man I trust with the safety of my... the safety of this car. I've told you how important this is to my niece."

"Speaking of your niece, what's she going to say about being cut out of her own deal?"

"Cat won't be a problem, I'm certain of that." He studied Bolt closely, his steel-gray brows lowering into the fierce frown that had helped earn him the nickname no one ever dared use to his face. Lucifer. "I could make it an order, you know."

"You could," Bolt agreed quietly. "Except that you're retired and I no longer have to follow orders."

"Just because you don't have to follow them doesn't mean you won't. *If* I was to make it an order, that is."

Bolt met the older man's gaze silently and didn't disagree. It was well-known that the general had always inspired in his men a willingness to go above and beyond the call of duty because he went above and beyond what duty required in his loyalty to them. His creed was that he never left a live body behind. Never. A nearly impossible feat in the high-risk world of Special Services.

Bolt had spent a decade in that world, nearly a third of his life. To him, Hollister was much more than a former commanding officer. He was the role model Bolt had strived to emulate. In spite of the fact that he'd failed miserably, he still felt a loyalty to the general that had nothing to do with active duty or obligation.

"So," he said finally, "are you making it an order, sir? Are you telling me my job with the firm depends on my agreeing to do this?"

"Not exactly. Then, even if you complied, you might resent it, and I wouldn't want you sliding behind the wheel in the wrong frame of mind. So let's just call it a favor and leave it at that, shall we?"

"Why not?" Bolt agreed resignedly as he reached for his king to make the only move left to him.

The general follow suit. "Checkmate," he said.

Bolt nodded, his slight smile cynical. "My thoughts exactly."

Chapter Two

She was graceful and full-bodied, at least compared to the leaner, more angular frames currently in vogue. She had the sort of curves that had first turned Bolt's head years ago, when he was still as much boy as man. They could still turn his head today, in spite of the fact that such lushness had supposedly gone out of fashion with trend-setting designers.

Fashion be damned. Just looking at her made his mouth water. He found himself so distracted, in fact, that he nearly forgot to ask himself what the hell she was doing tossing luggage into the trunk of his car.

He'd arrived in Montreal late last night and had found the Chevy he'd been sent to fetch exactly where the general had told him it would be, in a private storage lot in a part of the city not frequented by tourists or anyone else who had a brain and some choice in the matter. As his very persuasive boss had made clear, Bolt had no choice.

The lot had been locked when he arrived at five-thirty this morning, eager to get the dratted chore over with.

However, even with no attendant on hand to provide him with the key as arranged, there had been no missing a '57 Chevy convertible. Cherry red with a white top and white interior, it gleamed as brightly as if it had just rolled off the showroom floor. Wherever the car had been for the better part of the past forty years, it had obviously been pampered.

It was a real beauty, all right. Bolt was surprised to discover that the animosity he felt about being there didn't extend to the Chevy. Although he'd yet to have the pleasure of slipping inside, he was beginning to understand what the general had meant about the car being a dream come true. He doubted there was man alive who wouldn't understand the possessive craving such a car could unleash, or who would blame him for already thinking of it as his baby, at least for the duration of the trip. Which brought him right back to wondering who the lady now making herself at home in the driver's seat might be.

She'd been nowhere around when he stopped by earlier of that much Bolt was certain. There would have been even less chance of his overlooking her than the Chevy, he thought, gazing appreciatively across the lot as she fiddled with the outside mirror. He'd left to have breakfast and go for a short jog in hopes of working out some of the kinks remaining in his legs from yesterday's long flight before he began the even longer drive south. When he returned, the Chevy had been moved to the front of the lot, its top rolled down, and this heavenly distraction in snug white shorts and a red tank top was dancing around acting as if she owned it.

Thanks to the dark glasses that concealed nearly half her face, Bolt hadn't yet determined whether the woman was as much a classic beauty as the car, but with an innate degree of macho insensitivity that he would never admit publicly, he could honestly say that with everything else she had going for her, it hardly mattered.

There was always the possibility that her sitting in the car he was there to claim could be a mistake, some sort of crazy mix-up where she'd been given the keys to a vintage Chevy instead of her own Toyota compact and simply hadn't noticed the difference. It was possible, especially if even a fraction of the blonde jokes he'd heard were based on fact, but Bolt wasn't naive or optimistic enough to seriously consider it for even a second. No, somewhere deep inside, he knew even before he began his inexorable move toward her that the woman was trouble.

He stopped beside the half open driver's door, lowering the black canvas duffel that contained several days worth of clothes and other essentials to the ground by his side. The battered leather flight jacket, that was as much old friend as clothing, remained slung over his shoulder. The lenses of his sunglasses were dark enough to hide the direction of his gaze and he wasn't near noble enough to keep from letting it follow the movement of her soft, smooth thighs as she experimented with the clutch.

"Morning," he said. Might as well approach this civilly.

She tossed her head back as she turned to look at him, distracting Bolt all over again with the way her hair glittered in the morning sunlight. It was the same deep rich gold as good ale, and long, the way he believed a woman's hair ought to be, fanning across her bare shoulders like a see-through cape.

"Good morning," she said. "Are you the mechanic the motor club sent to check out the clutch?"

"Not exactly."

Elegant tawny brows arched above her dark glasses, registering her amusement. "Do you mean they didn't exactly send you or you're not exactly a mechanic?"

"Both." Bolt frowned and peered into the car, her long, tanned legs forgotten in his instantaneous rush of concern over the clutch. "What's wrong with it?"

"I think it's sticking."

"Mind if I have a try?"

"That depends. You did say you're not from the auto club?"

"That's right. But I do know about clutches. And I'm here—their man isn't."

She caught her bottom lip between her teeth as she glanced toward the glass-walled booth, where the young attendant was talking on the telephone, and then down the narrow street that ran alongside the lot. There wasn't an auto club truck in sight.

"All right," she agreed, sliding from behind the wheel. "I suppose it can't hurt for you to take a look."

Wordlessly, Bolt dropped his jacket on top of his bag and took her place, using his right foot on the brake and depressing the clutch pedal with his left. He let it up slowly, frowning.

"See what I mean?"

He nodded curtly. He depressed it a second time, again letting it up in small increments, cocking his head to the side like a safecracker listening for the proper fall of the tumblers. He pumped it hard several times and looked up at her as she leaned over the open door to watch.

"It sticks," he announced.

Her brows arched eloquently once more. "Thank you for confirming my diagnosis, Doctor. Any suggestions as to what I should do about it?" Her voice was soft and a little raspy in an almost girlish way, so it took a few seconds after she delivered her one-liner for him to realize he'd been zapped.

Without replying, Bolt reached for his duffel bag from where he sat and unzipped one of the numerous side pockets to pull out a can of automotive spray lubricant. He didn't care how much it was worth or how well it had been pampered, an old car was still an old car. Things were bound to stick and grind a bit here and there, and he had come prepared to at least handle the sticking.

Swinging his legs from the car, he half crouched, half laid across the wide front seat and liberally sprayed the metal shaft that disappeared into the opening in the floorboard, being careful not to get any lubricant on the clutch pedal itself. There was no telling how rubber that old might react to a chemical assault.

After giving the spray a few seconds to work, he twisted upright behind the wheel once more and again pumped the clutch, then turned to her with a grin.

"Feels good. I think it's going to live a little longer."

"Thank goodness," she exclaimed. "I was afraid I'd gone and broken the darn thing before I even started it up."

"Broke it?"

"Right, you know, the car."

Bolt nodded. "I just never heard it put quite that way before, as if breaking a car was about the same as breaking a lamp or a window."

"Isn't it?" She shrugged. "Cosmically speaking, that is. Anyway, thank heavens it's working...and for doctors who make house calls."

As she spoke she leaned over the door and reached across him for her purse, laying on the passenger seat. Her long wavy hair spilled across his forearms in a silky tickle. The delicate sensation coupled with the scent of flowers that clung to the woman made Bolt light-headed in a way he wasn't accustomed to feeling so quickly or unexpectedly. Sure, women turned him on, but these days it was at his convenience, only when he was in the mood to be turned on and never when he had something much more pressing on his mind. Like now.

"What do I owe you?" she asked him.

Bolt, his awakened senses momentarily overriding his common sense, didn't immediately comprehend. "Owe me?"

"For fixing the clutch."

"Nothing. It was nothing."

"That spray you used isn't nothing. At least let me pay you for that," she offered, holding a ten-dollar bill out to him.

Bolt shook his head. "I mean it, I don't want money from you." He climbed from the car, carefully shutting the door behind him, and stood with one hip resting against it. "Just your name will be payment enough."

She pushed her hair behind her right ear, her mouth curving upward in a smile. Her mouth was gorgeous, full and mobile, giving rise to more politically incorrect thoughts on Bolt's part.

"Just my name for payment," she repeated softly. "How very romantic."

Romantic? Bolt didn't see anything so romantic about trading a shot of silicone spray for information he badly needed to know, but if she wanted to think of it that way, so be it. Just so long as she told him her name and they got this thing settled soon. At this rate the early start he'd hoped for was going to be early afternoon.

"Your name," he prodded.

"I mean it, you're very sweet to ask, and to go out of your way to help me, but I'm afraid it's a case of bad timing. Mismatched karma. I'm leaving Montreal this morning. Any minute, in fact."

Bolt barely registered the fact that she had mistakenly assumed he was trying to pick her up. All he heard was that she was leaving Montreal this morning. Not a good sign.

"Where are you going?" he asked.

"Home," she replied. "To Florida. That's all the way—"

"I know where it is. Your name," he said again.

Her smile faded. She studied him from behind her dark glasses for a moment, then shrugged. "Catrina. Catrina Amelia Bandini."

She said it defiantly, her chin lifting as if challenging him to dispute it.

Bolt frowned. She was making it up. She had to be. Who would name a kid Catrina Bandini? He couldn't recall by what name the general had referred to his niece, if he had even mentioned her name at all, but he was certain it wasn't Catrina Bandini. So she either wasn't his niece, after all, or she wasn't as trusting and foolhardy as her uncle feared. At least she knew enough not to give her real name to a stranger in a parking lot.

"But my friends call me Cat," she added suddenly, her smile reappearing as if she couldn't help herself. "Satisfied?"

He wasn't. Not by a long shot. No man would ever be satisfied with just knowing her name, which was why she shouldn't part with it so easily. Part of Bolt wanted to take off her glasses and look into her eyes, to lean close and see if she really smelled as good as his first impression, to tuck her hair behind her other ear and trace the exposed line of her jaw with his fingertips.

Another part of him wished she would just disappear into thin air, because while Catrina Amelia Bandini didn't ring any bells for him, the much simpler Cat had his head chiming like a church belfry on Easter morning.

Cat. He remembered now. That's what Hollister had called his niece.

"No," he replied, wishing that he hadn't recognized the name and that the woman before him had turned out to be a car thief. It would have made everything so much simpler. "As a matter of fact, I'm not satisfied. Tell me, do you happen to have an uncle by the name of Henry Hollister . . . General Henry Hollister?"

"What is this?" she countered, her lips pursed in bewilderment as she shoved her sunglasses to the top of her head and stared at him suspiciously with eyes the color of wild violets.

Not beautiful, that was Bolt's first thought as her glasses came off. Her nose was a little too long and her startling eyes a little too close-set for her to be called classically beautiful. Even her cheeks were a bit on the round side. The expression "baby fat" prickled at the back of his mind.

But if she wasn't beautiful, she sure was something. Even when she was frowning and looking riled, as she was now, there was a spark in her expression, a sense of excitement in the tilt of her head and the flutter of very long, very dark lashes that drew your attention and held it.

She was Hollister's niece, all right, Bolt could feel it in his gut. And he wished with all his might that she was a thousand miles away, back home where she was supposed to be, where the general was supposed to see to it that she stayed, while he, Bolt, played her errand boy.

He could see now that things were even worse than he'd thought on the flight up here, and even then irritation had simmered like red heat at the edges of his mind. Forget the indignity of being drafted to do busywork and play delivery boy—he'd been sent here to be a bloody baby-sitter. He hadn't felt such an urge to shoot a particular U.S. general in a long time.

"How do you know my uncle?" she demanded.

"Fate," he retorted, his tone and smile acerbic. "Mismatched karma, to use your words. Bottom line...I know him because I'm cursed. So are you, it would seem."

"What do you mean?"

"I mean, lady, that we've got a big problem here."

Catrina Amelia Bandini regarded him as she might any madman who stopped her on the street to ask for a quarter or for directions to Venus. "How can *we* have a problem? I don't even know you."

"You're about to get to know me in a hurry," he said, a cynical curve to his lips. "Like it or not. My name's Hunter. Bolton Hunter."

Bolton Hunter. Cat ran the name through her mind a second time as she automatically reached to shake the hand he offered her. His grip was, not surprisingly, firm and strong. Bolton Hunter. It wasn't a common name, and it took her only a moment to recall where she'd heard it recently.

It had been during her phone call to her uncle the night before last. Hunter was the name of the man he'd been playing chess with when she'd phoned to tell him about this trip. The question was, what was he doing here, carrying a duffel bag and glaring at her as if she was the fly in his own personal jar of ointment?

It was testimony to her close relationship with her uncle that it took Cat far less than a moment to come up with the answer to that question. First she shuddered. Then she saw red.

"So tell me," she said, leaning against the car, her arms folded across her chest in a very misleading suggestion of calmness, "of all the parking lots in all the cities in all the world, what brings you to this one?"

He eyed her darkly. "Do you really need to ask?"

"No, I think I can guess. Uncle Hank asked you to come here and tag along with me for my own protection. Right?"

"You're warm. As I recall there was precious little asking involved in my being here."

"Of course," she countered with a disgusted shake of her head. "Giving orders comes so much more naturally to my uncle."

"So, it seems, does the sin of omission. The general didn't say anything about your being part of the deal."

"What are you talking about?" She waved her hand impatiently at the car beside them. "This is my deal."

"Not anymore... at least, not this end of it. Your uncle asked me to come up here and drive the car back to Florida so that you wouldn't have to. And that's what I plan to do."

"Don't be ridiculous. My uncle doesn't have any say in the matter."

"Tell him that. I'm just the delivery man."

"Oh, really? And while you're busy driving the car I was hired to drive, just what am I supposed to do?"

"Fly home," he suggested, lifting his duffel bag and tossing it along with his jacket into the backseat of the Chevy. "Relax, sit back and collect your fee for work I'll be doing."

Cat wasn't sure whether to scream or laugh. She settled for a frustrated groan somewhere between.

Hunter's expression of grim determination didn't waver as he said, "My sentiments exactly."

"So you're not particularly thrilled to be doing this?"

"Oh, I am, I am," he retorted, his short laugh lacking the smallest measure of amusement. Cat followed as he moved to the back of the car and crouched down to check out the rear tires. "Hell, I don't believe I've looked forward to anything this much since boot camp."

"Then why are you here?"

With one booted foot he kicked the left rear tire a lot harder than she thought necessary. "It's my job, lady."

"Wrong," she snapped. "This is *my* job."

"Like I said, not anymore."

"Why?" she demanded, rolling her eyes. "Are you a charter member of the chauffeur division of Volunteers in Action?"

He shot her a quelling glance. "Not quite. But I am on the payroll at Hollister Associates and, as the general made abundantly clear to me, this is all part of the job. Part of keeping it, anyway," he added under his breath as he bent and tightened an air valve cap.

The lethal feelings that had been stirring inside her flared higher. "Are you telling me that Uncle Hank threatened to fire you unless you did this?"

"Threaten is a little harsh," he said, moving to check the front tires. "Promised, was more like it."

"And you believed him?" Cat scoffed, following along. "Trust me, I speak from experience when I say the man is ninety percent bluster."

He swung his gaze around to her, staring for so long that Cat was tempted to pull off his sunglasses so she could see what was going on behind them.

"Maybe," he said finally. "But since I don't happen to be his precious niece and all my experience has been with the other ten percent of the man, I think I'll just go on playing it safe."

Cat bristled. "Look, Hunter, I didn't ask him to send you here to interfere with my life...exactly the opposite, in fact. I warned him to stay out of this."

"Fine. You warned him and he ignored you. Your family squabbles don't concern me. All I know is I'm here because this is what the general wants. I like my job...most of the time, anyway, and I'm good at it and I'm not taking any chances on screwing things up."

"You don't have to," she assured him, watching as he felt inside the front grille and released the hood. He removed his sunglasses and dropped them in the pocket of his clean white T-shirt before leaning over the engine and removing the oil stick. "I'll handle everything," she assured him.

Without straightening he slowly shifted his gaze from the engine to her face.

"Just how do you plan to do that?" he inquired.

"You go on home and I'll call Uncle Hank and tell him I was the one who sent you away."

He quickly shoved the oil gauge back into place, slammed the hood shut and straightened to face her with his arms folded across his chest. He looked fierce. It wasn't hard for Cat to believe he'd served under her uncle. The short hair, straight-arrow posture and willingness to follow orders he didn't like all added up to one thing. Military madness. Bolton Hunter was clearly the type. And to think that only a few moments ago she had thought him sweetly romantic. And sexy.

She ran her gaze over him quickly. She had to admit, he was still sort of sexy.

"Smile," she urged, smiling herself. "You're off the hook."

"Let me see if I've got this straight. You're going to call the general and tell him that you sent me away and that's supposed to take care of everything?"

"Yes. Of course I'll also explain—for the umpteenth time, I might add—that I know what I'm doing and that he doesn't have to worry about me."

"Forget it."

"Why?"

"For starters, forget the fact that you're still practically a kid, without enough sense in your pretty little head not to go telling your name to a stranger who approaches you in a parking lot in a lousy section of town. Looking the way you do and dressed the way you are, I'd say there's plenty to worry about with you taking off alone in a car."

"My pretty little head?" Cat repeated in outraged disbelief. "Of all the stupid, condescending—"

"Let me finish," he broke in. "Forgetting all that, which really isn't my problem, if I showed up back at the office with a lame excuse about letting a woman...no, a *girl,* send me packing, I'd fire my butt before the general had a chance to."

"I can see why you like working for my uncle," she said, flipping her glasses into place. "You two have so much in common. You're both pigheaded, overbearing, arrogant bullies who can't adjust to the fact that the Cold War is over and it's time for all good little soldiers to take their tanks and go home." She lifted her chin defiantly. "Life is not a battlefield, soldier."

"Finished?"

"Absolutely."

"Fine. Let's not make this any more difficult that it has to be, all right?"

"Sounds good to me."

He held out his hand, palm up. "Just hand over the keys and I'll help you unload your things from the trunk. In fact," he added, with a quick grimace at his watch, "if you move it, I'll even drop you off at the airport."

"No, thank you," Cat replied, her smile warm, but her cordial tone sliding steadily into the range of cracked ice. "I think I'd prefer for you to just get your bag from the back seat and get the hell out of my way so I don't have to run you over on my way out of here."

"I knew it," Hunter said, leaning against the closed driver's door and shaking his head at the sky. "I just knew it."

"Knew what?" she asked in spite of the urge to utterly ignore him. The silent treatment, in any shape or form, had never been her weapon of choice.

"I knew that dealing with you was going to be one gigantic pain in the—" He paused mid-growl and glared at her. "Neck."

"You mean simply because I want you to mind your own business and let me do the job I was hired to do?"

"This is my business," he insisted. "Your uncle—my boss—made it my business. I didn't go looking for the assignment, I sure as hell don't want it, but lady, there's no way I'm going to walk away from it . . . not even with your permission," he added, his mouth twisting in a sardonic smile. "I'm driving this car to Florida."

"Over my dead body."

He shrugged. "Would you settle for bound and gagged?"

"You wouldn't dare."

"In a second, if it becomes necessary," he snapped, spearing her with a look so quietly threatening Cat had to quell an urge to take a step backward. His eyes were gold and shadowed, like hammered brass, his jaw dusted with yesterday's whiskers, and his tall, lean body tense and absolutely still. The old fight-or-flight battle was raging full force inside Cat when he relaxed suddenly and gave another of those careless shrugs. "But it won't come to that," he said.

To be dismissed with such indifference really got to her, making her reckless.

"You don't say?" she murmured. "How about keys? You can't drive without keys."

His look was the sort you might direct at a not-too-bright child, which is what she suddenly felt like for goading him so foolishly. "That's why I'm going to give you about another minute and a half to hand them over before I take them off you," he replied.

Cat instinctively thrust her hand in her shorts pocket and realized even before his gaze followed the movement and lingered that it had been another mistake. She couldn't help it. He made her nervous.

"If you take this car," she said slowly and determinedly, "I'll call the police and report it stolen. You'll be caught before you're out of the city."

"I don't think so," Hunter replied. "Because you're smart enough to know that if you do report it and the police stop me, I'll refer them straight to the general. I already have a letter of reference from him on me," he added, patting the back pocket of his faded green army fatigues. "And we both know that the general has more contacts and influence with the officials in Canada and the U.S. than anyone, except maybe God."

He was half right. She did know all that, she just hadn't been thinking straight enough to realize it until he pointed it out. She knew from experience that if the authorities became involved, Uncle Hank would find some way to persuade or pressure them into doing things his way no matter how many rules had to be bent in the process. Complaining about it would be like shooting herself in the foot. If she caused enough flap the newspapers might even pick up the story. She could see the headline now. General Stops Niece from Seeing the USA in a Chevrolet. How long until word of the whole embarrassing mess filtered back to Tony LaCompte, who was, according to Gator, a real nervous Nellie when it came to his classic car collection?

There was no telling when a real career opportunity would turn up and she could stop depending on odd jobs like this one to support herself. In the meantime, Gator was an invaluable asset. He seemed to either know everyone in Florida who needed something done or know someone who knew them. She wanted to impress him with her ability to handle whatever problems might arise and get the job done in spite of them, not give him cause to think she was too much trouble to bother with in the future.

No, damn Uncle Hank and the brass-eyed henchman he'd sent to do his dirty work. That wasn't going to happen. She was going to handle this, by God. Cat slanted a glance at Hunter, who was watching her expectantly, as if certain that any minute she would come to her senses and hand over the keys like a good little girl. She was going to handle him, too, she decided. In the only way available to her at the moment. Distasteful though it might be.

Smiling her most conciliatory smile, she pushed her glasses to the top of her head, the better for him to see the sincerity glowing in her eyes.

"How about a compromise?" she suggested.

His eyes narrowed. "What do you have in mind?"

Tying you to the rear bumper and dragging you across the border, Cat thought.

"I drive the car to Florida, as requested by the legal owner," she added pointedly, "and I let you come along for the ride."

"Out of the question. I prefer to travel alone."

"So do I, as it so happens. Do I have to define the word compromise for you? Think about it, Hunter," she urged, switching to a more cajoling tone. "I'll be taking care of my responsibilities and so will you. The only reason Uncle Hank sent you here is because he's worried that something will happen to me during the long drive alone. Now I won't be alone." She couldn't quite suppress a grin. "And what could possibly happen to me with someone as menacing as you along? Sorry, sorry," she continued hurriedly as his jaw snapped shut on whatever he had been about to say. Why couldn't she have stuck with sweet and cajoling for a few minutes longer?

"It's still out of the question," he told her.

"Why?"

"Because I'm not a damn baby-sitter, that's why."

"And I'm no one's baby."

"Tell that to the general. There's another reason, too," he continued without giving her a chance to speak. "The fact that you can't give in and accept that your uncle has a right to be concerned for you proves to me that you're exactly the sort of selfish, spoiled brat I expected you to be, and truthfully, I can't imagine spending a few hours alone in a car with you, never mind days."

"Is that all?"

He shot her an incredulous look and ran his hand over his hair. "Look, just give me the keys before I say something else I'll probably be sorry for later."

"You haven't said anything to be sorry for. My feelings have survived being called worse things than a spoiled brat."

"I was thinking I'd be sorry after you ran back and told the general what I called you."

"In case you haven't noticed, I don't run to the general with my problems. Not that it stops him from meddling."

"What can I say, he loves you."

This time his shrug suggested definite uneasiness. Cat couldn't tell if it was having to say the L-word or her anguished sigh that had made him suddenly uncomfortable. She tried the sigh again, adding the slightest catch at the end to hint at tears just barely held back.

"I love him, too," she said softly. "But just once I'd like to prove I can handle things on my own. Do you have any idea how it feels to be treated like some sort of bird in a gilded cage?"

"No."

"It feels horrible."

"Yeah, well, you'll probably feel a whole lot better once you get back home," he said awkwardly. "Go shopping, sleep late—there must be something you'd rather do than watch hundreds of miles of highway go by. Hell, most people would leap at the chance to make money for nothing."

"This isn't only about money. It's not even entirely about proving I can do it."

The silence stretched between them as he shifted his weight from one foot to the other. Finally he asked. "What is it about?"

"It's about a once-in-a-lifetime chance for a job I really want."

"You mean driving other people's cars around the country is what you want to do with your life?" He sounded perplexed.

Cat dipped her head to hide her urge to giggle. "I'm not talking about this job. This is just to pay the rent until I find something permanent. I studied to be a photojournalist."

"That's right. Your uncle mentioned something about that."

"What my uncle doesn't know is that a magazine I'd do anything to work for has given me a tentative go-ahead for a project I pitched to them." A bit of an exaggeration, Cat thought, but she had to use what she had at her disposal. This was war, after all, and he had experience and brute strength on his side.

"This ought to give you some extra free time to work on it."

"It would, except that the work I have to do is in four or five different places along the east coast. I was counting on using this trip to get where I need to go to take the shots I need for the project. I couldn't afford the necessary travel any other way, not to mention that my old clunker of a car would never make it." She stared into the distance, her teeth closing on her trembling lower lip. "Getting this job was the answer to my prayers."

"Does your uncle know all this?"

Cat shook her head vehemently. "And I don't want him to know. Not until the editor gives me a definite yes. I've had too many false starts lately, and I think poor Uncle Hank takes the disappointments harder than I do. I want to spare his feelings at all costs."

There. Call her a spoiled brat, would he? Keeping her head down, she slipped her finger beneath her glasses and dabbed delicately.

"How many stops do you need to make?" he asked in a rough tone.

"Five definite stops. Maybe a sixth."

"You're sure they're all on the way?"

"Positive."

"How long will they take?"

"Long enough to shoot a couple of rolls of film and ask a few questions. A couple of hours each if all goes well."

"It better all go well," he grumbled.

"Does that mean you agree to my compromise?"

"It means I'll do the driving and you can ride along and do whatever it is you have to do."

"Thank you, I mean it. I know you're as much a victim of Uncle Hank as I am in this thing." She withdrew the key from her pocket and tossed it to him. "Shall we go?"

"Do we have a choice?"

Cat was a bit surprised when he walked around the car to open the door for her. Then she realized she shouldn't be. Opening doors and picking up the check would come automatically to a man like Hunter. It was what lay underneath the superficial gallantry that she suspected he would have a problem with. Somehow she couldn't imagine him having the interest or inclination to learn what was really going on in a woman's "pretty little head."

He circled around the back of the car to his own side. Half turning in her seat, Cat could see him shaking his head, and she swore she heard him muttering something about being a damn baby-sitter.

Clearly, the man did not relish the prospect of being her traveling companion.

"Would it make you feel any better," Cat inquired after he'd climbed in beside her and started the engine, "to think of yourself as a bodyguard rather than a baby-sitter?"

He gave her a chilling look. "No. It wouldn't."

With a shrug she settled back against the seat. She felt like telling him he didn't need to worry. If he was as much like her uncle as she suspected, he would never renege on their deal, and he would certainly never abandon his boss's niece somewhere along the highway.

Unfortunately for him, the boss's niece had no such compunctions. At the first rest stop they visited, Bolton Hunter was history.

Chapter Three

Ten years of active duty in the Army's elite Special Services unit had qualified Bolt as an expert on a number of subjects. Women wasn't one of them.

Back at the parking lot he'd been convinced Cat was on the verge of tears and was stunned by the depth of his reaction to her distress. He'd been around enough to witness a lot of things more worthy of tears than a botched chance to write for a magazine, and yet for some reason this woman's disappointment had really gotten to him. He hadn't been able to walk away from it. Or from her.

Driving southeast from Montreal, he told himself it was simply because he'd grown up with three brothers, raised by a father who'd been widowed when they were all still in grade school, in a house devoid of female touches of every definition. Women had been something of a foreign species to him back then and still were in some ways. On occasion Bolt would find himself mysteriously and embarrassingly undone by the sight of something unabashedly feminine, a crystal perfume decanter or a fluffy pink powder puff lying on a lover's dressing table. Didn't it follow that he could be similarly affected by a woman's tears?

Whatever the reason, in the end he had ignored common sense and experience and agreed to bring her along. He'd even agreed to the blasted stops she wanted to make, even though they meant delays that were simply going to prolong this sorry road show. He'd expected her to be pleased by his acquiescence to her wishes, and she was. He just hadn't expected the speed and completeness with which her mood change had occurred.

To look at her now, humming along with the oldies station that was all she'd been able to tune in on the car's tinny-sounding AM radio, you wouldn't think she'd been trembling with emotion just a short while ago. Bolt didn't even see any trace of the anger and resentment she'd displayed when she'd first found out about her uncle's little plan. Heck, he'd known about it for days now and he was still seething inside. He had expected her to at least protest the fact that he expected to do the driving. Were women so much better at dealing with their feelings? he wondered. Better at hiding them maybe? Or simply better at pretending?

She bent forward to rummage in the straw bag at her feet. The bag reminded Bolt of a gunnysack with handles. It looked big enough to hold everything anyone might need for a few days on the road. He couldn't imagine what she had seen fit to pack in all the bags and suitcases he'd watched her stow in the trunk.

He took his eyes from the heavy morning traffic on Canada's Highway 15 long enough to see her shoving aside plastic cases and bottles, magazines and a bright yellow cassette player with headphones. A tube of lipstick, several candy bars and a bag of cheese popcorn fell to the floor. She tossed them back into the bag and sat up holding a small notebook.

Flipping it open, she studied the first page in silence for a minute.

"According to the directions," she said at last, speaking loudly to be heard over the combined noise of the wind and music, "we should hit customs in just a few miles, right around where we pick up U.S. I-187."

"Is that a map you have there?" he asked, more interested in the contents of the notebook than in directions he had already studied and committed to memory.

"It's not really a map," she explained, holding the notebook closer so he could glance at it. The traffic was too heavy for him to do more than take note of the blocks of printing, all neatly numbered, one to seven. He had a hunch the next page would pick right up with number eight, and he wondered where it might end.

"Although I do have a real map in there somewhere, too," she assured him, nudging the gunnysack with her bare toe. She had slipped off her sandals the second they were on the road. "This is the list of directions Gator gave me. He got them from Tony... Mr. LaCompte. He's the guy who owns the car."

"I see. Who's Gator?"

"A friend. He put the deal together for me. He knew LaCompte wanted this car brought to Florida and he knew I needed the money. *Voilà.*"

"So what's in it for Gator?"

"Nothing," she replied, shrugging as if the thought had never occurred to her.

Bolt slanted her a cynical look. "Nothing?"

"That's right," she said, a defensive edge to her tone. "He just did it to be nice."

"If you say so," he replied. He kept his eyes fixed on the road ahead and wondered what this Gator character wanted of Catrina Amelia Bandini in exchange for his help. Bolt didn't claim to have much of an imagination, but once you'd seen the lady, it didn't take much of one to come up with an answer.

"You don't believe it?" she asked, toying with the heavy gold barrette she'd used to pull her hair back. Even so, loose tendrils blew across her face.

"Sweetheart, I don't believe anybody does anything without a reason."

"Don't call me sweetheart unless you mean it."

He glanced at her in surprise. "How can I mean it? We barely know each other."

"That's the point, soldier."

"All right then," he said, a smile tugging at his lips, "if you insist on formality, I guess I'll just have to call you Catrina Amelia."

"Whatever," she said placidly, as if it hardly mattered to her what he called her provided it wasn't "sweetheart."

"Nah," Bolt said, intrigued by her reaction. The woman was all spitfire one minute and almost disinterested the next. "Takes too long to say all that."

"Then call me Cat."

He turned to eye her consideringly, then shook his head, more to draw a response from her than anything else. "No, you just don't strike me as the Cat type."

"Head for the left lane," she instructed as they pulled within sight of the customs stop for entry into the United States.

"All the cats I've ever known were quiet and lazy creatures, and you don't strike me as either. Anyone ever call you Trina?"

"No. Left lane," she directed again.

"How about Lia? Short for Amelia."

"No," she snapped. "Are you listening to me? I said get in the left lane."

"Does it make a difference what lane I'm in?" he asked, veering to the left because it just happened to have the shortest line.

"It does to me. This is the lane specified in the directions."

"The directions even tell you which lane to drive in?"

"No, but they do suggest I use the far left lane in going through customs."

"Why?" Bolt asked, his suspicion piqued.

"Who knows? I told you, LaCompte is a fanatic. All I know is that I promised Gator I'd follow the directions to the letter and I'm going to...make that *we're* going to," she added pointedly.

"All right, the left lane it is," he drawled as they pulled forward, only two cars remaining between them and the uniformed customs agent at the head of the line. "No need to get excited... Tiger."

She scowled at him.

"Yep, that's it, all right," he said. "Tiger. Fits you like a glove."

"I won't even dignify that with a response."

"Good," he told her, chuckling. "That way you can concentrate all your energy on digging in that bottomless sack of yours for your papers."

"Papers?"

"Right. I'm really hoping for your sake that your little book of directions included a reminder that you need proof of citizenship to get back into the country. Birth certificate, passport, voter registration card."

"I forgot all about that," she exclaimed.

"That's a shame. I'm sure going to hate leaving you here at the border."

"You wouldn't dare."

Bolt just smiled.

"Not that it's an issue," she said. "I meant that I forgot I would need to show it at customs. Of course I have my birth certificate with me."

She was sure she had it. She just wasn't exactly sure where she had tucked it for safekeeping. It might be in the bag at her feet or it might be packed away in a suitcase. Sometimes she even hid things inside one of her camera cases. All she had to do was think. Something easier said than done with him watching her that way. At times his gaze was so intense it was as if he was touching her with it, and it made her very uneasy.

Doing her best to ignore the effects of his scrutiny, she bent and searched through her bag, saying a little prayer and coming upon the envelope containing her birth certificate just as the customs agent finished with the car before them. She pulled it from the envelope and waved it triumphantly at Hunter.

"There," she said. "Will this do?"

"Nicely." He took it from her and scanned it quickly. Holding it in his left hand along with his open passport, he used his right to steer the car forward in response to the agent's wave.

"Good morning, sir," the man greeted Hunter as he took the papers from him and glanced at them. He was short, with wire-rimmed glasses and thinning hair. "Did you enjoy your stay in Canada?"

"About as much as I expected to," Hunter replied, removing his sunglasses.

"Very good, sir," the agent said in the crisp, uninvolved tone of a government servant just doing his job. "And the lady? Ms. Bandini?" he said, shifting his gaze to Cat.

"That's right," she replied. "My stay in Canada was fine."

"Were you out of the country for longer than forty-eight hours?"

They both shook their heads.

"You may or may not be aware that in that case there will be duty due on any purchases you might have made. Do either of you have anything to declare?"

"I don't," Hunter told him, then glanced at Cat.

She shook her head again. "Me, either."

"Very well," the agent said, smiling. "May I see the registration for the car? Then we'll take a quick look in the trunk and you'll be on your way."

Cat opened the glove compartment and pulled out the registration, reaching across Hunter to hand it to the agent.

He scanned it quickly. "I'm envious, Ms. Bandini," he said. "This is a beautiful car. You don't see too many in this condition."

"Thank you," she said. "It is beautiful, isn't it?"

"How does it run?"

"So far so good," she told him.

"How long have you had it?"

"Only a few months."

Cat saw the surprise that flickered in Hunter's eyes as he listened to the exchange, his gaze fixed on her the entire time, and she kept her fingers crossed that he wouldn't say anything stupid. When the customs agent leaned into the open car to return the registration, he quickly put up his hand to intercept it, giving it the most cursory of glances before passing it to her. His eyes met hers.

"Now for the trunk," the agent said.

Cat was glad for the interruption. She certainly didn't owe Hunter any explanations for the car being registered to her, but something warned her that he was going to demand one as soon as they were away from here.

She hurriedly slid her feet into her sandals and climbed from the car, standing by as Hunter unlocked the trunk and opened it. The agent shifted her suitcases around inside and then pointed to one of her black camera bags.

"Will you open this, please?" he requested.

"Sure," Cat replied, unzipping it and peeling back the flap. "It's a camera. There are several others in here," she added, waving her hand at the open trunk. "Along with a small fortune in film. I'm a photographer."

"I see. Was any of this equipment purchased in Canada?"

"None of it," she assured him. "I've owned most of it for years. Except for the Nikon, that is. That was a graduation present from my uncle this past June."

"You have proof of purchase for all of it, I assume? Receipts? Something?"

She shook her head, frowning. "No. At least not on me at any rate. Uncle Hank probably has the receipt for the Nikon, and the others must be back home in my apartment. Somewhere," she added feebly.

"You have the cameras, but not the receipts?" the agent queried.

She shrugged.

The man sighed.

"Is that a problem?" Hunter asked him.

Without answering, the other man pushed aside the bags in the trunk and stared inside it once more. His hands were planted on his hips, his expression unreadable. Finally he looked up, glanced across the lane to where a fellow agent was engrossed in poking through the backpack of one of a carload of teenage guys, and shook his head.

"No, I think we can safely let it go this time," he said. He turned to Cat. "But from now on when you leave the country with anything of value, make sure you bring proof of ownership with you."

"Oh, I will," she promised. "And thank you."

The agent returned to Bolt both his passport and her birth certificate, and after wishing them a pleasant journey home, waved them through.

Once they were safely on American soil, Cat rested her head on the back of the car's well-padded seat and hissed a relieved breath through her teeth. "Boy, am I glad that's over."

"Me, too," Hunter agreed.

"For a minute there I was a little tense, to say the least."

"Only for a minute? Lucky you. I still am a little tense. To say the least."

Cat immediately glanced over her shoulder, half expecting to find that the official had changed his mind about her lack of receipts and sent a posse of customs agents chasing after them. "Why, for heaven's sake?"

"This whole thing doesn't feel right, that's why."

She twisted around, her arms folded stiffly across her chest. "I take it you've had extensive experience driving cars for other people so you would know how it should feel?"

"No," he conceded with no hint of humility. "But I've had a bellyful of experience knowing when things don't feel right, and I'm never wrong."

"Well, you're wrong this time," she said dismissively. "This 'whole thing,' as you put it, is no more complicated than it seems."

"Oh, no? Then why is this car registered in your name instead of the real owner's?"

"To make things less complicated, that's why. Gator said that LaCompte felt it would simplify matters all along the way if the car was temporarily registered to me. He plans to switch the registration to his name as soon as I get back."

"How about the bill of sale?" Hunter pressed.

"What about it?"

"Is that in your name, too?"

"I have no idea."

"It would have to be in order for you to register the car," he pointed out.

"Then I suppose it is."

"But you don't know for sure?"

She shook her head, determined not to let him see that his questions had rattled her. "I told you, LaCompte handled all the details. I'm just the driver." She made a face and added, "At least I was supposed to be the driver."

"I'm also wondering why you were told precisely which customs lane to use."

"Who cares? As long as we made it through without a hassle, I'm happy."

That more or less summed up her philosophy of life, and she refused to let his suspicions and obsession with details spoil the trip for her, not even for the short time she planned to have him around.

"I'm glad you're happy," he muttered, "because I'm not at all."

"For Pete's sake, quit grumbling. We made it through just fine. Stop obsessing about it. It's bad for your blood pressure."

He eyed her warily. "I have a feeling that you're going to be bad for my blood pressure."

"Relax. If Gator and LaCompte were a little concerned about customs it was probably only because of the Cuba thing."

His knuckles went white as his grip locked onto the wheel. "What Cuba thing?"

His words were so curt they made Cat think of bits of gravel hitting the windshield. She instantly wished she'd kept her mouth shut. "Nothing, really. Just that that's where the car was before they had it shipped to Canada."

"Cuba?"

That sounded more like a rock slide than a bit of gravel.

"Don't shout. Yes, Cuba."

"I knew it. I could feel it."

"Feel what?"

"That this was bad news from the start."

"Just because the car came from Cuba?"

"Yes, because the car came from Cuba. You are aware that this country has a trade embargo against Cuba?"

"I suppose. I don't see where it's such a big problem, though."

"You can't see why smuggling is such a big problem?" he demanded, incredulous.

"Smuggling seems a little strong a word. After all, the car was made here in America. Just think of it as having been temporarily misplaced."

He glanced at her in disbelief. "Temporarily misplaced? For thirty some odd years?"

She shrugged.

He shook his head as if dazed. "I can't believe I just smuggled a car across the border."

"Don't be so dramatic. Smuggling conjures up images of boxes of cigars hidden in suitcases."

"Maybe I ought to have another look at your suit-cases."

She ignored his sarcasm. "We simply drove across the border. There's no law against bringing a car here from Canada, is there?"

"Yes. If the car came from Cuba originally."

"Oh. Well, then."

Silence filled the car. She could feel his anger simmer-ing.

"I guess that explains why Gator kept telling me to be careful not to draw any undue attention to myself coming through customs."

"And that didn't set off any bells inside your head?"

"Bells are always going off inside my head. I simply thought he was warning me because he knows that at times I can be a little... flamboyant."

"How very reassuring," he drawled.

Cat was silent for a minute or so, trying to decide if she really wanted to hear his answer before she posed the question. What the heck, she decided finally. Things could hardly get much worse.

"So what do you plan to do now?"

"Do? You mean about the car?"

"Yes."

"Are you asking if I plan to turn you in at the nearest police station?"

Her shrug was regally unconcerned. Her heart was pounding. Actually she hadn't considered that possibility at all.

"It's an option," she said.

"True. But then I'd have to go back and explain to the general how I played a part in your serving five to seven in a federal slammer. I think I'll pass."

Cat breathed a sigh of relief and decided to quit while she was, if not exactly ahead, at least not behind bars. She could see now that she really should have checked out this whole Cuba angle more thoroughly.

He wasn't as eager to let it drop.

"Do you have any idea what the general would say if he knew you were involved in something like this?"

"I wouldn't really say I was involved," she began, breaking off in the face of his pointed stare. "All right, maybe I am involved, but I'm not responsible for where the car came from, for pity's sake.

"As for what Uncle Hank would say," she continued, "he would say, 'That's all right, Cat, do better next time.'"

Hunter rolled his eyes. "That explains a hell of a lot. What he ought to tell you is why the embargo exists in the first place, about all the men who..."

Cat listened to the entire lecture on foreign policy in silence.

"Does any of that mean anything to you?" he demanded at the end.

"Of course it means something to me."

"What?"

She smiled a smile so sweet no one could possibly doubt her sincerity. "It means I'll have to try harder next time."

He threw up his hands, reclaiming the wheel just in time to keep the car from sliding into a passing Jeep.

With not much left to say on the subject, they drove in silence for a few moments. After a while Hunter picked up her birth certificate from where he'd placed it on the seat beside him and handed it to her.

"Better take care of this before it blows away," he suggested, giving it another quick glance as he handed it to her. "Born in seventy-three, hmm? That makes you—"

"Twenty-two," she supplied. "Plenty old enough to know better."

"Better than whom?"

"Better than guys who think the way to a woman's heart is to call her names and cast aspersions on her motives . . . if not her intelligence."

If she'd expected him to deny it or apologize in an attempt to soothe her feelings, she would have been sorely disappointed.

"Trust me, Tiger," was all he said, "I'm not looking for a way to your heart."

Cat felt her cheeks grow warm. "It was meant as a joke. I'm sorry if it sounded as if I'd jumped to the wrong conclusion."

"No need to go getting all huffy. It's no reflection on you that I'm not interested. You're simply too young and not my type."

"I see. Exactly what is your type?"

"For starters, someone born a decade earlier and who's not old Lucifer's niece."

"Lucifer?"

"Sorry," he said, wincing slightly. "I probably shouldn't have said that to you."

"But you did, so you might as well explain. You call Uncle Hank *Lucifer?*"

"Not to his face. It was sort of an inside joke in our unit. No one knew what the L stood for in Henry L. Hollister, so one of the guys tagged him with Lucifer and it stuck."

"Lucifer. Now there's a nickname that fits like a glove...at least in some of Uncle Hank's darker moments. Does he know you call him that?"

"No. And it better stay that way," he warned.

"I don't know, I think maybe you should tell him. I'm sure he'd prefer it to what the L really stands for."

"What's that?"

"Leopold."

He laughed.

"I guess I shouldn't have told you that," she said ruefully.

"So now we're even ... both vulnerable and both armed to retaliate."

"Right," Cat echoed, "now we're even."

The problem was, she didn't feel even. She felt confused. As they came upon the first rest stop, she was also feeling undecided, so she let it go by without asking him to stop as she had intended. Sometimes, especially when he turned and gave her that half-smile that had mischief written all over it, Hunter seemed less like a soldier and more like someone she didn't mind having around. She wasn't worried about making the long drive to Florida alone, but she wasn't a loner by nature and couldn't deny that it would be more fun to have someone along, someone to talk with and share meals with and point out things of interest. But it ought to be someone of her own choosing, she reminded herself, and in spite of that smile, Bolton Hunter would not have been her choice. If she'd wanted someone around to lecture her and second-guess her every move, she would have brought along Uncle Hank. By the time the next rest stop came into sight she legitimately needed to use the facilities, and she'd talked herself into going with her original plan.

"Hunter, there's a rest stop coming up in about a mile and I really need to stop."

"No problem."

He signaled to move to the right lane and steered into the rest stop parking lot.

"Make it quick," he told her as she stuck her feet into her sandals and reached for the door handle.

Cat turned to him in surprise. "Aren't you coming in?"

He shook his head. "I'm all set for now."

Damn, Cat thought. "You ought to at least get out and stretch your legs. I know my legs are feeling cramped and I haven't been driving all this time. There's no telling how long it will be before the next stop."

"They're usually pretty regular on the interstates."

"Don't you at least want something cold to drink?"

He appeared surprised that she'd thought to ask. He considered it for a moment and nodded. "That does sound good."

"Great," she said, hoping her sunglasses hid most of the giddy relief that swept through her.

"Just bring me whatever you're having," he told her.

"No way," she shot back, irked. "I may not be doing the driving right now, but that doesn't make me your errand boy."

"If there's one thing I would never dream of wanting you to be," he countered, amusement heavy in his deep voice, "it's a boy. Errand or otherwise."

"Very funny. You can still fetch your own drink."

"Fine. I'll go in as soon as you get back. That way we won't have to put the top up," he explained before she had a chance to question him. "Besides, I don't much like the idea of leaving this car unattended in a public parking lot where anybody can walk by and break something."

"It's nice to see you take my responsibility so seriously," Cat muttered as she climbed out and slammed the door behind her. "I'll be back in a jiff."

"Take your time," he said.

Cat glanced at him. "What happened to 'make it quick'?"

"I shouldn't have been so impatient with you. Go ahead and stretch your legs and freshen up or whatever it is you need to do. There's no hurry."

Not for you, maybe, she thought as she started up the tree-shaded path to the building, which housed rest-room facilities as well as an assortment of fast-food counters where the hungry and road-weary could get everything from gourmet chocolate chip cookies to tacos.

Cat made her quickest visit ever to the ladies' room, then stopped to buy a pretzel and a diet soda on her way out. The pretzel was for later. At the moment she was too apprehensive to eat, and her hands, which she had just dried on a paper towel, were damp and slightly unsteady.

"Your turn," she said brightly to Hunter when she returned to the car.

He stepped outside and stretched mightily, drawing her unwilling attention to his broad shoulders and the well-defined muscles in his arms. He was deceiving, she observed. Her first impression had been that his build was lean and rangy, like a runner's, more suited for speed than power. She could see now that his long limbs and easy grace belied real strength, consciously honed strength, she was sure. It wasn't hard to imagine him doing an obscene number of push-ups each morning. And probably at an ungodly hour, as well, when most normal people like herself were still tucked under the covers.

"I won't be long," he told her. Halfway across the sidewalk he stopped and turned to her. "Catch," he called and waited for her to lift her hand in anticipation before tossing her the keys. "Might as well leave those here," he said. "Just don't try anything stupid."

Cat's eyes blinked rapidly behind her dark glasses. "Stupid?"

"Right. Like playing the radio without starting the engine. No telling what shape the battery is in."

"I won't," she promised. She had no intention of making any stupid mistakes. That's why she hadn't mentioned to him the extra key in her purse and why she now waited until he had disappeared into the building before carefully placing the cardboard carton containing her drink and pretzel on the floor of the passenger side.

Reaching into the back for his jacket and duffel bag, she arranged them carefully on the sidewalk where he was sure to see them when he returned. A small flutter of guilt caused her to hesitate as it occurred to her that someone else might come along and steal his things before he got back. She forced herself to shrug it off. That probably wouldn't happen, and if it did, he needed a new jacket anyway. The fact that he was one of the high-paid consultants recruited by Uncle Hank left her no doubt that he could afford one.

Her conscience appeased, she hurriedly slid behind the wheel.

"At last," she exclaimed, chuckling under her breath. Grinning broadly, she adjusted the outside and rearview mirrors so that she was able to see, fit the key into the ignition and turned it. There was no rough purr as there had been when Hunter had started the engine. There wasn't even a sputter to suggest life under the hood.

Cat frowned. Then she fiddled with the key, pumped the gas and crossed her fingers as she tried again.

Chapter Four

Once inside the rest stop, Bolt didn't hurry. In this case, time was as good as rope, and he wanted to give Cat plenty to hang herself with if that was her intent. If they were going to be traveling together, he needed to know for sure where he stood.

He found a phone booth away from the main concourse and placed a call to the general at his office. Hollister's secretary had obviously been instructed to put him through right away.

"Hunter, how's it going?" the general asked by way of greeting.

"About as you expected, I'd say," Bolt replied in a dry tone. "I've had a few surprises, though."

"Such as?"

"Catrina Amelia Bandini."

Hollister chuckled. "I did tell you she had a mind of her own."

"Yes, you did. What you failed to tell me was that she would be in Montreal when I got there. Just like you neglected to tell her that you'd arranged for me to take her place."

"I couldn't tell her," he explained with no hint of contrition. "She would never have agreed to a scheme like that, and to give her advance warning would have only created more problems."

"So you left it to me to break the news to her?" Bolt demanded, exasperated.

"I didn't have any choice." The general's voice dropped to a cautious note. "How'd she take it, anyway?"

"Let's just say I have a feeling she likes me even less than you predicted."

Hollister found that very amusing. Bolt rolled his eyes as he waited for his chuckling to stop.

"I'm sure she was madder than an old wet hen when you told her that you were taking her place," the general said at last, "and believe me, I know from experience that Cat can be a handful when she's angry. I also know how resourceful she can be when she wants her own way. That's why I picked you for the job. I told myself that if there was a man alive who couldn't be hoodwinked by her tears or her sweet talk, it was you."

Bolt kneaded the spot between his eyes where a dull throbbing had begun. "Thanks for the vote of confidence, sir, but—"

"No buts," he interrupted. "And no false modesty. Just tell me one thing—did you make sure she got safely to the airport?"

"No, sir," Bolt replied. "There was no need to take her to the airport, because she made it clear she didn't have any intention of flying home."

"Wanted to stay and see the sights up there for a few days, did she? All right, no harm in that, I suppose. I'll just call her hotel and—"

"No, sir, she didn't stay in Montreal. Your niece is here with me. Well, not exactly right here in the phone booth," he amended. "Actually she's outside in the rest area parking lot."

"What the devil is she doing out there?" the general demanded in a thundering tone.

"Unless I've lost my knack for anticipating trouble, right about now she's tossing my stuff on the sidewalk and getting ready to take off and leave me here in the middle of nowhere."

"Alone? She's going to take off alone? And you're letting her? I thought I made it clear—"

"Relax, General, I disconnected a few wires before I left her with the car."

"You did? Of course, you did. I knew you'd stay one step ahead of her. But how the dickens did you end up bringing her along in the first place?"

Good question, Bolt thought. "It's a long story," he replied wearily. "Let's save the details for when I get back, all right?"

"All right," Hollister agreed, reluctance in his tone. "But I'm not sure I like it. A young girl traveling all that way with a man she doesn't even know. This isn't what I had in mind, Hunter."

"I don't especially like the arrangement myself, General Hollister, and I venture to say she isn't all that thrilled with it, either. But I don't see as any of us has much choice at this point."

"All right, I'll accept that. But I still don't relish the idea much. The only reason I'm going along with it at all is because I know that you're a gentleman, Hunter, and I know that you know I expect you to keep that in mind at all times."

"Oh, I will, sir," he replied, wondering if the gentleman's code ruled out gagging her as an option to quiet her should the need arise. "Now I better go. I wouldn't count on a few disconnected wires to stymie your niece for very long."

"Smart man. Go ahead then, but check in with me again from time to time."

"Will do."

"And remember one last thing, Hunter. That's my little girl you have riding shotgun. Take good care of her. Or else."

After witnessing the aplomb with which she'd handled things so far, Bolt was of the opinion that his "little girl" was a lot more capable of taking care of herself than her uncle thought. Still, if only in the interest of his own job security, he vowed to take the general's warning to heart.

Stopping in the men's room, he automatically chose the sink at the far end of the long row of stainless steel fixtures and gray tile wall and bent to splash water on his face. When he straightened, beads of water still blurring his vision, he caught a glimpse of something red close beside him and instinctively flinched. He blinked rapidly to clear his eyes and figured out that it was just the plaid shirt sleeve of the guy using the sink next to his.

Bolt leaned on the sink, head down, and drew a deep breath. Three years away from the game and he still didn't like people coming up on him without warning.

Rinsing the soap from his hands, he slanted the man an annoyed glance. At least two dozen sinks not being used and he had to pick that one.

"Doing some traveling?" the man asked, grinning at Bolt in the mirror.

Bolt studied his reflection without returning the smile. The man was about his height, but with considerably less muscle beneath his long-sleeved shirt. He looked to be in his thirties, old enough in Bolt's opinion to have outgrown the shaggy blond ponytail and gold hoop earring he was wearing.

"That's right," he replied tersely.

"Got some nice weather for it," the man remarked.

Bolt said nothing.

"So where you headed?"

Turning away to reach for a paper towel, he said simply, "South."

The man whistled through his teeth. "South, huh? I hear it gets pretty hot down there this time of year. How far south you going?"

Bolt patted his face roughly with the paper towel and tossed it in the trash, his tolerance for polite chitchat completely expended. Ignoring the question, he took a step toward the door and was forced to draw to a sudden halt when the other man turned so he was blocking his path. Was it intentional, Bolt wondered, thinking that if it was, the man wasn't only unkempt, he was a fool.

"You traveling alone?" the man asked him.

Again Bolt said nothing. Then, giving him a long, hard warning look, he stepped around him and headed for the exit.

Well, I'll be damned, he thought as he walked away. He'd been a lot of places in his life, high spots and hellholes alike, but this was the first time anyone had ever come on to him in a men's room. If that was really what it had been about, he thought, shrugging off the incident. Maybe northerners were just a lot more friendly than people gave them credit for being.

He bought a cup of coffee to go at one of the food counters and checked his watch. He'd been gone eight minutes, plenty of time for Cat to attempt a getaway if she was going to. If it turned out she hadn't, he would gladly admit to himself that his suspicions had been wrong, and maybe he would be able to relax for the remainder of the trip. On the other hand, if she had, they had a few things to get straight before they went any farther.

Heading outside, Bolt figured that his first glimpse of Cat would tell him everything he needed to know. If she was sitting docilely in the passenger seat waiting for him, he would know he'd been wrong. If not, if her temper was burning a hole in the pavement, then chances were his hunch had been right. He considered a third possibility, that she might have tried to start the car and, upon failing, immediately figured out what he was up to. In that case she might parry by pretending nothing had happened, hoping to lull him into a false sense of security while she bided her time and watched for another opportunity to get away.

He rejected that scenario outright, chalking it up to too many years of having to second-guess everything and everybody in order to survive. If he was right about Cat, then docility, even phony docility, wasn't in her nature. He hadn't pulled the nickname Tiger out of nowhere. No, he was quite certain that if Cat realized she'd been thwarted, he was going to feel her wrath. And soon.

The one possibility he hadn't considered was that she might not be alone when he returned. He wasn't at all prepared to see her standing shoulder to shoulder and hip to hip with some young guy in jeans and a black T-shirt, the two of them bent cozily over the engine of the Chevy. And he didn't like it.

The car's raised hood partially blocked his approach. Not that it mattered, he noted with annoyance. They were too absorbed in what they were doing to look up. He drew close enough to hear the man give a small triumphant whoop.

"Here's your problem right here, sweetheart. The alternator wire is loose. Hell, it's not just loose, it's completely off."

"I don't understand. The car was working fine before I stopped here."

The man shrugged as he fiddled with the wire. "It might have been jogged loose. Been over any rough roads lately?"

"No," Cat replied. "It's been highway all the way."

"Well, it's fastened back on there good now."

"I don't know how to repay you."

I do, Bolt thought. Silently cursing the man's interference, he managed to control the surprising rush of resentment the little scene had provoked. He ran his gaze from Cat's sandal clad feet to the soft stretch of thigh that disappeared into her snug shorts. He should have known some guy would come panting to her rescue the minute his back was turned. Maybe the general wasn't so far off base about her needing a baby-sitter, after all.

The young hero was still smiling at Cat and shrugging off her profuse thanks as Bolt stepped closer.

"Would you like me to try starting it up for you?" the man asked Cat.

Bolt immediately stepped to her side and slid his arm around her waist in a blatantly possessive manner. "What seems to be the problem, sweetheart?"

She stiffened at his touch, her expression a mixture of annoyance and something more lethal. "The car wouldn't start."

Bolt shook his head in gentle admonishment. "Were you going to surprise me by picking me up at the door?"

She smiled tightly. "Yes, sweetheart, I was. Surprise."

Their gazes locked in silence.

After a few seconds, the helpful stranger cleared his throat. "She couldn't start it because the alternator wire was off."

"Imagine that," Bolt said without taking his eyes off Cat.

"Yes," she said, "imagine that."

"Must have been jogged loose by a rough patch we hit on that side road a while back," he added.

"What side road?" Cat demanded, frowning.

Bolt laughed softly and ran his hand up and down her arm affectionately. "I forgot, you were dozing." He touched the tip of her nose. "Sleepyhead."

"Funny, I don't recall dozing any more than I recall being on any side road." She punched his arm. "Honey-bunch."

"I guess you were still worn out from last night." He glanced at the other man and added confidentially, "We're on our honeymoon."

Cat flinched. "In a pig's—"

Bolt squeezed her elbow to silence her.

The stranger eyed them very suspiciously. "Honeymoon? How long have you been married?"

"Years," came Cat's sarcastic response at exactly the same time Bolt replied, "Just one day."

She smiled tartly and added, "I guess it just feels like years."

"Yeah, well." The man was still regarding them oddly. "Where are you headed on your honeymoon?"

"South," Bolt replied, thinking it was as good an answer as any and wondering why everyone around there was so curious about where he was headed.

"Well, congratulations," the man said, backing away. "And have a good trip."

"We will," Bolt replied. "Thanks for your help."

"Call it a wedding present," he said over his shoulder as he headed across the lot.

Bolt watched him stop beside a black Mustang and then was distracted by Cat's sudden wrenching free from his hold. She was definitely in a huff, he observed as she threw herself into the front passenger seat and slammed the door. He also noted that she had the good sense to wait until he had retrieved his things from the sidewalk and tossed them into the backseat before lashing out at him. The anger in her eyes was like lightning in a deep purple night sky.

"How dare you set me up like that?" she demanded, twisting in her seat to confront him face-to-face.

Bolt followed suit, resting his back against the door, his arm stretched comfortably along the back of the seat. "What are you talking about?"

"I'm talking about that cheap little stunt with the wire . . . disconnecting it that way."

"Who says I disconnected it?"

Her eyebrows arched, expressing disdain more eloquently than a sailor could with a string of epithets. "Are you denying it?"

"Not at all." He smiled. "I make it a point never to lie to a lady."

"Just to set traps for her, is that it?"

"You didn't have to step into it," he said pointedly. "We had a deal."

"The only deal I care about is the one I made to drive this car to Florida. Alone."

"Are you sure about that?"

Her eyes narrowed and her bottom lip curled in on one side the way he'd already noticed it did when she was uncertain. "What are you suggesting?"

"Only that I was under the impression you cared at least as much about the magazine story you want to do."

"Of course I care about it. It's my project. Fortunately it doesn't in any way depend on having you along."

"I am along, Tiger. That's a fact, so you might as well face it right here and now. I gave your uncle my word that I would see this through, and I won't go back on it no matter how much trouble you cause for me or how badly you make me wish I'd never agreed to do it in the first place. However, I'm not masochistic enough to want to prolong my own misery."

"Get to the point."

"The point is that while you don't have any say in my being here, you still get to make a choice."

"Lucky me."

Ignoring her, he went on. "You can choose to make life easier for both of us. Just bow out now and I'll drop you at the nearest airport and see to it you get safely on a plane headed home."

"Or?"

"Or you can insist on coming along with me. In which case you get to make one more choice."

"I can hardly contain my excitement," she said with a bored sigh.

Bolt's mouth twitched. "Do your best. If you choose to come along, you can be a good girl and cooperate, in which case I'll make whatever stops—within reason—you want to make. Or you can go on being a pain in the butt and force me to make the drive the way I planned to in the first place, straight through with only enough stops to grab an hour or so of sleep right here behind the wheel when I get so bone tired I can't keep going."

"What about eating?"

"Ever heard of drive-through restaurants?"

"Yes, but I've never heard of drive-through showers," she retorted. "How do you propose to bathe?"

He leaned forward. "I don't. I estimate that driving flat out I can be in Florida in less than four days. I've gone a lot longer than that without soap and hot water."

"Ugh. That's disgusting."

"But highly effective. I figure that the more time I spend moving, the less I'll have to spend worrying about you taking off."

"Why should you have to worry? You're such a whiz at disconnecting engine wires."

"Because I have a funny feeling there would always be some young, virile good Samaritan around who would be more than willing to help you out," he remarked in a dry tone. "And sooner or later, I wouldn't make it back in time to stop you. Even if there wasn't anyone to help, I don't expect it would take you long to figure out how to reconnect a few wires all by yourself. I can see it now, by the time we reached Georgia I'd have to sleep with the whole damn engine under my pillow just to make sure you stayed put."

He saw her mouth twitch, then curve upward in a smile of pure pleasure at the image that presented.

"It would serve you right," she drawled.

"It might, at that," he conceded, "but don't get your hopes up because it's not going to happen." Without thinking he reached out and took her chin in his cupped hand, squeezing gently to make her turn and look at him. "You have to give me your word on this or you're history," he told her.

She lifted her chin defiantly, looking a whole lot calmer than she really was. Bolt knew because he could feel the delicate racing of her pulse beneath his fingertips.

"If I give you my word, then we can stop and eat and sleep and shower like civilized people. Is that the deal?"

He grinned. "More or less. What do you consider civilized?"

"Three real meals and at least once a day on the showers."

"I think I can go along with that."

"All right, then," she said, trying to pull free. "I give you my word, no more escape attempts."

He kept his hand on her jaw. "Not so fast. Before you promise, I think it's only fair to warn you that I'm not playing some college kid's game of hide and seek here. If you run, it won't matter how fast or how far. I'll find you before you make it home." He looked deeply, purposely into her shadowed eyes. "It's what I'm best at, Tiger."

He regretted the slight shiver that he felt pass through her as she nodded, but he understood the apprehension behind it and decided that under the circumstances a little healthy fear was in order.

"So it's settled?" he asked softly.

She nodded once again. "Yes, it's settled."

He dropped his hand to the seat between them. "Good. Now let's have a look at that Bible you're carrying around. The book of directions," he explained in response to her quizzical look.

She pulled it from her tote bag and handed it to him. Bolt flipped through it, amazed at the details included in some of the instructions and the crazy things they pertained to.

"Your friend Gator is right," he remarked. "This guy LaCompte really is a fanatic. But at least the route he recommends is the same one I planned to follow anyway."

"Except for my stops," she reminded him.

"Right. But you said they were all on the way." He folded the notebook open to the first clean page. "Do you have a pen handy?"

She fished in her bag and handed him one that wrote with bright purple ink. "What can I say?" she said, shrugging, when he gave her a critical look. "It happens to be my favorite color."

"All right, shoot. Tell me exactly where you need to stop," he instructed.

"Exactly?"

He nodded.

Her smile became slightly sheepish. "Exactly is a little tough to say, exactly. At least for a couple of the stops. I can tell you that the first one is exactly in Wilmington, Vermont."

"Wilmington?" he echoed before she could go any further. "Wilmington, Vermont, is clear in the middle of the state, isn't it?" He reached for the map in his duffel bag.

"That's possible," she said, blinking rapidly.

"I thought you said these stops were all on the way."

"Vermont is on the way," she insisted. "If you just look at the map you can see that it's right there on the road between Canada and Florida."

"Between Canada and Florida covers a lot of ground," he pointed out, his tone rough with impatience. "That doesn't mean every two-bit town in the eastern third of the country is on our way."

"So it's a little off the beaten path," she retorted, reaching for a tube of lip balm and rubbing it across her lips. "It's still in Vermont. How far out of our way can it be?"

He unfolded the map, scanned it quickly and pointed out to her their current route and the town of Wilmington.

"See that," she exclaimed, her tone jubilant. "It's hardly even an inch away."

"What are you talking about? That's two inches anyway," he insisted, then stopped and shook his head. "What am I saying? We're traveling miles, not inches. Wilmington is over a hundred miles out of our way."

Her lips puckered distractingly as she gave a long, soft whistle. "My goodness, maps really can be deceptive, can't they?"

"Yes." Again Bolt shook himself. "I mean no. A map is very straightforward. It's drawn to scale, for Pete's sake. You just have to translate the inches to miles."

She pushed her glasses to the top of her head and lifted one bare shoulder in a shrug. "I guess I'm not very good with maps."

Maybe not. But in that instant, as he sat smack in the focus of the wide violet eyes she had no doubt uncovered just for his benefit, watching the seductive sweep of her long, dark lashes, Bolt understood that she was very good indeed with things much more potent than maps. Soft, intangible, manipulative things of which he knew little, least of all how to defend himself against them. Even as his mind computed miles and lost time, he saw Wilmington in his future.

He frowned at the map. "It's worse than just out of our way," he grumbled. "To get there we have to take something called the Molly Stark Trail."

"So?"

"Think about it."

She sat silently for a minute before shrugging and saying again, "So?"

"Let's play word association," he suggested, his tone mocking. "When I say expressway, I think speed. When I say trail, what do you think?"

"Horses. Now I get it. Isn't there an expressway we can take instead?"

"No, expressways don't go to quaint little places like Wilmington. That's how they stay quaint. Isn't there someplace along the expressway you could stop and take pictures instead?"

She shook her head firmly. "No, there really isn't. I know it's going to cost us time and I hate to be stubborn, but I really need to go to Wilmington. I'll be glad to do all the extra driving involved along with my regular turn. Please, Hunter, this really means a lot to me."

The sudden glistening in her eyes might have been real or contrived. For the effect it had on Bolt, it hardly mattered. There was just no way he could look into those eyes and say no.

"Forget about the extra driving," he said, the roughness in his tone mostly due to his annoyance with his own weakness. "I can handle it."

"But there's no reason you should have to. After all, I was prepared to drive all the way to Florida alone. Granted, I wouldn't have given up a hot bath to squeeze in a few more hours, but I can certainly do my share. Especially since I'm the one who's adding on extra miles."

"Don't worry about it," he said, studying the map. "I might even be able to save a little time by cutting over here near Saratoga Springs."

"And you'll let me help with the driving?" she persisted.

"Maybe later."

"All right. Just for the record, trails are my specialty."

He couldn't help smiling, and was surprised to discover that when he did, a little of his frustration and the urge to pound the steering wheel with his fist went away.

"I'll remember that. In the meantime," he continued, holding the open map out to her, "how about if you take charge of map folding? When I need a break from the road, I'll let you know. Okay?"

"Okay," she agreed.

Bolt believed there was an art to folding a map correctly and he had to suppress a wince at the haphazard way she went about doing it, ending up with a wrinkled wad about twice its original size. Ordinarily he would have grabbed it back from her and folded it himself, properly. But she was humming softly as she carelessly tossed his map into her bottomless pit of a bag, and for some reason he didn't want her to stop.

"All set," she said, glancing at him with a smile he thought it best to ignore.

It was just a smile, he chided himself. With a bit of an overbite, at that. But somehow, when she turned it full force on him, it made his thoughts skip like a worn needle on an old record album.

"Good," he said, his voice unexplainably gruff. "Then let's get going. If we're going to add hundreds of miles onto the trip at a pop, we can't afford to waste time at rest stops."

Chapter Five

To his annoyance, Bolt discovered that it wasn't easy to make up for lost time in a '57 Chevy. He coaxed the speed as high as he dared in view of the car's advanced age, and they drove for several miles before Cat's quiet chuckle broke the silence.

"What's so funny?" he asked her.

"I was just thinking about the look on that guy's face when you told him we were on our honeymoon. He looked . . . flabbergasted."

"I'd say more likely disappointed," Bolt suggested dryly. "I showed up and spoiled the big move he was planning to put on you."

She shook her head. "I don't think that was it. I mean it, he seemed downright shocked. I guess we must look like the original odd couple or something."

"Maybe. I still think he was disappointed."

"Why did you tell him we were married in the first place?" she asked, turning so she was half facing him, her legs curled up on the wide seat.

Bolt glanced at her, letting his gaze sweep from her face to her bare legs for as long as was safe. "So he'd be disappointed," he admitted.

"No, really."

"Really."

"Why? Were you afraid if he got the idea we were simply traveling together he might challenge you to a duel or something?"

"A duel?" he asked, his eyes narrowing as he glanced at her.

"Right, a duel. You know, with swords and the glove and—"

"I know what a duel is," he broke in, "and to be honest, the prospect never crossed my mind. It was just an impulse, that's all."

"Do you always act on impulse?"

This time he took his eyes off the highway for longer than was safe. "No. Never."

She leaned against the door and appeared to contemplate that.

"Now it's my turn to ask you a question," he said after a few minutes.

"All right, go ahead."

"How come you didn't tell that guy back at the rest stop not to call you sweetheart unless he meant it?"

"What?" she countered, laughing bewilderedly.

"That guy called you sweetheart," he reminded her, "and you let him. When I did it, you told me not to call you that unless I meant it."

"Oh, that. I was hardly going to quibble over what he called me when he was going out of his way to do me a favor."

"He was going out of his way to do you a favor?" he growled in disbelief. "I walked away from my own work, flew clear out of the country to drive a car that's nearly forty years old hundreds of miles so you wouldn't have to, and now I'm headed for Wilmington, Vermont, for some reason I'm not even sure of. If you think he was doing you a favor, what do you call this?"

"All right, all right," she said, laughing. "I admit you have gone out of your way for me. But you have to remember that at the time I told you not to call me sweetheart, I was pretty ticked off. I thought you were just one of Uncle Hank's automatons who was interfering in my life and being a real pain in the butt about it in the bargain."

"And now?"

"I still think you're interfering in my life," she said cautiously. "As for the rest..." She shrugged and said, "I may have been a little overzealous in my original assessment."

Bolt shot her a grin. "Don't count on it."

Again they rode without speaking, the only sound the soft strains of jazz that Cat had somehow coaxed from the radio. After an hour or so even that faded to static and she reached to turn it off. The quiet felt good. Earlier, he had feared she might turn out to be a real yakker. She had the sort of sparkle and exuberance he associated with women who couldn't go too long without hearing the sound of their own voices. But Cat was clearly just as comfortable with the silence as he was. Perversely, that made him want to talk to her more than he would have otherwise.

But about what?

He suddenly realized how little talking he did to women. On a date, he always relied on whatever woman he was with to keep the conversational ball rolling. She would usually talk about herself for most of the evening, which suited him fine. It meant he was only required to respond with smiles and an occasional expression of interest or, even better, fascination. Eventually they reached the stage of the evening when instinct took over and talking wasn't what was required of him at all. When, after a few dates, a woman moved on to the next stage, where she wanted and expected more from him emotionally, he ended it.

Once in a while he met a woman who would try to draw him out. Invariably she went away frustrated. He just wasn't given to the sort of honest, soul-baring exchanges that seemed to come so easily to most women. He disliked talking about himself, and given his preference avoided most talk altogether. That was probably the reason he was having so much trouble coming up with something to say to Cat now.

"So, tell me about this project of yours," he urged after a great deal of concentration. Work seemed like a safe topic for openers.

"It's sort of complicated," she replied hesitantly.

Bolt smiled. "That's not a problem. We've got plenty of time on our hands for you to explain it to me."

"I guess we do, at that," she said with a laugh. Again she curled up on the seat and faced him. "Well, for starters, have you seen any of those coffee-table books that have come out recently with titles like *How They Met* or *Fabulous Gifts* or *The First Time?*"

"No."

"Hmm. This could be even more complicated than I thought. You see, these books are about celebrities, movie stars and famous people in general, and they feature lots of photos and some text about how the famous person met their mate or the most memorable present they ever received or the details of the first time they made love."

"How does whoever writes these books find out this stuff?"

"They interview the celebrities, of course."

"You mean they tell someone all this, about how they met or the first time they made love, knowing it's going to be in a book for anyone who wants to read about it?"

"Uh, that's sort of the point of the whole thing."

"Whew." He shook his head. "Sounds weird to me."

"You mean you think it's weird to ask someone that sort of question?"

He nodded. "Asking. Answering seems even stranger. Even wanting to read the book strikes me as a little like stopping on the highway to gawk at an accident. Some things just ought to stay private."

"I agree."

"So is that what your project involves?" he asked, his brows lowered in a frown. "Asking celebrities about their love lives?"

"I would hardly admit it now if it did," she retorted. "But actually it's not that, at all. Although you might still think what I have planned is an invasion of privacy. I was just using those books as an example because they were half of my inspiration."

"And the other half?"

"That came from a decorating magazine I was looking through one day."

"Let me guess, we're driving a hundred and some miles out of our way to take pictures of some big shot's bathtub for a book on bathrooms of the stars."

"Sorry, that's been done," she said, laughing.

Bolt groaned. "Of course."

"Actually I'm going there to photograph the library of a woman I consider one of the greatest American poets ever."

"A library?"

"That's right. You see, the magazine I was telling you about featured a layout on a famous interior designer's Manhattan apartment, and in one of the shots the photographer caught about half of the built-in bookcase in the den. I found myself turning the magazine sideways so I could read the titles of the books on the shelves and I was utterly frustrated by the fact that no matter how much I strained and squinted, most of the printing in the picture was too small to read.

"I kept muttering to myself about the photographer not pulling in closer for the shot," she continued. "I mean, the room was beautiful, but let's face it, we've all seen plenty of Oriental rugs and Louis the Thirteenth chairs. What fascinated me was the chance to see which books this very successful woman chose to keep around. There were books on interior design and fabric and antiques, of course, about what you would expect. But there were also novels and biographies, and suddenly it came to me."

"It did?"

"Yes. I decided that if I was that curious about which books accomplished people read, then it stands to reason others might be, too. I mean, wouldn't you like to know which cookbooks a famous chef keeps on the shelf in her kitchen? Or if a master of the horror genre ever curls up with a book of poetry? Or, in this case, what on earth it is that inspires Madelaine Van der Court's beautiful images?''

"Who's Madelaine Van der Court?"

"The poet we're going to Wilmington to see," she explained. "She was the first person I wrote and told what I had in mind and asked for permission to photograph her library."

"I sure am hoping she said yes."

"Of course, she did. Do I strike you as the type of person who would drive hundreds of miles out of the way on a whim?"

He glanced sideways briefly. "Was that a rhetorical question?"

"No, but since you needed to ask, I'd prefer you didn't answer it. I'll have you know that Ms. Van der Court was extremely gracious and encouraging. She said she's often wondered herself what sort of books influenced the people she most admires and she can't wait to see my article when it's published. She even invited me to stay with her. Remind me to get some background comments from her on the house itself while we're there, will you?"

"Want to run that past me again? The part about inviting you to stay with her?"

"That's right. She told me she lives in an old carriage house just outside of town and she loves having company. Not exactly what you'd expect from a poetess, is it?"

"I really don't know a whole lot of poetesses. Poets, either, for that matter."

"Neither do I, but I always assumed they'd treasure their solitude. I can't wait to meet her."

"So what did you say?"

"To whom?"

"The poetess. When she invited you to stay with her?"

"I said yes, of course," she replied in a tone that seemed to question his grip on reality. "Did you really think I would pass up a chance to stay with Madelaine Van der Court?''

"No. No, I was pretty sure you wouldn't."

"Oh, I get it," she exclaimed, leaning forward to touch his arm reassuringly. "You're worried about coming along with me unannounced. Don't be. When we last spoke I was still hoping to bring a friend along, and Madelaine said that was no problem. She'll just assume you're my friend."

"As opposed to your bodyguard?" he asked, eyebrows lifted.

"As opposed to whatever." After a moment, her voice more subdued, she asked, "So what do you think? Of my idea, I mean."

"I think it's a great idea," he told her. "Ingenious, actually."

"You don't have to say that just to be nice."

"Trust me. I wouldn't. Those other books you told me about seemed to me to appeal to the lowest common denominator in people. A little on the sleazy side, even. Your idea isn't like that. I never thought about it before, but you're right, I would have liked a chance to browse around the private libraries of some of the famous people I admire, see what they kept on the shelves."

"Really? Like whom for instance?"

"Jefferson. Benjamin Franklin. General Patton."

"Sorry, none of them are on my list."

His mouth curved into an easy smile. "Then I guess I'll have to wait for the sequel."

"Please, right now all I'm shooting for is one little article in a small-circulation magazine."

"Maybe you should aim higher. I mean it," he said in response to her skeptical look. "Heck, if those other books you mentioned can find their way into print, yours ought to be a best-seller."

"I honestly hadn't thought about trying a book," she replied thoughtfully. "I just assumed that as a novice I'd have to pay my dues and work my way up to that point."

"Sounds to me like you've been working. You've sure done your homework, at any rate. I don't know anything about the book business, but I know all about getting trapped inside your own expectations. All I'm saying is, don't sell yourself short.''

"A book," she murmured, as if the word was a piece of rare marble she needed to consider from every angle. ''All right, I'll think about it.''

Bolt nodded. For his part he was doing his best not to think too hard about the night that lay ahead. He had already resigned himself to the fact that with Cat along he would have to stop to sleep sooner or later, but he'd assumed they would be staying at motels along the interstate.

If you couldn't be home, motels were the next best thing. Motels were easy, the rooms small and boxlike, easy to scope out with a glance. If you needed to, you were free to go outside before you turned in for the night and walk the perimeter just to see what was out there. Just to reassure yourself that nothing and no one was waiting out there in the darkness. He didn't have much experience as a houseguest, but he had a hunch that sort of behavior wasn't de rigueur.

In a motel you could also keep a light on all night if you wanted to and run the air conditioner full throttle to cover the noise in case it was a bad night and you awoke with a scream in your throat. Even if you did scream, there was no one to whom you owed an explanation.

It would be different in someone's home, with Cat and the poetess sleeping in nearby rooms. He'd never actually seen a carriage house, but he envisioned something big and old and full of moving shadows. A place with creaking floorboards and countless nooks and crannies and long curtains that would dance in the New England night breeze as soon as he turned the lights out and tried to sleep. Madelaine Van der Court might be one hell of a poet and hostess, but he sure wasn't looking forward to spending the night with her.

He was still brooding over the prospect when he caught sight of the black Mustang in his rearview mirror, about four cars back. The front windshield of the car was tinted, making it hard to see who was inside, but that didn't affect Bolt's gut instinct in the least. It was twanging wildly as he signaled a move to the slow speed lane and kept watch in the mirror.

"What's wrong?" Cat asked a few minutes later, just as the Mustang shot into far left lane, doing close to ninety as it sped past them.

"Nothing," he replied distractedly.

"Then why have you been glaring in the rearview mirror for the past five minutes?"

"I was noticing that car," he said, nodding at the Mustang's disappearing rear end. "That was your buddy from the rest stop driving it."

"How do you know?"

"I remember the car. And I caught a glimpse of him as he passed us."

"That's not really a surprise, is it? I mean, we are both on the same road, headed in the same direction, right?"

"Right. Except that we killed quite a bit of time before leaving the rest area," he reminded her, "and since then we haven't exactly been setting any speed records with this baby. I'd have thought he'd be miles ahead of us by now."

She shrugged. "Maybe he had car troubles of his own."

"That doesn't explain why he was hanging way back there until I slowed so much he was forced to make a move."

"It might. Maybe he wanted to be sure everything was working right before he floored it."

"Maybe," Bolt allowed. "But then how about the fact that the guy riding with him just happens to be the same guy who really went out of his way to be friendly to me back at the rest stop? I recognized his shirt," he explained.

"So you recognized his shirt. What are you implying? That these guys might be following us?"

"The thought crossed my mind," he countered grimly.

"Why on earth would they do that?"

"I don't know." He flicked her with a quizzical glance. "Got any suggestions?"

"Yes, I suggest that you have a very suspicious mind. Has anyone ever told you that?"

"No one has to tell me."

"Relax, Hunter. I'm sure it's all just a coincidence."

"Maybe," Bolt said.

Maybe, he said again to himself. Except he didn't believe in coincidence.

Strange man, Cat decided as she rested her head against the seat and turned to gaze out the window. Fortunately years of being around Uncle Hank had acquainted her with his particular form of dementia, the tendency to think the world was filled with bad guys, most of whom were out to get him and those he loved. She knew enough not to take it too seriously. The very idea of being followed by a good Samaritan and some guy who committed the sin of being too friendly...sheesh.

With her eyes drifting closed, the tall trees covering the surrounding hills became a blur of bright and dark greens. She imagined the sight a month from now. In late September the colors on the hillsides would be very different, the green giving way to flaming hues of gold and orange and rust. She'd seen pictures of the famed New England fall foliage, but had never witnessed it firsthand.

Someday she would, she vowed. Someday she would love to shoot these hills in their full autumn regalia...and covered with snow in winter and dotted with spring wildflowers. There were a lot of things she wanted to see and places she wanted to visit, and photography was going to provide her with a way to do it. If she could just get so much as a toe on the first rung of the ladder, she thought hopefully.

It wasn't always easy to keep her hopes up. Sometimes when she got very discouraged, she weakened and even considered asking Uncle Hank to help. Fortunately she'd always come to her senses before she actually acted on the insane impulse. She got more than enough help from that quarter without asking. No sense inviting more interference. No, this was all hers, her career, her future, her freedom, and it was going to stay that way no matter how long it took her to get to all the places where she wanted to go.

It was ironic, she thought, and not for the first time in her life. Most Army brats—which was more or less what she had been since she'd gone to live with her uncle when she was five—were routinely dragged along from one Army base to another, often living in seven or eight places throughout the world by the time they were grown and on their own. Such a life-style might not provide much in the way of stability and long-term friendships, but at least those kids got to see the world.

Uncle Hank had decided at the start, however, that all that uprooting was no good for a little girl who had already lost both her parents. And so while he had spent weeks and sometimes months at a time away, commanding the mysterious, top-secret missions upon which he thrived, she remained safely at home in California, looked after by a series of kind, well-referenced housekeepers who meant well but wouldn't dare deviate from her uncle's severe restrictions about where she went and with whom she associated.

His rules forbidding sleep overs and unsupervised play had resulted in her having few really close friends as a child. She learned early to entertain herself, to figure things out for herself, to rely on herself. As an adolescent, she had found the restrictions unbearable, however, and at sixteen had finally rebelled in a wild, weekend-long declaration of independence that brought Uncle Hank tearing back from the Middle East to drag her home from a crowded beach house in Venice Beach.

More closed-minded than actual ogre, he had eventually calmed down and listened to her complaints, recognized a few of his mistakes and loosened the strings a little. Still, a leopard can't change his spots no matter how much he may want to, and when it was time for college, Cat's selection of a school clear across the country had been motivated as much by thoughts of escape as academics.

She had come fully into her own at the University of Florida. That is, after a couple of wasted semesters catching up on all the partying she'd missed out on over the years. When she did settle down to her studies, she discovered that the self-reliance and self-knowledge she'd been forced to develop at an early age gave her a real advantage over most of her classmates. Impulsive and headstrong she might be, but after her very first course in photojournalism, she knew what she wanted to do with her life. No matter the odds, she believed with all her heart that sooner or later she would make it.

In part, she had Uncle Hank to thank for her stubborn determination. It made her love him more than ever, and by the time he announced he was retiring to Florida to be closer to her, she accepted the inevitable with only mild annoyance. Of course, Cat mused, turning to glance at the man seated beside her, this latest stunt of his could change that state of affairs considerably.

Hunter glanced at her.

"I thought you were asleep," he said.

"No. Just thinking."

Cat waited, expecting him to follow up the way most people would, by asking her what she was thinking about.

"You should sleep," he said instead, taking her by surprise. "It'll be a couple of hours anyway before we reach Wilmington, and then you have to go to work."

"That's true," she said, appreciative of his concern and his unexpected lack of nosiness. "Maybe I will close my eyes for just a little while."

Her eyes were barely closed when she felt herself drifting off to sleep, lulled by the warm sun on her face and the steady drone of the old engine. When she opened her eyes again they were on the Molly Stark Trail and, according to Hunter's best guess, about ten miles from Wilmington.

"I can't believe I conked out like that," she exclaimed, running her hands through her hair, thankful for once for the stubborn natural wave that made it possible to simply shake it into some semblance of presentability. "You should have woken me to help with the driving."

"There was no need," he told her. "I'm fine."

"At least you can look forward to a good night's rest."

"Right," he said.

There was something enigmatic about the small smile that accompanied his reply. Not having his willpower when it came to not being nosy, Cat was about to ask about it when he continued.

"Did your poet friend happen to mention which side of town she lives on?" he asked.

"Let me see." She pulled her leatherbound daily planner from her bag and, being careful not to spill any of the numerous cards and notes slipped between the pages, she found the directions Madelaine had given her over the telephone.

"It's on Route 9 east, just before you reach Wilmington," she told him.

"Then you better start looking," he advised. "Do we have a number? Color? Anything?"

"It's green with black shutters, and set back on the right-hand side of the road. There's also a sign," she added. "Craven House."

"Craven House," Hunter echoed less than a minute later. "Here we are."

Cat strained to see through a thick curtain of maples and weeping willows as he turned into the narrow pebbled drive.

The temperature seemed ten degrees cooler beneath the overhanging branches. Cat, the product of California and Florida sunshine and the long, low style of architecture that abounded in those states, stared in fascination at the gambrel-roofed carriage house with its narrow windows and glossy black shutters that actually closed on hinges.

"It's so...rustic," she said on a soft breath.

"That's the word, all right," Hunter responded, more than a hint of sarcasm in his tone. "Think there's indoor plumbing?"

Cat turned to him and rolled her eyes. Opening her door to get out, she said, "I think that if there isn't, it will make our stay even more of an adventure."

"Swell," Hunter muttered, joining her on the drive. "If there's one thing I never get enough of, it's adventure."

The front door of the house opened and a petite women hurried toward them, smiling. She was wearing white slacks and a lacy black tunic, her shoulder-length silver-blond hair pulled into a knot at the back of her neck so that only a few wispy curls framed her heart-shaped face. Squarish wire-rimmed glasses were perched on her nose. In her late fifties, Madelaine Van der Court was still a very pretty woman, and Cat recognized her instantly from the photo on her book jacket.

"Hello, you must be Catrina," she said, with only a hint of the French accent of her youth. Extending both hands to grasp Cat's warmly, she went on, "How wonderful to finally meet you."

"I'm the one who's thrilled to meet you, Ms. Van der Court."

"Please," the other woman said with a laugh. "I told you when we spoke on the phone, you will make me feel too old if you call me anything besides Madelaine."

"All right," Cat agreed, "Madelaine it is. And I usually go by Cat."

Madelaine turned to Hunter with a smile. A good foot shorter than he was, she had to tilt her head back to meet his gaze. "And this must be your traveling companion, am I right?"

That covered it pretty well, Cat thought.

"Yes," she replied. "This is Bolton Hunter. Hunter, Madelaine Van der Court."

"You will please call me Madelaine, as well," she said to him, smiling broadly as he removed his sunglasses before shaking her hand. "And Cat calls you Hunter?"

"Cat's a little...stubborn about some things," he replied, slanting an amused glance her way. "Most folks call me Bolt."

"Bolt." Madelaine said the name as if tasting it. "I like it. It fits you, strong and to the point." She glanced at Cat. "I am right, aren't I?"

"Strong and to the point," she repeated. "I guess I can't argue with that."

"Fine, then," Madelaine said, turning to take them both by the arm. "Enough keeping my guests standing outside. Come in, please. I've made lemonade. I thought you might want to take your pictures before the sun sets. Later we'll have dinner. I should warn you that I have my nephew and his young friend staying with me at the moment as well,'' she went on exuberantly. "I did tell you that I love having company."

"Yes, you did. I'm grateful that you're so generous with your beautiful home."

"It is beautiful," Madelaine agreed without a trace of false modestly. "Come, I'll give you the grand tour, as I call it. Max, that's my nephew, and his friend Andrew are sixteen and off somewhere with an old wreck of a car they are determined to fix up. Just wait until they see your car. It is very old, right?"

"Very old," Cat agreed. "It's a '57 Chevy and it's not actually ours."

"Of course," she said. "You did tell me that was your reason for making the trip, to drive the car for a friend."

"Right," Cat confirmed, deciding that was more or less the situation.

They started their tour in the front hall, where a grand turning staircase with polished oak treads and the aged patina of the pale yellow walls set the tone for the rest of the house. Worn and comfortable, with a timeless elegance and an eclectic mix of furniture and treasures, the house reflected the many shifting moods that drew Cat so strongly to Madelaine's poems. The artist was thrilled when Cat told her so.

She led them through the entire house, from the wicker and chintz filled living room to the comfortable upstairs bedrooms. When they passed the bath with its tempting claw-foot tub, Cat poked Bolt, as she had succumbed to calling him, in the ribs. He retaliated a few minutes later by nudging her into the sun room and quickly pulling the door shut while their hostess's back was turned.

"Cat," Madelaine called, her brow furrowed as she looked for her.

Cat emerged sheepishly from behind the curtained French door. "I guess I made a wrong turn," she said.

"See why I can't let you drive," Bolt intoned, deadpan.

Cat smiled a silent promise to deal with him later.

"And now," Madelaine was saying, "I have saved the very best for last." She made a sweeping motion of her arm to urge them into a spacious room opposite the living room at the front of the house. "My library."

Here the walls were painted a restful dark green, and brass floor lamps were positioned near two overstuffed chairs that begged you to curl up in them. A stone fireplace dominated one wall of the room, but it was the other three walls that commanded Cat's attention. Books, thousands of them, lined the floor-to-ceiling shelves. Some of the bindings were of fragile leather with the gilt printing worn away in places; other books looked as if they had hardly been opened, as if they had been acquired for only a moment's inspiration, or to glimpse a single illustration, or in the hope they would deliver something wonderful that might or might not have come to pass.

Cat was suddenly filled with dozens of questions for Madelaine, the same sorts of questions she hoped to inspire in readers when her article appeared in print.

Bolt helped her carry her equipment from the car and set up the lights. Then he moved out of the way while she went about taking the shots she'd been planning in her mind for months. Long views and close-ups, experiments with angles and lights, she quickly used up several rolls of film. At first she was surprised that Bolt seemed to sense when she was ready to change lenses or needed a fresh roll of film and would magically appear by her side to help. He returned cameras to their cases and labeled film canisters according to her instructions. After a while, she ceased being surprised and they simply worked together almost as easily as if they'd been at it for years. In a way, she thought very briefly, too involved with her work to think much about anything else, the easiness between them was another surprise.

Afterward, they sat and had the lemonade Madelaine had offered and Cat got a chance to ask her all the questions bubbling inside her. Madelaine was a delight to interview, witty and forthcoming, and by the time Cat excused herself to go upstairs to change for dinner, she was feeling elated with the success of her first official shoot.

"Do you think this is an omen?" she asked Bolt when he trailed her to the bottom of the stairs even though he had expressed no interest in changing his own clothes.

"I'm the wrong man to ask about omens," he replied.

Cat frowned worriedly. "Why? Do you sense something? You think maybe this is a bad omen? Oh, I knew it was too good to be true. What do you sense?"

"Hysteria setting in," he said in a dry tone. "Will you calm down?" He caught her hands in his, probably to stop her from waving them around frantically. "I said I'm the wrong man to ask because I don't believe in omens."

"Don't believe in omens?" She eyed him incredulously. As far as she was concerned, that was like saying he didn't believe in four-leaf clovers or lucky numbers. "What else don't you believe in?"

"The Easter bunny," he shot back, his smile droll. "Now get upstairs and change before Madelaine finishes whatever she's doing in the kitchen and calls us for dinner."

"But you did think it went well, didn't you?"

"Yes, I thought it went great."

"I mean, that room should photograph beautifully, all that contrast between the dark walls and white woodwork. And the light from those amber lamps..."

"Beautiful," he agreed, laughing. "Perfect. You're a genius, Tiger. Now get out of here."

He squeezed her hands and let her go and all the way up the stairs Cat felt his gaze on her. It made her spine tingle in the same alarming way his gentle squeeze had left her fingers tingling. Why should that be? she asked herself, recognizing sexual awareness when she felt it. At the top of the stairs she turned, knowing he would still be watching her and knowing why, and not knowing at all what to do about it.

She showered quickly and dressed in a black cotton knit dress that was actually little more than an elongated tank top, and black sandals. The dress laced up the back, ruling out even the skimpiest bra, and always made her feel sexy.

Something that common sense warned she should have no interest in feeling around Bolt Hunter.

He might be a more decent guy than she had been willing to concede twelve hours ago, but he was still as far from being her type as a man could be and still be classified a Homo sapiens. They were going to be traveling together in close proximity, she reminded herself, and there was no sense in tempting fate or starting something that had absolutely no future as far as she was concerned. Which was why she wasn't wearing the dress for him, she decided, smiling with satisfaction at her reflection in Madelaine's pedestal mirror. She was wearing it for herself.

Dinner was deliciously New England, with baked stuffed lobster fresh from the neighboring state of Maine and grilled vegetables from a farm just down the street. Dessert was strawberry shortcake made with berries the size of plums, which Madelaine had sent Bolt to pick in her patch out back. Her nephew had phoned earlier and said that he and his friend wouldn't make it home for dinner. Cat, who was looking forward to meeting the young man and perhaps gaining another perspective on his poetess aunt for her piece, hoped he would return early enough for them to talk for a while.

After dinner, she insisted on helping Madelaine with the dishes, and Bolt offered to bring in logs to build a small fire in the fireplace in the library. She was hoping to take a few additional shots of Madelaine in her favorite chair, a glowing fire in the background.

Cat was in the process of carefully drying a Majolica platter, which Madelaine told her had been in her family for years, when what sounded like a gunshot shattered the early evening quiet.

"My goodness," Cat exclaimed.

"Relax," the other woman urged with an indulgent smile. "That's simply Max and that old bomber of his. Believe me, I've gotten quite familiar with the sound of a car backfiring over the past two summers."

The sudden tightening of Cat's shoulders had just begun to ease when she heard someone shout.

"Help," cried a male voice from somewhere outside. "Somebody help."

"Get down," snarled another man. "Down."

She turned to Madelaine, whose eyes were wide and fearful.

"That sounded like Bolt," Cat said.

Together they ran for the door, Cat shoving the platter onto the counter, Madelaine's hands dripping soapy water. They followed the direction of the shouting to the oversize barn that was now used as a garage. A black electric lantern hanging from a wooden rafter provided the only light, and it took a moment for her eyes to adjust to the shadows. When they did, she saw Bolt standing over two men—no, two boys—who were lying facedown on the dirt floor. He was leaning with his hand on the neck of one, his foot planted squarely on the back of the other.

Cat knew without asking that the boys were Madelaine's nephew and his friend. A dented and rust-spotted car with its hood up told her that they had been in there working on it. She couldn't in her wildest dreams imagine what Bolt was doing.

"My God, Bolt, what are you doing?"

"He's crazy," cried the boy he was holding by the neck. "He charged in here and jumped us with no warning, Aunt Maddy."

"Is that true?" Madelaine asked, her voice shaking. Then, more firmly, she added. "And I'll thank you to please let those boys up. Now."

Bolt looked over his shoulder at the women, his expression fierce. Something in his eyes sent a shiver through Cat. She could easily understand why the kid thought he was crazy.

"Is this your nephew?" Bolt asked.

"Of course, he's my nephew," Madelaine replied. "Who else do you suppose would be working out here in my barn? Max, darling, are you hurt? How about you, Andrew?"

"I'd be all right if this jerk would get his hands off me," Max shouted.

Sensing support, both boys began to struggle in earnest and Bolt straightened and released them. They scrambled to their feet, chests heaving angrily, and glared at Bolt.

"Who are you?" Max demanded. "And what the hell do you think you're doing?"

He was the taller of the two boys, a handsome kid with broad shoulders and thick, dark brown hair. His friend Andrew was a couple of inches shorter and at least twenty pounds lighter. He had a stringy blond ponytail and an earring.

Andrew brushed dirt from the sleeves of the red plaid shirt that hung loose over his baggy jeans. "You're a sicko, man. Sneaking up on people that way. I think you broke my back or something."

"Oh, no," Cat exclaimed, instinctively taking a step forward to see if she could help him.

Bolt froze her with a look.

"If your back was broken you wouldn't be standing up," Bolt told him in a monotone.

"Yeah, well, it's no thanks to you if it's not broke. What the hell were you trying to do?"

"Yeah, what are you doing here anyway?" Max demanded.

"He's one of my houseguests for the evening," Madelaine spoke up. Both boys stared at her in amazement. "And I'm sure he can explain whatever happened out here." She drew herself up and Cat recognized in her manner the same unyielding strength that marked her work. "You will explain this to us, Bolt."

It wasn't a question.

Bolt nodded to her, then faced the two boys. "I apologize," he said, his tone like sandpaper on cement. "I made a mistake."

It wasn't an explanation, not really, but it looked to be all they were going to get. Turning, he stalked from the barn.

"That's it?" Max shouted in angry disbelief. "He made a damn mistake? End of story?"

"What a jerk," Andrew muttered.

"I'm sure there's an explanation," Cat said feebly. She wasn't sure of anything at that moment, least of all what had driven Bolt to attack two kids who were minding their own business on their own property.

But she was determined to find out.

"I'll talk to him," she said and hurried out of the barn in the same direction he'd gone.

She found him leaning against the car, breathing as if he'd just run a long, hard race.

He didn't look at her as she approached and stood leaning against the car beside him.

"I'm sorry," he told her.

"So you said. It's not enough."

"Sorry, it's all there is."

"I don't think so."

"I don't care what you think."

"Obviously. You obviously don't care what anyone thinks, or about other people's feelings or rights, or about little things like good manners and gratitude."

He spun to face her in the thick darkness. Cat couldn't see more than the angry glitter of his eyes. Judging from the fury in his tone, it was just as well.

"You think I wanted to hurt those kids?" he demanded. "You think I wanted to repay Madelaine's hospitality by jumping her nephew? You think I wanted to screw up your visit here, knowing how much it means to you? And make a damn jackass out of myself in the process?"

"Then why did you?" she asked, her tone softly pleading to understand. As he spoke, the anger in his voice had broken and given way to a heart-wrenching contempt that she sensed was directed at himself alone.

He shook his head. "You wouldn't understand. None of you would."

"Try me."

She heard his sigh, saw him arch his neck and lift his hand to knead the back of it as if it hurt.

"I thought I saw that car again," he said at last.

"What car? You mean the same car from the rest stop?"

"Yeah."

"Where?"

"Out there." He tipped his head toward the road. "Pulling past real slow. I watched for a while, but it didn't come back. I was carrying the wood inside when I heard the shot."

"That was just the car backfiring."

"Yeah, I figured that out," he said, contempt in his voice. "Right after my foot connected with that kid's back."

"Why on earth did you jump them?"

"I don't know." He shook his head and looked at the sky. "I heard the shot—what I thought was a shot—and I wondered where you were. When I ran into the barn, the first thing I saw was that damn red plaid shirt, just like the one that guy back at the rest stop was wearing. And the other kid, Max, you have to admit that from the back he looks like the guy who helped you with the wires."

"So you thought—"

"I didn't think," he interjected. "I acted. That's what I do, what I was trained to do. That's why your uncle sent me here in the first place. I act, and react. And sometimes it doesn't work out quite the way I expect, all right?"

"No," she snapped. "It isn't all right at all. I don't care what you were trained to do. You're not in the Army now and you can't just attack two innocent kids because you imagine you saw a car that you think might be following you."

"I didn't imagine it," he said firmly.

"Even if you did see it, it's no excuse for your behavior."

"I know that. I said I was sorry."

"And I said sorry's not good enough."

"What do you want me to do? Give the kid a back rub?"

"No, but I want more than lip service. I want you to show a little remorse."

"You want remorse?" he demanded, reaching out and grabbing her by the arms and yanking her close to him. Now she could see his expression clearly and her heart began to pound furiously. "Lady, I'm carrying around an ocean of remorse. More than you could ever understand in your worst nightmares. More than I would wish on my worst enemy." He loosened his hold slightly. "I said I was sorry I scared those kids, and I know what I feel. If you can't see it, that's not my problem."

When he let her go, Cat took a step back from him and stood rubbing her arms for a moment. Finally she said, "I'll go inside and try to explain it to the others, smooth things over somehow."

"All right. Get your things while you're in there," he added.

"Get my things? Why?"

"We're leaving."

"Tonight?" she asked in disbelief.

"Tonight."

"That's out of the question. After what just happened I can hardly add insult to injury by refusing to stay the night as planned . . . if we're still welcome."

He stepped close to her, crowding her against the car without even bringing his body in contact with hers. The heat and strength she sensed in him held her motionless. She sensed something else, as well. Desperation, Cat realized. She thought that, all things considered, she probably ought to be afraid. But she wasn't. Instead she felt a crazy urge to put her arms around him and pull his head to her shoulder and just stand there in the darkness holding him. The way she'd so often longed for someone to come out of the darkness to hold her.

"I can't stay here tonight," he said quietly.

"Because you're embarrassed by what happened?"

His laugh was a harsh, bleak sound. "Embarrassment doesn't have anything to do with it. I just can't stay in this house."

"But why?"

"Remember when you first told me you had to make these stops along the way?" he asked.

Cat nodded.

"I agreed to go along with you without knowing any more than that." He hesitated, then added, "I'm asking you to go along with me on this now the same way. No questions asked."

Cat bit her bottom lip, trying to think what she should do.

If she did as he asked and left with him now, it would mean getting in the car alone with a man she barely knew and driving away on dark, lonely country roads that stretched for miles in all directions.

She could refuse, she told herself. He probably wouldn't leave without her or he would have already done so.

She could go inside and call Uncle Hank and demand to know just what kind of man he had sent to watch out for her.

Or she could follow the small, steady inner voice that told her she already knew what kind of man Bolt was. Over the years she'd spent a lot of time alone, listening to that voice, and she'd come to trust it more than she did most things in life.

"All right," she told him finally. "I'll get my things."

Chapter Six

It was all new to Bolt, this sensation of wanting to vanish into thin air. Granted, there had been moments in his colorful past when the ability to vaporize and disappear would have come in handy. It definitely would have saved him from some sweaty palms, a few physical poundings and several broken bones.

As painful and frightening as those other moments might have been, however, he had never before actually wished he could just fade away into nothingness. It wasn't his style. Fighting his way through the fear within and the danger outside, now, that was more his style. Act and react and save the second thoughts for later, just like he'd told Cat. He'd never been one to even consider slinking from sight as an option.

Until now. He wouldn't mind slinking out of this one. Unfortunately, the old Chevy, as spacious as it was by current standards, still didn't provide for a whole lot of slinking room between the driver's and passenger's seats. He resisted the urge to turn and glance at Cat. He'd done that only once in the half hour or so they'd been back on the road, and the watchful, almost wary way she'd been looking at him, as if he was something in a petri dish that might lunge at any second, left him in no hurry to turn her way again.

Back at Madelaine's, before he'd followed her inside to repeat his apology and help carry their things to the car, Cat had asked him if he was embarrassed by what had happened in the barn, if that might be the real reason he didn't want to stay as planned. He supposed it was a natural assumption, but he'd been telling the truth when he denied it. He regretted his behavior because it had been a mistake, a failing on his part, not because the impulse was wrong or because of what Madelaine and the boys might think of him as a result.

The fact was, he didn't much care what they thought of him. He shouldn't care what Cat thought, either, he told himself. But for some reason he did. The realization that he had screwed up badly in front of her, that he'd come off looking like some sort of overzealous, trigger-happy goon, was what made him want to vanish from her sight. Just thinking about it left his skin feeling too hot and his gut too cold. Was this what it felt like to be embarrassed? he wondered, not liking it. Not liking it at all.

"Would you like to talk about it?" Cat asked softly.

Bolt felt his grip on the wheel tighten. "About what?"

"You know, about what happened back there."

"I thought we already did."

"I mean about why it happened."

"I told you, I made a mistake. It was a case of mistaken identity."

"I think it was a little more than that. Be honest, Bolt, you were obsessed with the idea that we were being followed. Now you're sitting there brooding as if you lost your best friend, and I'm sitting here trying to figure out why."

He stiffened, and his gaze, locked on the road ahead, turned savage.

"All I mean," she continued, the words hitting him like relentless drops of scalding hot water, "is that it doesn't take Sigmund Freud to see that you're still very upset. If you ask me, you overreacted to something that even you call a simple mistake, and I just thought you might like to talk about whatever it is that's bothering you."

"No. Thanks anyway," he retorted. "That's something else we probably ought to get straight right now. I don't talk about what bothers me. Not to Sigmund Freud and not to you. Not to anyone. Not ever."

"Fine, have it your way."

Even though she barely moved, he could sense her withdrawing from him, battening down the hatches somewhere deep inside. That was exactly what he wanted, for both their sakes. So why was the relief he felt mixed with something else, a feeling of loss that was unfamiliar and sharp?

Another new feeling he didn't like.

Fine, have it your way, she'd said, all the sweetness gone from her voice. *It's not my way,* he wanted to tell her. *It's just the way it is.* He didn't know how to tell her that without telling her more, more than he ever told anyone. So he said nothing.

After a while, she spoke again.

"I really think we ought to look for a place to stop for the night."

"Why? I'm doing fine," he said. He was in no mood for stopping and trying to sleep in a strange room.

"Well, I'm not. I'm exhausted."

"So sleep."

"I can't sleep when I'm worried you might join me and drive us into a pole at any time. How can you possibly still be going strong after all these hours on the road? You're not taking anything to stay awake, are you?"

"No," he retorted, annoyed at the suggestion. "Unless you consider willpower an illegal substance. Believe me, I've had to will myself to stay awake for longer stretches than this in the past, and under much worse conditions."

"How admirable. Pity you don't have such absolute control over all your impulses."

Bolt figured he deserved that and declined to rise to the bait.

"So are you going to look for a place to stop?" she asked.

"Eventually." Like tomorrow night, he thought.

"I see a motel with a vacancy sign just up ahead," she pointed out a minute later. "Let's pull in there."

Bolt frowned at the small roadside motel. "Wouldn't you rather wait and look for something bigger after we get back on the interstate?"

"Bigger?" she echoed.

"And maybe nicer."

"Why?" she retorted, shrugging. "I'm not planning to raise a family there, simply grab a few hours' sleep. This place looks fine."

Swallowing a frustrated sigh, he slowed and turned into the motel parking lot. He parked in front of the office and they both got out.

Inside, they registered separately, to the unmistakable amusement of the night clerk who couldn't seem to take his eyes off Cat in that black dress. Old coot probably thought asking for separate rooms was just a cover and that they'd be sharing a bed within the hour, Bolt thought irritably. He wasn't sure exactly what irritated him more, the old man's smug smile or the fact that he was so flat-out wrong about them.

Bolt had to admit that looking the way she did in that dress, it wasn't a stretch for any man to link thoughts of Cat and a warm bed. The way the dress left the center of her back exposed and clung to her nice round butt tempted him to forget things he'd sworn not to, like the fact that she was hardly more than a kid and that she was the general's niece. Not to mention that he was supposed to be looking out for her, not wondering what it would be like to unlace the back of her dress and peel it from her shoulders. He hated bony shoulders and hers were anything but bony. They were softly rounded and tanned and smooth-looking.

He did his best not to think about her shoulders or any other part of her as he moved the car to the other side of the lot and followed her to the door of her room. His willpower must be overtaxed, because he wasn't very successful.

"I'll take a look inside your room and check it out for you if you like," he offered as she unlocked the door.

"Thanks."

He stepped inside and flipped on the light, walked to the bathroom and did the same there, pulling aside the shower curtain for a glance at the tub.

"Looks all right," he said.

Cat stood inside the open door watching, her lips curved with amusement. "Did you really expect otherwise?"

"I always expect otherwise. Good night, Cat."

He sensed more than saw the patronizing roll of her eyes as he passed. After waiting to make sure she locked the door behind him, he walked the few feet to the door of his room next door. As soon as he got inside and tossed the bags he was carrying onto the bed, he realized he still had Cat's as well as his own.

He turned toward the entrance, hesitated and moved instead to the door connecting the two rooms. Unbolting it from his side, he knocked and called her name. "It's me, Bolt," he added.

It was a minute before she undid the lock on her side and opened the door.

"Yes?" she said quizzically.

"I forgot to give you this." He held out the tote bag, which matched the suitcase now open on the bed. Already a silk nightgown was tossed across her pillow and intriguing-looking bottles and jars, full of what he hadn't a clue, were scattered on the dressing table beside her.

"Thanks," she said. "I'll need this in the morning."

"No problem. If you like, you can keep this door unlocked. Just in case you need me or something during the night."

"I won't," she said.

"All right. It was just a thought."

"Night, Bolt."

"Just one more thing." He rested his shoulder against the door and tried to disguise his uneasiness with a smile. "Do you need a hand with your dress? Getting out of it, that is. I mean, with the laces." He made a fumbling motion at the back of his own neck. "I wasn't sure if you could reach them."

"I can. Thanks. I'll be just fine."

She was smiling faintly at him, a smile that said she saw right through him and didn't find him much of a challenge. Bolt suddenly felt as if he was years younger than her instead of the other way around.

"Okay, then."

"Good night," she said again.

"Right." He turned and saw the book on the edge of the dresser. The woman on the glossy cover had laces on her dress, too, only hers were in the front and they looked as if they were popping open from the pressure of her ample breasts. She even looked a little like Cat, long blond hair and lots of soft curves. But the woman on the cover didn't look as if she was telling the man leaning over her that she didn't need help with her laces. Quite the opposite.

Without thinking, Bolt reached for the book and picked it up.

"Knight of Passion," he said, reading the title out loud. "Any good?"

"I think so."

He smiled at her. "Now I know where all that duel talk came from earlier."

She shrugged, her gaze direct. "You have to admit it seems a more honorable way to solve differences than jumping people without warning."

Bolt winced. "It does, at that. I wonder why duels ever went out of style."

"I guess because, for the most part, everything else about the world they represented went out of style. Things like honor and chivalry and loving someone enough to die for them if need be."

"Don't forget wearing your lady's token into battle," he added. "You see, I do know a little about it."

"Why are you chuckling?"

He shrugged. "Natural reaction, I guess. I mean, I'm sure it makes for a great story, but who would take any of this seriously?"

"I would," she said, removing the book from his hand. "All of it."

She began to close the door on her side, purposefully bumping the toes of his boots in the process.

"I'm going, I'm going," he muttered. "I didn't mean to offend you or anything."

"Trust me, you didn't. I hardly expected a man like you to understand my philosophy of life, much less agree with it."

"A man like me?"

She met his gaze with a lofty expression. "That's right."

It was late and he really wasn't sure he was up to hearing her view of his manhood. "Yeah, well…there is one more thing."

"What now?"

"About tonight…" He stopped and rubbed his jaw with his palm, looking at the bed behind her and the ceiling above before finally meeting her impatient gaze. He spoke quickly. "I sometimes have dreams, all right? Bad dreams, I mean, and there's a chance I might shout or something. I just thought I would warn you so you won't be scared if you hear anything."

"Thank you," she said softly. Just as he stepped into his room, she added, "Bolt, I think maybe I would feel safer after all if we left the connecting doors unlocked. Is that okay?"

He caught her gaze, her hint of a smile maddeningly perceptive, as if she knew him better than he knew himself. Bolt felt that same uncomfortable feeling twisting inside him, as if roles were suddenly reversed and he was the one who needed protection and she was taking care of him.

"Whatever you say, Tiger," he replied, managing a cocky grin for her benefit. "Sweet dreams."

Sweet dreams. The wish trailed him into his room, lingering in his mind as he kicked off his boots and attempted to punch the paltry motel pillows into shape. Were there still such things as sweet dreams? It had been so long since he'd had any that were even remotely sweet, he couldn't be sure. He either didn't dream at all or woke up sweating. No in-between.

Which was fitting, he supposed. At any rate, he preferred things that way, black or white, all or nothing, no in-between. To Bolt, in-between implied halfway and compromise and concessions. Concessions left room for error. Something he'd learned the hard way.

He stretched out on the sagging mattress with the bedside lamp still on and closed his eyes experimentally.

Immediately he descended into the middle of an explosion of heat and streaks of red light, bloodred. The noise filled his head and he was diving, diving through glass and blackness, hitting the ground hard and hurting, hurting bad, then running, running as fast as he could to get clear of the smoke and see where he was. He had to find his way inside the house, only the pain in his chest kept stopping him, making him fall again and again, and finally he was flat on his belly, looking back and seeing there was no house left to find, not anymore, and he was crying out because he knew that with the house had gone the woman he had just found to love, the woman he thought had loved him, and then he was just lying there, facedown in the dirt, dying in some godforsaken corner of a country he didn't understand and mostly hated and not knowing the half of it.

He knew now, though. He knew it all now. Knowing it, knowing the truth about Angelina, and about himself, was what brought the real screams from some private hell deep inside him.

Jerking upright, away from the memory, he swung himself off the bed. This wasn't going to work. Not tonight. Maybe it was being overtired or Cat's talk of knights in shining armor. Whatever, there was no way he could risk falling asleep in that room tonight. Noise and motion and the sense that he wasn't alone in the darkness, that's what he needed to sleep in peace.

Since that wasn't an option for tonight, he needed instead to shake off some of the languor that was already setting in. A walk seemed in order. Cool night air might have helped refresh him, but the air outside was still warm and heavy. He prowled more than walked, circling the small motel twice. That wasn't enough, so he also walked a distance down the road and back. Whenever a car approached, he was careful to look away from the glare of the headlights, wanting vision sharp in case a black Mustang happened to pass.

As he rounded the corner into the motel parking lot, the first thing Bolt saw was the old convertible gleaming like cherry ice in the moonlight, and he smiled in spite of his dark mood. As he drew closer, the urge to just slip behind the wheel and take off rose up strong inside him. It would be so simple, Bolt told himself, just him and the Chevy and the old man in the moon who already knew all his secrets anyway. He could drive away and leave all his problems behind.

He glanced at the darkened window of the room next to his, the curtains tightly drawn on the other side. Problems like Catrina Amelia Bandini, for starters.

It sure was a tempting thought.

He had no doubt she'd get home safely without him. She was a big girl with a wallet full of credit cards. She could take a taxi to the airport and be home by tomorrow afternoon. Of course, the general would be all over him about deserting her here, but by then both she and the car would be safely where they belonged, and everyone knew that in the end, results were what mattered most. The general understood that even better than he did.

If he didn't leave now, if he stayed and continued at the unhurried pace Cat clearly intended, the trip was only going to get harder. Harder in all kinds of ways that he didn't even want to think about. And more complicated. He knew that in his gut. One look at Cat in that black dress had seared that truth into him in a way he wouldn't be forgetting in a hurry.

The hell with chivalry. The smart thing to do would be to take off. If he went now, everyone would be happy in the end. Him, the general, Tony LaCompte. Okay, maybe not everyone. But the only one who wouldn't be happy was Cat. At least she'd be getting paid for her trouble. She wouldn't, however, get to take her damn pictures.

So, Bolt reasoned, her project would simply have to be put on hold for a while, until she could afford to travel on her own. And if the magazine editor lost interest in the meantime, well, Cat was young. Very young, chided a small voice in his head. There would be plenty of other projects for her.

Not, he reminded himself, that any of that was his problem.

Nope, it wasn't his problem at all, he decided, sighing as he turned toward his room. Not even remotely his problem. If he wanted to, he could have his stuff in that car and be out of there in a heartbeat.

He entered the room and closed the door quietly behind him, not wanting to disturb Cat. His mouth curved reluctantly at the memory of the sleepy yawn she'd tried to stifle when bidding him good-night a while ago.

Still moving carefully so he didn't make any noise, he turned the room's only chair, which easily qualified as the ugliest and most uncomfortable vinyl-covered chair ever manufactured, so that it faced the small television. He turned the set on with the volume low, cranked the air conditioner to high, kicked off his boots once again and spent the night slouched awkwardly in the chair, thinking about the woman sleeping next door.

Cat was surprised when Bolt readily agreed to let her take the first stint behind the wheel the following day. Pleasantly so. Uncle Hank would never ride in a car while a woman did the driving, and Bolt went up a notch in her estimation for not being quite that obsessively macho. Of course, after last night and the debacle in Madelaine's barn, he still had a long way to go.

The man was clearly the victim of too many of her uncle's top-secret missions. She'd seen the signs before in some of the men who visited Uncle Hank from time to time. Wary and guarded, quick to suspicion and slow to laughter. Special Services burnouts, she'd dubbed them, to her uncle's dismay. There was a time, she knew, when Uncle Hank had cherished a hope that she would someday settle down with a man in uniform, preferably one hand-picked by him from his corps of elite officers. She'd long since disavowed him of that silly notion. She loved her country and had the utmost respect for the soldiers who dedicated their lives to defending it, but she could never live with one.

Cat knew exactly what kind of man she wanted to share her life with. She'd known since the days when she'd sat on her uncle's lap and listened rapturously to his stories of how her beautiful ballerina mother and handsome magician father had met and fallen head over heels in love and run away to get married because they just couldn't bear to be apart for even a minute. Her mother had given up her dream of dancing professionally to become the stage assistant of the Great Bandini.

Together they developed the act and took it on the road, more often than not leaving their only child with a friend, and together, on one of those road trips to a string of small-town gigs, they had died, their souls now bound for all eternity. To Cat, it was the most romantic story ever, far more so even than her favorite fairy tales about Cinderella and Rapunzel.

She may not have been able to put it into words at first, but even back then she had known there was a Prince Charming in her future. The man she was waiting for was creative and daring and wildly romantic, a man who needed her and wanted her and respected her, a man to cherish her and build his world around her. A man exactly like her mother had found, she mused, thoughts of the parents she'd barely known tugging at her heartstrings, as always.

None of the men she'd dated had ever come close to fulfilling her requirements. Not surprisingly, since her requirements were so demanding. She knew that and had no intention of compromising one iota. If her mother and father could find their soul mates, then so could she. Even if it took her a lifetime. She'd already decided that she would prefer to share a short while with the man who was created for her alone than to waste eternity with some runner-up.

For a while, when they first met, she'd thought Gator might have been the man for her. Now the very idea made her giggle. Gator was creative, all right, and even daring in his own off-the-wall way, and he certainly knew how to make her laugh, another must. But he utterly lacked the inner strength and compassion she was looking for. He was a great friend, but no more her soul mate than... Bolt Hunter, she thought, giggling even louder at that. Bolt might be as strong and stubborn as the lock on Fort Knox, but wrong for her in every other way she could conceive of and probably a few she couldn't.

Besides being surprised by Bolt's agreeing to let her take the wheel this morning, she was also secretly relieved to be driving early in the day. Of course, she would ride strapped to the bumper before admitting that to him. She knew for a fact that she would never have been able to drive anywhere near the number of miles he had covered yesterday and she certainly would never have been in any shape to consider going on after they left Madelaine's. She had to admire Bolt's fortitude, which he had dismissed as a simple matter of willpower.

Actually, that would explain it nicely. She didn't have enough willpower to resist a jelly doughnut or splurging on a sweater she couldn't afford, much less enough to will her eyes to stay open and focused after a long day on the road.

That's why she was happy to do her share of the driving now, while she was fresh and alert. She'd fallen asleep as soon as she hit the bed last night and had only been dragged back to consciousness when Bolt banged none too gently on her door at the ungodly hour of six o'clock. She felt great now, wide-awake and full of energy. Which was more than she could say for her copilot.

She darted a quick sideways glance to where he'd been sleeping soundly ever since they'd stopped for breakfast just outside Albany. So far he'd slept through tolls and a rush-hour traffic jam and the quick pit stop she'd made to tank up on gas and coffee. Now they were approaching the New York City area, which Gator had taken pains to warn her about, and in spite of a selfish wish that he might awaken in time to take over the driving before the upcoming route changes and heavy traffic, Cat didn't have the heart to disturb him.

If she had been making the trip alone, as planned, she would have had to handle the tough driving on her own, she reminded herself. And Bolt didn't appear destined to rejoin the living anytime soon. She chuckled to herself as she carefully followed the signs directing her to bear left at the split ahead. Apparently yesterday's hard drive and the incident at Madelaine's had taken more of a toll on old Captain Invincible than he would ever admit. Now that she thought about it, he'd started out today looking worse than he had when he went to bed last night.

Some of it was due to the fact that he hadn't bothered to shave, and two days' worth of dark stubble made him look grouchy and vaguely menacing. But the circles under his eyes and deep grooves by the sides of his mouth with which he'd greeted her this morning had nothing to do with whiskers, only fatigue. It was obvious he needed the sleep and even if it meant risking a detour through the heart of Manhattan, Cat was going to see that he got it.

She wasn't sure why she felt so kindly to him all of a sudden. After all, at this time yesterday she would have cheerfully left him hog-tied by the roadside if she could have managed it. For reasons she couldn't explain, Bolt got to her in a way she would never have expected. He made her feel almost protective, which was totally absurd, she thought, smiling wryly. Even if she hadn't known that he was one of her uncle's legendary warriors, after one day in his company she could tell that Bolt Hunter was as tough and resourceful as they came. The man needed her protection about as much as a cobra needed protection from a butterfly.

All he needed was sleep. And since he was going out of his way to help her, she supposed she owed him that much. Besides, she thought, sneaking another peek his way, the man looked adorable when he slept. Not exactly cuddly, but definitely less fierce and irritating than he did when he was awake. He even snored nicely, she decided, listening to the soft, snuffly sound of his breathing. It was deep and rhythmic and reassuring on some elemental level, like listening to someone's heartbeat.

And, she thought, tightening her grip on the wheel as she approached the Garden State Parkway, she could use all the reassurance she could get about now.

By taking it slow and paying attention, she managed to make it through the heaviest traffic without a single close call or wrong turn. She felt quite triumphant and proud of herself. Baltimore, their next stop, was still over four hours away, but Cat figured that with a quick trip to the ladies' room and another cup of coffee, she just might be able to make it all the way.

This time Bolt stirred when she pulled into a rest stop, parked and turned off the engine. He groaned, rubbed his jaw sleepily and turned to peer at her with a heavy-lidded expression that made her pulse race for no good reason. Good Lord, what was the matter with her?

"Where are we?" he asked, his voice husky.

"New Jersey," she replied proudly.

That opened his eyes in a hurry. "You're kidding, right?"

Cat smiled and shook her head.

"Damn," he muttered. "I didn't mean for you to drive this far. I must have really zonked out."

"You did. Which means you really needed the rest."

"Maybe," he replied. Cat decided that was probably as close as he would come to admitting she'd been right. "I'm fine now, though," he went on, "so I'll take over from here."

She nodded agreeably. She was proud, not stupid, and her neck was getting stiff from driving.

"All right," she agreed, stretching her arms over her head before reaching behind her for her bag. "But first I need to wash my face and grab a cup of coffee. Do you want to take turns using the facilities?"

"I think we should, just to be on the safe side," Bolt said, scanning the parking lot.

"Looking for a black Mustang, by any chance?" she teased.

He shot her a look. "Why? Do you see one?"

"At ease, soldier, it was a joke." She shook her head ruefully. "So who goes first?"

"You can," he said, reaching for the door handle. "I'll get out and stretch my legs a little while I wait."

"Okay. Back in a jiff," she said as she walked away.

Bolt followed her example and stretched his arms over his head as he watched her go. Didn't the woman own any slacks? he wondered, scowling at the back of her long legs as she hurried up the walk. Sure, it was hot, but he was wearing jeans, wasn't he? It wouldn't hurt her to do the same and it would sure help him to concentrate on his driving. Maybe he'd suggest it to her for tomorrow. A shirt with sleeves wouldn't be a bad idea, either.

He grinned suddenly, his quiet chuckle drawing a strange look from a couple passing by. He couldn't help it. The thought of Cat's reaction should he try to tell her what clothes to wear made him laugh out loud at himself. Something he didn't do very often these days.

He shook his head. Slacks and a long-sleeved shirt in the middle of August. Why not go ahead and suggest a baggy overcoat while he was at it? No, on second thought, he'd better just keep his mouth shut about her clothes, which was more or less what she would tell him to do anyway if he was stupid enough to broach the subject. All in all, it would be easier to shut up and put up with the distraction her bare legs presented than to put up with her temper. They still had a lot of miles ahead of them, he reminded himself grimly.

He checked his watch, feeling restless. Now that he was fully awake he was anxious to get moving. He stretched his legs, took a look at the map and rearranged the trunk, which, crammed as it was with Cat's brightly colored assortment of bags and other junk, reminded him of a teenager's bedroom.

He checked his watch again, astounded as he had been most of yesterday by how long it could take a woman to splash some water on her face and order a cup of coffee.

Cat had never seen anything as cute as the handmade stuffed rabbits with floppy bodies made of ivory muslin rather than the usual fur. Their embroidered faces were amazingly expressive, and each one was dressed uniquely in hand-sewn clothes. There was a dignified lawyerly rabbit in a pin-striped suit, with tiny black wire spectacles perched on his long nose, and a rabbit chef with an apron, a ladle and a pot labeled People Stew. But the one that stole Cat's heart was the soldier. She smiled, thinking it looked disarmingly like another soldier she knew, right down to the black whiskers and steely gaze.

Reaching out, she picked it up and gave it a gentle squeeze. Just as she suspected, soft as a marshmallow on the inside.

"Adorable, isn't he?" asked the woman behind the makeshift stand, which had been set up in the spacious lobby of the building. There were two teenage girls behind the table with her. Students, most likely, since a banner behind them announced that the rabbit sale was a fund-raiser for the home-economics department of a local high school.

"Absolutely adorable," Cat agreed with the woman. "I'll take him."

She shook her head at her impulsiveness as she fished money from her purse and waited as the woman slipped the rabbit into a bag for her. What on earth was she going to do with a stuffed soldier? Cat had no idea. She just knew the instant she saw him with his ferocious expression that there was no way she could walk away and leave him there.

The lawyer and chef bunnies had obvious fine points and would easily find homes, but not many people would bother to check out the soldier's soft heart. He needed her, she told herself, shaking her head all over again as she walked away, bag in hand. And she needed to hurry up. This was supposed to be a pit stop, not a shopping excursion.

Sometimes there were lines in the ladies' room, Bolt reminded himself. Cat had told him so only yesterday. A flimsy excuse if he ever heard one, he groused to himself, arms folded across his chest as he leaned against the car and waited. He'd never stood in line to use a men's room and he'd told her so. She'd had an answer to that, too, of course. She had an answer for everything and, to his surprise, he liked hearing them. Partly because she was irreverent enough to make him laugh and partly because she had the guts to speak up and say whatever was on her mind no matter what he might think about it. Cat was the most guileless woman he'd ever known, and he liked that, too.

It's only because she's still young, he reminded himself with the same masochistic streak it would take to prick himself with a pin. He'd discovered he didn't like dwelling on the age difference between them. Fourteen years. And a lifetime of experience, he added to himself grimly. The fact that she was young explained why she might not have yet learned the tricks women were so good at. Then what about Angelina? came his next thought. She'd been young, too, just about Cat's age, and by the time he met her she'd already mastered every trick in the book. He had a hunch some women were born knowing all the tricks. Did it follow then that other women went a lifetime without bothering to learn?

He checked his watch again. What the hell could be taking her so long?

The line inched forward. Cat wished Bolt was there to see it. No, on second thought, she didn't wish that. The thought of Bolt in a ladies' room was scary and comical at once. It would be nice, however, to prove to him that there was such a thing as a line for the ladies' room. He insisted there was never a line for the men's room. Cat watched with a sympathetic smile as yet another mother struggled to zip, button and marshal to the sinks two small children and thought that was probably because men had so much less to worry about when they went to the john. Zip, zip, in and out. No rambunctious toddlers, panty hose, lipstick application or bad hair disasters to slow them down.

Two women squeezed past her to reach the exit and she moved up exactly two spaces in line. At least there was a nice measured predictability to the whole affair. You counted the stalls, counted the bodies ahead of you and could more or less estimate the length of your wait. Kids counted as two, of course, because they took so long, and senior citizens . . . forget it. Cat had observed that for some elderly people on the road, rest room visiting qualified as a hobby.

Take this lady, for instance, Cat thought, watching a heavyset woman making her way to the door. Definitely the type who had to check all the stalls to find the cleanest one, then swath every square inch of the interior with squares of bathroom tissue, after which she would attempt to perform the feat itself while clutching her purse, lest the occupant of the next stall reach over the dividing wall and snatch it from the door hook. That would be a time-consuming procedure even for someone more spry.

Cat pressed herself against the wall to give the woman as much leeway as possible as she passed. Everything would have been fine if it hadn't been for the bag in her hand. Afterward she swore that soldier bunny had poked his boot through the plastic and snagged the woman's purse on purpose.

The purse snapped open, and contents equal to the goods at a medium-size yard sale rained down on the tile floor. And it was all Cat's fault. The woman didn't actually say so, but the angry look she flashed her made Cat feel that way.

"Oh, no, oh, no," the woman cried, as people stepped around her in their hurry to get out the door. The line moved forward around Cat who stood frozen in place.

What choice did she have?

"Here, hold this for me," she said to the woman, thrusting the bag with the bunny at her as she stepped from line. "I'll pick up everything for you."

Crouching down, she quickly began to gather the combs, sucking candies, pennies, matches, keys and other accumulated necessities that were scattered across the floor. Since her own bag held about the same number of many of the same things, she really couldn't even get angry.

"Oh, thank you, thank you," the woman was saying now, tossing in an occasional "Bless you" for good measure whenever Cat had to crawl under a sink or reach behind the trash receptacle.

By the time she'd picked up everything, the woman was beaming at her in a way that made Cat glad she had helped, even if her knees were dirty and she was four places farther back in line.

Bolt glanced at his watch again, then in the direction of the walk to see if maybe he could spot Cat coming back, then at his watch. This waiting was really beginning to get to him. Heaving his shoulders in disgust, he paced to the back of the car and for at least the tenth time since he'd been there he ran his gaze the length of the crowded parking lot, checking to see what was around him.

This time, when he caught sight of the Mustang parked at the far end of the lot, he wasn't surprised at all. The car had been backed in to the parking spot so as to afford a clear view of Bolt and the Chevy to anyone sitting inside who might be watching. And someone was. He knew it. He could feel it.

In a matter of seconds he was around the car and across the grass median strip that divided the parking lot into sections, running full speed toward the back of the lot and the Mustang.

He was sure he saw movement behind the tinted windshield. An instant later he heard the car's engine start.

"Oh, no, you don't, you sucker," he growled under his breath. "You want to play games with me, this time we play my way."

He veered sharply to head them off and didn't even see the kid doing the balancing act with the ice cream cones until he was on top of him. Literally.

The kid was screaming, the mother was shouting at him, and he was elbow deep in rapidly melting chocolate ice cream and colored sprinkles.

Worse, the Mustang was getting away.

Bolt lurched to his feet and sprinted after it, but it was useless and he knew it before he was halfway across the lot. Cursing soundly, which earned him a few more dirty looks, he hurried back to pay the mother for the spilled ice cream cones. He even offered to take the kid inside to get replacements, but she refused, grabbing the little boy's hand firmly and pulling him safely behind her. Under the circumstances he could understand her reaction.

He brushed off as many of the sprinkles as he could as he headed toward the car. He was going to need a wet paper towel to get rid of the ice cream. Better yet, he decided, he was going to need a clean shirt. He opened the trunk and pulled one from his duffel bag, then looked around, realizing that Cat still wasn't back. He'd heard all the jokes about women and rest rooms, but this was ridiculous. She'd been gone much too long.

The implications of that settled over him with all the subtlety of getting a bucket of ice water in the face on a winter day. Where the hell was she? All he could think about as he started up the walk at a trot was that she'd been gone for too long and that the black Mustang had taken off. The two thoughts chased each other around in his head, threatening to link together and create a nightmare he couldn't afford to think about right now.

He was supposed to be watching out for her, damn it. He was supposed to have been watching out for Angelina, too. That was different, he thought frantically. This was New

Jersey, not Colombia. Cat wasn't the sister of the head of a major drug cartel, preparing to testify against him. Supposedly preparing to testify.

Not now, he thought frantically. He couldn't let himself get all tied up in that now. He had to find Cat.

By the time he pushed through the crowd gathered around a table just inside the door, he was once more running full speed. There were lots of kids with ice cream there, he noted, dodging them and the strollers and the little old ladies from the tour buses as best he could. He ran past the ladies' room to the food court. He guessed that she would have used the ladies' room as soon as she came in and should have been out of there long before now. He circled the perimeter of the food court, noting hopefully the long lines at every counter.

What was she wearing? What was she wearing? he asked himself frantically. Shorts and a sleeveless top, that's all he could remember. No wonder women complained that men were only interested in one thing. Concentrate, he ordered himself, his eyes raking methodically over the crowd. He'd been trained to notice details. Shorts. What color? Blue, he decided. Denim cutoffs. And the top? Concentrate, concentrate. Yellow. That was it. Bright yellow on top, much brighter than the soft gold of her hair, and denim on the bottom.

His examination of the crowd became more focused, but no more fruitful. There was lots of yellow and there were lots of blondes, but none of them were Cat. Could she have been in the Mustang? Could someone have forced her out there without his seeing? And why? Why didn't matter now, only actions. But could they have done it without his seeing? Was he that rusty? If last night was any indication, maybe he was.

No. No, he told himself again, more firmly. Oh, sweet heaven, please, no.

His heart pounding ferociously, he turned toward the ladies' room. Maybe she was sick. Not a pleasant thought, but at that moment a very welcome one. Definitely preferable to what was quickly becoming the only logical alternative. That she was gone.

He stood directly outside the rest room, one leg flexing anxiously as he watched the door open and woman after woman, girl after girl, emerge. None of them Cat. Bolt ignored the indignant glares he was drawing by keeping such close watch. The rest room was set up with double doors so that he couldn't even sneak a look inside when someone came out to see if Cat might be bent over a sink in there. Surely if she was sick someone would send for help. Wouldn't they?

Wouldn't they?

He couldn't afford to count on the kindness of strangers, he decided abruptly. He had no choice but to ask the next woman who stepped out to check and see if Cat was in there.

The next woman out had blue-tinted hair and a hearing aid. It didn't matter to Bolt. Nothing short of a Seeing Eye dog by her side would have discouraged him from asking her to go back and take a look inside for Cat.

"Excuse me, ma'am," he said, approaching and reaching out to her without thinking.

She screamed.

There was no other way to describe the sound she made. Bolt was only thankful her advanced age made her a little short on oxygen so it wasn't loud enough to draw the attention of more than, say, the two or three hundred people in the immediate vicinity.

He stubbornly pressed on, trying to explain what he wanted, but she hurried away from him as if he was the devil himself. At that moment he caught a glimpse of his reflection in the shiny metallic front of a snack machine and winced. He couldn't blame the woman. The way he looked, unshaven and desperate, his own mother wouldn't feel safe around him.

Any minute he expected the rest-area security police to descend upon him, alerted to the troublemaker who ran into kids and accosted old ladies outside rest rooms. They would want explanations at the very least. He didn't have time for that or to stand around waiting for someone to help him.

Grabbing the handle of the ladies' room door, he yanked it open, doing the same to the one inside it, slamming it back against the tile wall with a bang.

"Cat? Cat, are you in here?" he shouted, looking around.

Holy hell, he thought.

Chapter Seven

He was surrounded by women.

Of course, he expected to find women in a ladies' room. Maybe just not quite so many of them, and all staring at him. Old, young. Tall, short. All kinds of women. Suddenly silent women, with their eyes and mouths open wide in surprise. Make that shock, Bolt thought. Women who within seconds recovered en masse from the shock of his sudden, wild-eyed appearance and began to scream and shout at him in unison.

It didn't matter. By then he had spotted Cat, standing at a sink with her back to him, and their eyes met in the mirror in front of her.

She was there. That's all Bolt could think. All that mattered. She was there and she was safe.

She was also mad as hell. He could see the anger flashing in her eyes as she hurried toward him with her hands still dripping water.

"Have you lost your mind?" she hissed.

"I think so," he replied, strangely light-headed with relief. He never got light-headed. "I think maybe I have."

She grabbed his arm roughly, stretching back to snatch a bag off the sink and clamping it to her side.

"Let's go," she ordered, pushing him backward through the door. "I can't believe you did that. I have never, ever in my whole entire life been so humiliated."

"Really?" He turned so he was walking facing front by her side. "You must lead a charmed life if that's the only embarrassing thing that's ever happened to you."

"I didn't say it was the only embarrassing thing that's ever happened to me," she corrected. "I said most embarrassing. Most, do you hear me? Which is saying a lot, seeing I was raised by a man for whom orchestrating embarrassing moments is second nature."

Bolt grinned. He wasn't just relieved. He was exhilarated, jubilant, walking-on-air relieved. Not even the mention of the general could bring him down. He wasn't even angry with Hollister any longer. Cat was safe. He hadn't screwed up out there. Heck, he just might be the happiest man alive.

"Hold on," he said, bringing her to a halt by the exit. "What about your coffee?"

"Forget it."

"Soda," he suggested. "Ice cream? One of those pretzels you like so much?"

"Nothing. All I want right now is to get out of here and to never see any of these people again."

"That may not be possible," Bolt said, trailing her outside. "You'd be amazed how the same people keep turning up at these rest stops."

"Then I just won't stop at one again."

"All the way to Florida?"

"That's right."

"What about when nature calls?"

"I'll exercise self-control," she retorted. The world around Bolt seemed to lurch briefly when her stormy, challenging gaze zeroed in on him.

"You're not the only one with willpower, you know," she snapped.

Bolt wouldn't argue with that. Not at the moment, at any rate, when he was feeling as if, where Cat was concerned, he'd run out of willpower entirely. Somehow the adrenaline rush of a few moments ago and his relief at finding her safe had become all twisted up inside him with another, much more basic emotion. Desire. It had been there from the start, but the panic of the past few moments had simply eclipsed his ability to ignore it. Now it was a warm, steady, insistent throbbing at his core as he followed her to the car.

"All right," she said, whirling at him as soon as they were there. "What do you have to say for yourself?"

Bolt broke off in the middle of a thought about how it would feel to have her stretched out above him, her hair spilling across his face and his throat, and just stared at her.

"About what?" he asked cautiously.

"About our foreign policy toward China," she snapped. "About that little scene in the ladies' room. What do you think about what?"

"I think you'd probably like my answer to the China question better."

Her head shook with frustration. "Why did you do it, Bolt?"

Bolt shrugged. "I got tired of waiting."

"That's it?"

"Just about."

"What about that crack about seeing the same people at every rest stop. Did you think you saw the Mustang again?"

"I don't think I saw it," he replied shortly. "I saw it."

"And?"

"You don't want to know."

"Tell me anyway."

He sighed and told her all of it, about chasing after it and about the ice cream cones and about how he'd been worried that something had happened to her. He glazed over most of the part about worrying. He didn't know the right words to explain how he'd felt when he thought she might be hurt or gone, any more than he had the words to explain how he was feeling now. Not even to himself. "Still think it's all one big coincidence?" he demanded when he was through.

"Yes," she retorted, frustrating him all over again. "What else could it be? I mean, why would anyone want to follow us?"

"Good question. If you come up with a good answer, let me know. In the meantime..."

He left the sentence hanging and moved around to the back of the car, opening the trunk and tossing things to the pavement. He mostly made a show of tossing things. It put a small dent in his frustration. He took special care with her cameras and other equipment, however.

"Now what are you doing?" Cat asked, standing a safe distance off to the side.

"Looking."

"For what?"

"I don't know. But if someone is following us, I'd stake my life it's not just because they have a crush on one of us. They're after something."

"What?"

"If I knew, I wouldn't have to look."

"This is ridiculous," she said. Then, a few seconds later, "Can I help?"

Bolt paused only long enough to tell her to check under the seats and in the openings between the seat back and bottom cushions.

"Be careful sliding your hand around in there," he warned. "You never know what you might find."

Once the trunk was empty, he pressed and tapped on every inch of it, checking out the sides and bottom and even the back wall. Cat was still examining the seats when he finished loading the trunk. Bolt got the flashlight from his bag. Dropping onto his back on the pavement, he slid under the car, and holding the flashlight in one hand, he used the other to check out every possible place where something might be concealed.

He was working cold, with no clue what it was he was looking for. Drugs, microfilm, everything he considered seemed preposterous. But then, so did being shadowed by two dumb punks in a flashy, impossible-to-miss sports car. Could this have something to do with the car coming from Cuba? Could the punks be CIA? Nah. Undercover Feds? He mulled that over and found it not quite as ludicrous.

He heard Cat rustling in the trunk above him, moving things around. Probably because he'd left it a little too neat for her taste, he thought, smiling reluctantly.

"Shall I shut this now?" she called to him.

"Sure, go ahead. I'll stick the flashlight in the glove compartment when I'm through."

A few seconds later she was beside him, flat on her back on the warm pavement.

Bolt turned the flashlight on her face. She smiled.

"What do you think you're doing?" he demanded.

"Helping."

"You're through helping. Get out of here. You'll scratch up your legs on this pavement." Not to mention the marks the gravel might leave on her soft beautiful shoulders. He had selfish reasons for not wanting that to happen. He was in love with her shoulders.

"I don't care about that," she said, brushing off his concern. "Did you find anything yet?"

"Nothing but oil and . . . damn."

"What?"

"Nothing but oil and some thirty-year-old grit," he grumbled. "I just got a piece in my eye."

"Let me help."

"No, I . . ."

"I can at least hold the flashlight."

"I can do it all—"

"Will you stop being so stubborn and manly and hand me the damn thing?"

Bolt reluctantly relinquished the flashlight and used the bottom of his T-shirt to wipe his eye. He blinked several times to make sure whatever had been in there was gone.

"All set," he told her. "Thanks."

"No problem. Even heroes need help sometimes."

Bolt stiffened, his tone turning low and harsh. "I'm not a hero."

"You're sure trying to be. Face it, Bolt, this is just an old car that some spoiled rich guy wants to park in his garage along with all his other old cars." Her tone had become one of pleading indulgence. "Don't complicate matters."

"I didn't complicate them," he said, turning to meet her gaze in the semidarkness. A minute ago he'd been choking on oil fumes. Now all he could smell was her, sweet, intoxicating, as if he'd stuck his face in a bunch of wildflowers.

"Oh, right," she drawled, "the guy in the Mustang is the one who's complicating things, is that it?"

"You've got it."

She blinked, her beautiful mouth softening prettily as she frowned at him. "Bolt, this is crazy."

"I know," he agreed, his voice dropping lower still as he tipped his head closer to hers. He lifted his palm to her cheek. "Insane. So's this."

He hadn't planned to kiss her. If he had, he would have planned to do it slowly and gently. This was neither slow nor gentle.

He parted her lips with the hungry pressure of his own, using his tongue to taste and learn and arouse. A craving for more of her, for all of her, roared in his head, blocking out any other sound and feeling.

He rarely surrendered himself to the moment, but he did so now. Completely forgotten was the fact that they were lying under a very conspicuous car in a busy public parking area. Her uncle and the Mustang and any sense of responsibility ceased to exist. There was only the soft warmth of Cat's mouth responding to his.

She did respond. Bolt's heart clenched and then soared at the realization. She slid her tongue lightly, almost experimentally across his lips and made a soft sound of pleasure far back in her throat that made him wild.

From somewhere far away, something, his conscience most likely, kept reminding him he ought to stop, but the pleasure of it kept dragging him back under, further and further away from that nagging voice. He was so far gone it was a miracle he could feel the urgency in the pressure of the hand Cat placed against his chest. And even beyond miraculous that he was able to heed the gentle urge to stop.

When he lifted his mouth from hers, she refused to look at him.

"I . . ." She wet her lips and seemed to find the sensation unsettling. "I think I need some fresh air."

Bolt let her go without saying a word. Then he stared at the car's blackened undercarriage without seeing it.

"Nice going," he muttered to himself.

"Did you say something?" Cat called.

"No. Just talking to myself."

Too bad he wasn't as good at listening to himself, he thought darkly. Then maybe he wouldn't have gone making an impossible situation even more so by doing something as crazy as kissing Hollister's precious niece. And liking it.

There was no denying that he had liked it. He'd liked kissing Cat more than he'd liked anything in a long time. How long, he wondered as he slid toward the front of the car, absently feeling behind wires and clamps for anything that didn't belong there, how long had it been since a kiss had left him feeling this good?

A while. A long while.

He finished checking out the car and got to his feet, dusting himself off and trying to look as if nothing significant had happened between them in the past few minutes. He noticed that Cat had combed her hair and applied lipstick that made her lips look all rosy and wet and made him want to drag her into his arms and kiss her all over again.

"Find anything suspicious?" she asked him.

He shook his head. "Nothing."

"So what's your next theory on why someone would want to follow us?"

"I don't have one," he admitted. "But I still can't shake the feeling that someone is."

"So what next?"

"A clean shirt," he replied, frowning at the sticky splotches of dried ice cream. "Think you'll be all right alone here while I run in and clean up?"

"I'm sure I'll be fine. Take your time."

Not likely, Bolt thought. He went as fast as he could, returning with two iced coffees as well as some sandwiches and French fries for them to eat on the road. Cat looked pleased, which thrilled him beyond reason.

She rigged a cup holder from the cardboard box the sandwiches were packed in and they ate as they drove. If their hands brushed when they reached for the same fry, he pretended not to notice the contact. He had a hunch Cat was doing the same. Pretending everything was the same as it had been, pretending they were just two strangers thrown together against their wills and straining to be civil, pretending that everything they'd felt lying under the car had been left back there in the parking lot. They seemed to reach for the same fry an awful lot.

They didn't talk much, however, and Bolt was comfortable with that. When they finished, she gathered the trash into a bag and tossed it into the backseat. They continued to ride in silence. After a while Cat rummaged in the tote bag at her feet and pulled out the paperback book he'd seen in her hotel room last night. Bolt frowned at the sight of it.

"I've been thinking, that is, I've been meaning to tell you," he began, strangely tongue-tied. He glanced sideways and found her listening intently and felt even clumsier. "Look, I'm sorry I made fun of your book last night, all right? If that's what you thought I was doing. I didn't mean to."

"Forget it," she said, shrugging and opening the novel to where her finger had kept her place. "It's only a book."

"Is it?" he pressed.

She flipped it shut and made a show of looking at the cover. "Yup. Sure looks like a book to me."

"What about what you said last night? About me not understanding your philosophy of life?"

"Oh, that."

"That seemed to be all tied up with that book."

"Maybe. Sort of."

"Tell me about it."

"About my philosophy of life?" she countered, a startled laugh in her voice.

"About why you got so upset last night."

"I didn't get—"

"You know what I mean. Tell me, Cat."

She hesitated a few seconds. He could almost feel her intensity.

"I can't," she said finally.

"Can't?" he asked, darting her a skeptical look. "Or won't?"

"Don't want to," she replied matter-of-factly. "How's that?"

"That's honest, at least. Do you not want to tell me because you're afraid of my reaction?"

She laughed, an easy, unencumbered sound that seemed to fill Bolt's lungs when he drew his next breath and spread to every part of him.

"Yes," she said. "I'm afraid if I tell you, you'll laugh and then I'll be forced to reach over and strangle you. I think I'd look awful in a prison uniform." She patted her hips. "Horizontal stripes, you know?"

He didn't think she'd look awful in anything, but her casual manner of self-deprecation made him want to smile. Almost as much as he wanted to know everything there was to know about her. He conquered the urge to chuckle, slanting her a sober look intended to reassure.

"And if I promise not to laugh?" he asked.

Cat stared at him, holding a deep breath that finally came out as a resigned sigh.

"All right, you win," she said. "Pull up a seat and I'll tell you all about my philosophy of life. Just don't blame me if you fall asleep at the wheel."

For the next few minutes Bolt listened with growing incredulity as Cat revealed her philosophy, if you could call it that. Fantasy was more like it, revolving entirely around love. Love of the starry-eyed, at-first-sight, violins-in-the-background, fairy-tale variety, which anyone with a grain of common sense knew didn't exist outside the covers of novels like the one she was clutching.

My God, he realized as he listened in silence, the woman was even younger and more naive than he'd first thought.

Young and idealistic and absolutely convinced that living happily ever after was only a matter of finding the right person to love. Her soul mate, as she put it in a tone full of wide-eyed conviction. She was, he realized bleakly, everything he was not. Not any longer, anyway, if he ever had been.

The whole true-love thing was clearly a subject very close to her heart, and as she spoke, she became increasingly more animated. The silver charm bracelet on her right wrist tinkled merrily whenever she waved her arm. He'd noticed the bracelet at breakfast that morning, and Cat had happily held out her wrist to show it off to him. Scattered amidst glitter-encrusted stars and moon charms had been a tiny silver castle, a unicorn, a heart with a key attached and a magic wand. Cute, Bolt had thought at the time, decidedly more interested in the plate of bacon and eggs the waitress put in front of him. Now he could see there was definitely a pattern at work in her choice of charms and that they held tremendous significance for her.

A man who believed in cutting to the chase as quickly as possible, Bolt didn't need to ask her to elaborate on any of the points she was making with such passion. It was obvious to him that the noisy little bracelet summed up her philosophy better than words ever could.

"Destiny," she concluded with a dramatic toss of her head. The quick glance he slanted her way revealed that her eyes were shining with excitement. "In the end it all comes down to destiny."

"Let me get this straight," he said, feeling as if he should say something by way of response after pressuring her to talk about it in the first place. "You really believe that everyone is preprogrammed to be right for only one other person in the entire world and that those two people are destined to meet somehow?"

"Yes, exactly," she said, nodding vigorously. "There are other people with whom they could get along, of course, and even fall in love to an extent. But there's only one man or woman who's absolutely perfect for each of us."

"Mr. Right?" he said, amused.

"Or Ms. Right, depending."

"On destiny?"

"Exactly. Go ahead, laugh," she said, sounding totally unconcerned. "I can already tell that you don't believe in destiny. Do you?" she prodded.

Bolt shrugged evasively.

"Be honest," she ordered.

"Hell, Tiger, I'm not even sure I believe in love. Destiny? That's a real stretch."

Now she did look concerned. Concerned, puzzled, a little stunned.

"How can anyone not believe in love?" she asked faintly.

Bolt wasn't about to explain. Nor could he have explained what made him suddenly reach out, flick her charm bracelet and add, "Just for the record, I don't believe in fairy tales, either. Or happy endings."

"Why not?"

"Let's just call it personal experience."

"But don't you see?" she countered, leaning forward eagerly. "That proves my point. If you've had a bad experience with love, and trust me, most people have, it's because you were in love with the wrong person... or rather you thought you were. You might have believed you'd found the woman for you, but obviously you hadn't."

"Obviously," he concurred sardonically.

"You have to keep trying."

"What are you?" he asked, one eyebrow arching speculatively. "Cupid's assistant or something?"

She smiled enigmatically and leaned her head against the seat.

"How about you?" he asked. "Have you had a bad experience with love?"

"Not really. But I think that's only because I've done so much thinking about the whole thing and figured it all out before I had time to make too many painful mistakes."

"Pretty clever, Tiger. Some poor suckers spend their whole lives trying to get a handle on love."

She laughed, either missing his sarcasm or ignoring it. "Destiny. That's the key."

"Just a matter of waiting for your soul mate to come along. Right?"

"That's right."

"What if he comes along and you don't recognize him?"

"That could never happen: When I meet him, I'll know."

"Just like that? No secret sign? No matching birthmarks to look for?"

Again she laughed, clearly above being teased or rattled on the subject. She really believed this, he marveled. Hook, line and little silver key to her heart.

"Just like that," she said. "When the right man for me comes along, our eyes will meet—"

"Across a crowded room," he couldn't resist interjecting cynically.

"Across whatever, and..." She smiled faintly, her gaze drifting off to some point in the distance. "I'll know."

Yeah. Right, Bolt thought. And he was the next King of Siam. But no sense spoiling everything by telling her that.

They reached Baltimore late that night. Too road-weary to be fussy, they checked into the first hotel they came to that had rooms available. Again they were given adjoining rooms, this time on the twenty-sixth floor, and again Bolt insisted on inspecting Cat's room thoroughly before leaving her alone in it.

Once he was gone, Cat deliberated only a few seconds before unlocking the adjoining door from her side. She wasn't sure if Bolt did the same, or if he was bothered during the night by the bad dreams he'd told her about. She couldn't even have described the decor of her room except to say it was considerably more luxurious than the last one and had a comfortable queen-size bed where she fell instantly asleep and didn't see or hear another blessed thing until morning.

This time she awoke on her own. For a while she lay in bed, indulging in long, lazy stretches and wicked thoughts about kissing Bolt Hunter. A subject that had been on her mind in one form or another practically nonstop since yesterday.

He was, without question, the most passionate kisser of all the men in her romantic past. Okay, so it was an admittedly limited romantic past. Cat was pretty sure that even if she'd had a much more promiscuous youth, Bolt's kiss would still have ranked above all the rest.

She was accustomed to the sometimes clumsy, sometimes tentative, sometimes drunken kisses of college boys. What happened under that car with Bolt had been something else. He had kissed her the way a man kisses a woman whom he desires greatly. No pretense. No games. His intensity was contagious, because she'd been struck by none of her usual mid-kiss concerns, such as where to put her hands and monitoring where his hands were straying that perhaps they shouldn't be and hoping her breath mints had worked. She hadn't thought at all, only felt. And what she'd felt had scared the daylights out of her.

She'd felt him wanting her and she had wanted him back. That in and of itself didn't scare her. Just because she was a little short on actual experience didn't mean she was a prude. She knew all about sex and how natural and potent a force desire was. What alarmed her was that, for the first time ever, her body had been tricked into feeling it for the wrong man. So strong and compelling had been her urges lying under that car that if Bolt wasn't so blatantly, undeniably wrong for her, she might be tempted to think he was the one she'd been waiting for all her life and throw caution to the wind.

She shook her head in amazement as she swung from the bed and fumbled for the cord to open the drapes on the sliding glass doors. Lust. What a crazy sensation. She was going to have to tread carefully around Bolt for the rest of the trip. For both their sakes.

The sliding doors opened to reveal a small balcony with a view of Baltimore's famous Inner Harbor only a block away. From there Cat could see the sail and pleasure boats gliding across the still blue waters beneath a blazing late morning sun. She'd had no idea they were so close to the harbor and gave a small exclamation of delight.

"Quiet, damn it," came the growl from the next balcony. Bolt's balcony.

She quickly moved closer and peered over the shoulder-high privacy panel separating the two balconies. Bolt was sitting there, huddled in a white patio chair, shirtless except for the blanket wrapped loosely around his shoulders, his eyes closed.

"Bolt," she exclaimed. "What are you doing out here?"

He opened one eye and didn't look particularly happy to see her. "Oh, it's you making the noise. I should have known."

"Who did you think it was?"

"Damn blue jays. They've been yapping all night. I thought birds only sang in the morning or for their supper or something like that."

She chuckled and shook her head. "Are you telling me you slept out here all night?"

"Slept might be going a little too far. Tried to, though."

"But why? What's wrong with the bed in your room?"

He shrugged. "I don't like sleeping in strange beds."

"Oh." She hesitated. "More bad dreams?"

"Do me a favor, will you?" he asked, standing and stretching, the blanket falling to the chair. "Forget I ever mentioned anything about that. It was stupid."

"I don't think so. If the dreams bother you, then—"

"They don't. So just drop it, okay?"

His harsh tone left her little alternative. "Sure, consider it dropped."

"Thanks." He ambled to the railing near where she was standing.

Cat gazed out over the harbor. "Pretty sight to wake up to, isn't it?"

"Beautiful," Bolt murmured.

Something in his voice made her turn quickly. She found him looking at her rather than at the harbor, his expression lazy and assessing, his bare chest much too close. It was hard and muscled, with a wide band of sleek dark hair running from breastbone to the open waistband of his jeans. She felt the same shiver of awareness she'd felt yesterday when his hand caressed her cheek.

"I was talking about the view," she told him.

"I know." He smiled slowly. "I wasn't."

She turned away, doing her best to hide behind the convenient curtain of her windblown hair. The sudden skittering of her pulse alarmed and confused her. She knew what it meant to feel this way and was certain she shouldn't be feeling it for this man.

"What's the matter, Tiger?" he asked, leaning closer so that Cat swore she could feel as well as hear the low-pitched timber of his voice. "Do I fluster you?"

"No," she replied, forcing herself to meet his probing gaze with a careless smile. "Of course not."

"Good. I prefer playing on a level field."

"Playing what?"

He grinned and picked up the blanket from the chair. "What time are we supposed to be seeing this Buchanan guy?"

James Buchanan was a Baltimore shipbuilder whom Cat also intended to feature in her article on private libraries.

"He said to come by around two. His condo is on the Inner Harbor, and since we're so close we could probably walk there. Playing what?" she asked again.

"Walking sounds good. I'm going to clean up."

"Playing what?" she demanded.

He slid the glass door open and hesitated with one foot inside the room. "For keeps."

"For keeps," Cat repeated, scowling. "What the heck is that supposed to mean?"

But Bolt had already disappeared inside and closed the door, leaving her to figure it out for herself.

It wasn't difficult. The only explanation that made sense was that because she had allowed him to kiss her, Bolt had reacted in typical male fashion and jumped to the conclusion they were now involved in some sort of seduction game. A game that, he no doubt had further concluded, would culminate in a little roadside fling.

Cat gave a mighty hurrumph just in case he was watching as she returned to her room.

All right, so maybe she hadn't merely allowed him to kiss her. She had kissed him back, and with regrettable enthusiasm. But she hadn't allowed it to go any further. She never would have. And she certainly had not meant to send him the signal that she was available to him in any way. Hadn't the man understood a word she said in the car earlier?

Cat went still, staring into her suitcase in the middle of trying to decide between white slacks and a T-shirt or a pale flowered sundress. Or had Bolt listened all too well? Had he understood the point she'd been making and somehow, mistakenly, concluded that she was the woman for him and vice versa? No. Impossible. Cat dismissed the idea with a grimace. No one could make that big a mistake. What Bolt had on his mind had more to do with a momentary desire than destiny.

As dedicated as he was to his own men, Uncle Hank had warned her often enough about soldiers in general, about men who blithely went from woman to woman as carelessly as they moved from base to base. Men who subscribed to the belief that the next best thing to being with the one you love is to love the one you're with. For all she knew, that was what Bolt was thinking right this moment.

Well, he could think again. She had no intention of allowing what was a business trip for her to become his personal joyride. Oh, no. One thing she did have ample experience doing was saying no.

Bolt might be older and more worldly than the guys she usually dated, but no still meant no. He would have to understand that. The fact that Uncle Hank trusted him assured her that even if he didn't like being refused by her, he would accept it. Forewarned was forearmed, as her uncle was fond of saying. When the time came, if it ever did, she would simply make it clear to him that while his attentions were flattering, they were unwanted.

Nothing to it.

If Cat wasn't so certain she had everything under control, she never would have been able to relax enough to handle James Buchanan, who turned out to be a very crotchety old man and a most unwilling subject for her camera. Cat couldn't imagine why he had consented to the shoot in the first place until he revealed that he'd written a book about his experiences at sea and as a shipbuilder and that his publisher thought his inclusion in her article would be good publicity. Buchanan made it clear the moment she arrived at his spacious waterfront condo that he expected her to plug his book in her piece. However, even Cat's ready agreement did little to sweeten his disposition.

It was Bolt who ultimately managed to do that.

Once again Bolt voluntarily acted as her assistant. For what it was worth. Although he could hardly be blamed for the fact that, dressed in snug-fitting black jeans and a loose, collarless shirt with the sleeves rolled to the elbow, he was as much a distraction to Cat as a help. The white of his shirt emphasized his olive skin and black whiskers, giving him the air of a pirate, something that appealed greatly to her romantic, swashbuckler-loving nature. Obviously Bolt's notion of "cleaning up" didn't include shaving, Cat noted. She wasn't ordinarily a member of the five o'clock shadow fan club, but even so she found herself dwelling on the memory of what it had felt like to have his rough cheek rubbing against hers as he kissed her.

Her traitorous, wandering imagination only added to the difficulty of the session. She struggled to concentrate while Buchanan resisted her best efforts to get him to relax and open up about his extensive collection of books on subjects ranging from wildlife to coin collecting. Not until Bolt made an offhand reference to his military career did the man display interest in something other than getting the ordeal over with as quickly as possible. Cat was beginning to feel anxious when Mr. Buchanan unexpectedly revealed to Bolt that he had done a long stint in the Navy.

A predictable exchange of their impressions and opinions of the various branches of service followed, with Buchanan gradually doing more talking and less questioning of Bolt. Cat might as well have been one of the tall ship replicas perched on the study shelves for all the attention he paid her. Irritating as it was, this didn't seem to be the time to try to raise Buchanan's consciousness about women's equality.

Cat wisely chose to simply listen and make herself and her camera as inconspicuous as possible as she moved about, quietly getting even better shots than she had originally planned. She counted it a bonus that in the process she learned nearly as much about Bolt's past as she did about her subject. For the first time she understood how exciting, and dangerous, a life he had led.

The big payoff of the afternoon came when Mr. Buchanan—or Jim, as he insisted Bolt call him—revealed to them that he also had a collection of nineteenth-century volumes on British maritime history that he kept on specially built shelves in his bedroom. He barely hesitated before saying yes when Bolt asked if they might see and photograph them, as well. Cat was afraid to act too excited by the prospect, half-suspecting the old coot would change his mind if she did. So she held her breath and got great shots of his private sanctum, with its carved mahogany shelving and antique brass ship fittings. Shots that she already knew would be the cornerstone of her article.

"It was a major coup," she told Bolt several hours later, as they sat on the outdoor deck of one of the restaurants that overlooked the busy harbor. A short distance away, a jazz band provided background music for what had turned out to be a very nice evening.

After finishing at Buchanan's, they had strolled around the picturesque harbor area that had been reclaimed from the city's once run-down waterfront. Now it featured flower gardens and trendy shops and a gigantic indoor farmer's market. They explored all of it, sampling the frozen yogurt and sparkling water hawked from street corner pushcarts and stocking up on enough snacks—both healthy and unhealthy—to last for the rest of their trip.

Other than offering her a hand up after a short rest on a stone wall or placing his hand gently at the small of her back when they moved through the jostling crowd inside the farmer's market, Bolt didn't touch her. Gone was the heavy, seductive implication of that morning. His manner now was that of an old friend. She might as well be having dinner with Uncle Hank, she thought at one point, slightly disgruntled as she wondered if perhaps she had imagined the exchange on the balcony.

Dinner had been fresh seafood eaten on the deck, and now they were lingering over their drinks. Scotch straight up for Bolt and a frozen margarita for Cat. Her third, actually.

"To you," she proclaimed, lifting her half-full salt-rimmed glass in a salute. "It was a coup and I owe it all to you." She giggled. "Coup and you. That rhymes."

"It sure does. Which means," Bolt said in a dry tone as he removed the glass from her hand and stood, "that it's time to go."

"Go?" she echoed, her brows lowering in a frown. "Not home? I'm having too much fun to go home."

"I know. But trust me, if you stay and drink any more, you won't be having much fun in the morning. Riding with a hangover is a real bitch."

She wasn't so tipsy she couldn't appreciate the truth of that. With a resigned sigh, she got to her feet and allowed him to lead her outside.

She really didn't want anything more to drink. She liked it just fine right where she was, a little silly, a little mellow, her senses in overdrive, acutely receptive to the caress of the light breeze that blew off the water and rustled the planters all around them, carrying with it a faint tang of salt and a hint of roses. But while she didn't want anything more to drink, neither did she want the night to end. The thought of saying good-night to Bolt and returning alone to her room wasn't appealing at all.

"Can you walk?" Bolt asked as they left the well-lit harbor area and started up the tree-lined hill to their hotel.

"Of course, I can walk. Watch."

She took a few steps in front of him, aware of her hair moving on her bare back and the soft cotton fabric of her sundress swishing around her thighs. Aware, too, that he was watching every move she made.

"Good," he responded in that same dry tone. "No offense, but it's been a long day and I wasn't looking forward to carrying you up this hill."

Cat paused, allowing him to catch up. "It does seem a lot steeper now than it did coming down, doesn't it?"

"It's not, though," he assured her. "Here, give me that bag."

Ignoring her protest that she could carry her own bag, he took it from her and added it to the camera cases and shopping bag already slung over his shoulder. She was left with only the bunch of daisies she'd bought on impulse from a street vendor, now looking in desperate need of water.

"I want to carry it for you," he insisted.

Cat smiled at the sidewalk, secretly as thrilled as she had been when Matt Rivers had asked to carry her books home from the bus stop in junior high, and for pretty much the same reason. Even at the tender age of thirteen she'd understood it meant Matt had a crush on her.

Did Bolt have a crush on her? She giggled to herself. Probably not. He was too cool and self-contained to feel anything so romantic. No, Bolt's intentions were probably a whole lot more physical than Matt Rivers's had ever been.

Cat supposed she shouldn't feel flattered by that fact, let alone thrilled. But she did. As impossible and shameless as Bolt's intentions were, there was something irresistible about being the center of a sexy man's attention on a moonlit summer night.

Chapter Eight

There was no denying that Bolt was sexy as sin. Not in the way that usually appealed to her of course. Still, Cat reasoned as she plodded along, just because a woman preferred champagne didn't mean she couldn't acknowledge the appeal of a glass of ale. Dark ale.

She once again giggled quietly at her own humor, wondering if any of this would seem as funny in the morning. Unconsciously she began humming "One Hundred Bottles of Beer on the Wall." She felt like singing, but since she was beyond counting backward, humming was as much as she could handle.

"That's not what I think it is, is it?" Bolt asked as they neared the end of their climb.

"I don't know. What do you think it is?"

"That stupid song about falling beer bottles?"

"That's it! Congratulations. I'll bet you're great at playing Name That Tune."

He made a disgusted sound. "That's one tune I'd rather forget, if you don't mind. It brings back too many memories of long bus rides and school field trips."

"Bad memories, I take it?"

He shrugged. "Not particularly, so don't go putting your amateur therapist's cap on."

"Do I do that?"

"No, I guess you don't," he said, his voice softening a little. "I've known women who have, though...who think psychoanalysis is a parlor game."

"Me, too," she countered, grinning. "Don't you hate when that happens?"

He glanced at her, looking a little surprised. "Yes, I do."

She bumped him teasingly with her shoulder. Intentionally, though the look he gave her suggested he thought it might have been the result of drunken weaving.

"So," she said, mostly in an attempt to convince him otherwise with her scintillating conversation. "Where did you go to school?"

Still looking slightly surprised, he named a small town in the midwest and then a large state university. In response to her query about whether he'd enjoyed it, he shrugged again. "School was school. I did all right, played a few sports without becoming a superstar at any of them. When graduation rolled around, I was glad to get out and enlist."

They'd reached the hotel grounds and followed the well-lit path around to the front entrance.

"What made you decide to go in the Army?" Cat asked with real interest. "And Special Services at that?"

For a minute, she thought he might not answer.

"I guess," he said finally, speaking slowly, "I was looking for something I could do better than anyone else. I come from a big family of superachievers," he explained, his tone a blend of affection and irritation that she suspected was an accurate reflection of his attitude toward them.

"Growing up it seemed as if everything I wanted to do had already been done by one of them and done perfectly.

My brothers were all-state basketball and football. Tough acts to follow. Now one's a doctor and one's a lawyer. Another one has become richer than Midas by managing other people's money. My sister writes children's books, very successful ones, I'm told." He mentioned the name of an author Cat recognized instantly.

"But none of them lived life close to the edge, so you set out to prove yourself by doing exactly that. Is that it?" she asked, as perplexed as she had been all her life by what drove a man to spend his days risking his life for causes that seemed to her to be constantly shifting.

"More or less."

"From what you told Buchanan today, it sounds as if you were very good at it."

"There was a time when I thought so," he said shortly.

Cat entered the hotel lobby through the door he held for her. It was late and there weren't many people around. She turned toward the elevator.

It was impossible not to sense how Bolt had become increasingly more curt and remote as their conversation progressed. Yet curiosity made Cat persist.

"I couldn't help noticing how you sidestepped Buchanan's questions about your final mission," she remarked.

Silence, but the reflexive stiffening of his shoulders was reflected clearly in the shiny brass elevator doors.

"I take it that's another thing you don't talk about," she ventured.

"That's right."

She risked slanting him a grin. "Not with Buchanan, not with me, not ever, right?"

He glared at her reflection in the doors, the set of his full lips forbidding until a smile slowly claimed them as he realized he'd been lampooned with his own words. "You're a pretty fast learner," he drawled.

"For a girl?"

"Yeah." His lips curved even further upward. "For a girl."

The bell above their head sounded the arrival of the elevator and the doors slid open.

Cat hesitated before stepping inside. "Just one more question."

His eyes narrowed warily. "What is it?"

"Your sister...does she by any chance have a library?"

Chuckling quietly, Bolt shook his head and gently shoved her into the elevator. "I'll ask her."

"Thanks."

Somewhere around the third floor, Cat began humming once again.

Bolt cleared his throat meaningfully.

"Oops," she said. "Sorry. It's one of those songs that sort of sticks in your head."

"Exactly."

She stared at the indicator light above the door, tapped her foot, fixed the strap of her dress, which kept slipping down over her arm. She looked up to see Bolt staring at her shoulder with a strange expression. Around the seventeenth floor she did it again without thinking. The damn song had a life of its own, Cat decided as she caught sight of Bolt moving forward, a determined look in his eyes.

"That's it," he growled. "Looks like there's only one way to get you to stop."

He swung around so he was facing her, his back to the doors, his open hand aiming for her mouth to cover it and silence her. Cat knew that was his intention.

What she didn't know was why, in the instant before his hand reached her, she tossed her head back, lifted her chin and said, "Oh yeah? What way is that?"

Her words, her look, the way she waved the daisies under his nose, it was all a challenge. She knew that, too, just as surely as she knew that a man like Bolt would never be able to ignore a challenge, especially not one coming from a woman.

She just didn't know why she had to go and do it.

If she'd had time for second thoughts, she might have taken it back or else laughed and tried to pass it off as a joke. But Bolt didn't give her any time, just as he didn't give her any room to escape as he dropped the bags he was holding to the floor and put both hands on her shoulders to push her against the back wall of the elevator.

"This way," he murmured in a husky tone, and then his mouth was on hers and he was kissing her and suddenly Cat knew exactly why she had challenged him.

She had done it so that he would meet her challenge. So that he would kiss her.

She wanted this, she realized, even as her arms lifted to circle his neck. She had been wanting it all day, longer, even. She'd been wanting him to kiss her again ever since she had stopped him yesterday.

She shouldn't be doing this. Nothing had changed, she reminded herself, as his tongue explored her hungrily. He was still all wrong for her. This couldn't go anywhere. Certainly it could never lead to where his hands, moving feverishly over her back and shoulders, told her he thought they were headed. She had to tell him so, and fast.

And she would, she assured herself, as he kissed her chin and her closed eyelids, the rough scrape of his whiskers unbelievably exciting to her senses. Any second now the elevator doors would open and he would have no choice but to back off. Then she would catch her breath and tell him exactly how things were between them. But in the meantime, what was the harm in one little kiss?

Too late she understood that what Bolt was doing to her bore as much resemblance to a little kiss as a tricycle does to a locomotive. That was what he was like, sleek and powerful, moving relentlessly forward, sweeping her along for the ride.

Again and again his mouth wandered from hers, to nibble at the tender spot behind her ear, to bite, none too gently, at the side of her neck. Cat trembled and shivered and clung to him, her whole body shimmering with a kind of excitement she'd never before felt.

The tequila, she thought helplessly. But it wasn't the tequila making her feel this way, and she knew it.

Always, just when she thought she might surface from the bottomless pool of her own wakening desire, he returned to claim her mouth all over again, making protest impossible.

His lips were smooth and firm, by turns coaxing and demanding. He leaned into her, pinning her against the wall with the heat and weight of his body. The daisies were crushed between them, releasing their faint scent, a heady perfume to be inhaled with each labored breath.

It was madness. His tongue at her ear, making her whimper, his hard hips rocking against hers, his hands moving under the loose skirt of her dress, pushing it higher and higher so that she felt the air fed from the vent above on her bare legs, its coolness a sharp contrast to the warmth of his touch. Madness, all of it.

Worst of all was the slow ebbing of her determination to put a stop to it once and for all. In this area, at least, she'd always had all the self-control required to stop things from going too far. Now she understood that her strength had been more a result of the company she kept than of character. It wasn't hard to be good when you had no urge to be bad.

She had the urge now, though.

She opened her mouth to Bolt's kisses, using her tongue to caress his lips and the soft flesh inside, letting instinct be her guide where she was lacking experience. When he kissed the curve of her bare shoulder, nuzzling her with his stubbled jaw, she arched with the fierce pleasure that ripped through her. He stroked the back of her thighs and her hips twisted restlessly against him. With each stroke, every heartbeat, the urge to surrender pulsed harder inside her.

Still, resistance was a lifelong habit. Cat clung to the knowledge that the elevator doors had to open soon as if it was a lifeline. In a way it was. She held out no hope that Bolt might stop of his own accord, and she was rapidly losing confidence in her resolve to call a halt.

His fingers reached the bottom of her panties, the only thing she was wearing under her dress. He toyed briefly with the leg band, slipping one finger beneath it, then another. When he had worked his whole hand inside, he cupped her soft cheek and squeezed.

Cat gasped and her eyes opened wide with shock and delight.

Directly in front of her was the floor indicator. The number twenty-six was lit, she noted, indicating they were at their floor, but the doors remained tightly shut.

While she dazedly pondered that, Bolt slid his other hand inside her panties, as well, and pulled her against him. His warm breath dampened her throat, his chin scraped her delicate flesh.

She felt her knees quiver and the earth tilt, and still the doors remained shut.

"Bolt," she said as his fingers moved higher, playing at the top of the sensitive cleft at the base of her spine. A sensation as electrifying as lightning shot through her. She grabbed his shoulders tightly, shook her head and repeated his name.

Bolt caressed her lightly in the same place. "Mmm?" he murmured against her throat. "Is that okay?"

"Yes. No. The elevator. It's stopped."

"I know," he replied without lifting his head. "I stopped it."

"You did? You can do that? How?" Amazing man, Cat thought. She hadn't even seen him move.

He drew back just enough to meet her gaze with a heavy-lidded expression of amusement. "By hitting the stop button."

"Oh." She glanced at the control panel an arm's length away and the red button labeled Stop at the bottom. "Then why aren't the doors opening?"

He smiled at her, his amusement turning to something closer to fascination, and kissed the tip of her nose. "Because I hit the stop button," he said again. "Not the door open button. I thought you'd prefer privacy. Was I wrong?"

"No."

"Good."

He tipped his head; his mouth was damp and reddened, sexier than ever. She watched his lips part slightly as he lowered them to hers.

Gathering her senses, Cat planted a hand firmly on his chest, in the process delivering the fatal blow to her poor daisies.

"No, wait, Bolt, please. We have to stop."

He smiled and her heart turned over. "Why?"

"Because..." It was hard to think of all the reasons with him rubbing the small of her back the way he was. "Because..."

He touched her lips with his tongue.

"Bolt, please. We have to stop before this goes any further and you get the wrong idea and think I'm leading you on or—"

"If this is leading me on, keep it up. I'm more than willing."

"No, please, you don't understand." She tried to wiggle free and only succeeded in moving his hands from her backside to her hips. "I'm trying to tell you that we have to stop because... because I'm a virgin."

He peered down at her. It was as if, for a moment, he didn't believe her. Then he nodded as if that made perfect sense. She couldn't tell if his grim expression reflected annoyance or regret or a combination of the two.

"Okay, we'll take it slow then. I promise I won't hurt you, Tiger, if that's what you're worried about." His hands moved on her hips, echoing the promise with an appropriately mild caress. "I'll be gentle, and real slow, and I won't take you in a damn elevator no matter how badly I want to right this minute."

Cat shook her head. "No, you don't understand. Bolt, I'm a virgin and I intend to stay one until the right man comes along."

He cocked his head to the side, his gaze dark and seductive. "Maybe I'm the right man. How will you know unless you give it a chance?"

"I know," she said as gently as possible. "You're not."

His eyes narrowed. "You're serious."

Cat nodded.

He laughed roughly as he yanked his hands from under her dress. She self-consciously smoothed it over her thighs.

"I don't believe it," he said. "You're feeling the same thing I'm feeling right now. I know you are, and I know you want it as much as I do, so don't deny it."

"I'm not denying it. I don't understand the way I'm feeling, but I'm not denying it."

His smile was nasty. "Shall I explain it to you?"

"No," she replied, focusing her gaze on the elevator floor.

"No, of course not," he drawled angrily. "You'd rather go on waiting for some knight on horseback to come riding along...some damn Prince Charming you've never even met, right?"

She lifted her head defiantly. "Yes."

"Did it ever occur to you," he asked quietly, reaching out to cup her chin in his hand so she couldn't look away, "that no man is ever going to come along who'll be able measure up to your fantasy?"

"Yes, he will. Eventually he will. He has to," she continued, her emphatic tone edging toward desperation, "because I have no intention of settling for second best."

"I see," he snapped, releasing her to punch the button marked Door Open. The doors responded instantly and he wasted no time getting out, barely glancing at her as he added, "Thanks for the warning."

Stupid damn starry-eyed kid. That's what she was. And he was even worse.

After all, Bolt fumed as he lay alone on his bed, not even bothering to turn back the covers or kill the lights, he'd known all along that she was too young and too naive and too much trouble, and in spite of that he'd let himself be...attracted. Attracted, hell—mesmerized was what he was. Was, past tense. He might be to blame for what had happened in the elevator, but he never made the same mistake twice.

He'd come damn close tonight, however. He should never have gotten carried away like that. Besides being too young, she was also Hollister's niece. Add that to the inconvenient fact that he was supposed to be looking out for her, not compromising her virtue in an elevator, and any fool would come to the only sane conclusion possible...that Catrina Amelia Bandini was strictly a hands-off proposition.

He'd known that, he thought, cursing himself again while he was at it. Even before he kissed her the first time, he'd known it was a mistake. The speed and intensity of his response to that very public kiss had only reinforced his resolve not to let it happen again. From that moment on he had been committed to playing it safe for the duration of the trip. Or so he'd thought. The problem was that he'd never been very good at playing it safe, and when he was around Cat that was truer than ever.

He wanted her.

There was no denying it. He wanted her and he couldn't have her. It was as simple, and as complicated, as that.

It was also a new position for him to find himself in, he reflected with a large measure of irony. New and not at all pleasant. Not that he was such a Don Juan, he thought with a self-derisive grunt. It was simply that as a rule he wasn't interested in women who weren't interested in him. As far back as he could remember, he chose women who made it clear up front that they would be receptive to his attentions.

Even Angelina had approached him first. Bolt braced for the inevitable wrenching in his gut as he recalled her coming into his room in the middle of the night, wearing something bare and lacy that did next to nothing to hide her ample curves, whispering to him about how she was afraid to sleep alone.

He gave a harsh laugh. What goes around, comes around. With a vengeance. Now he was the one who was afraid to go to sleep, afraid to descend alone into the Netherlands between dream and memory. And all because of Angelina. No, he thought sharply, redirecting the blame and bitterness to where it rightfully belonged. It wasn't Angelina who was to blame for his messing up. She was what she was. He was the only one to blame for what had happened. He was the one who had forgotten what he'd been sent to Colombia to do, the one who had put desire and something he'd mistaken for love ahead of responsibility. He was the one who had let down his guard and caused the best friend he'd ever had to pay for the mistake with his life.

Bolt jumped from the bed and stalked outside, trying in vain to escape the memory of that night and the always hovering echo of the explosion that had killed his friend and, for all intents and purposes, ended his career in the military.

It would be hard to escape anything on a balcony as small as that one, he thought. In spite of the fresh air and the stars overhead, he felt closed in. Trapped. He let his gaze slide to the adjoining balcony and the room beyond. He was trapped, all right, between a rock and a hard place. With a hell of a lot of miles to go before he was free.

It was a long night, but at least he managed to get a few hours of sleep. Frustration must be a hell of a sedative, he decided in the morning, because the hours of sleep he'd gotten had left him feeling a whole lot better. Physically, at least. The rest was something he chose not to dwell on.

He showered and dressed, deliberately not shaving. His beard had marked Cat's soft skin the night before. He'd winced at the sight of the red lines and smudges on her delicate skin and had made a silent vow not to let it happen again. He hoped the whiskers would be a physical reminder to keep his hands off her.

He ordered breakfast from room service and placed a quick call to Cat's room to make sure she was up and advise her to do the same. He wasn't in the mood for chatting over croissants and coffee this morning. He wasn't in the mood for chatting, period. Something he made clear to his chipper little copilot within a few miles of hitting the road.

She seemed determined to act as if nothing had happened between them last night and he wasn't buying it. Something had happened, damn it. And neither one of them could afford to forget it. When she finally got the message that strained politeness was to be the order of the day, at least on his part, she gave up trying to make conversation and reached for her junk bag with an exasperated sigh that Bolt found particularly rewarding. No fun being frustrated alone. After doing her usual rummaging routine, she pulled her book from the bag, shot him a defiant look and proceeded to read in silence, leaving Bolt to his own thoughts.

He'd been so sure that was what he wanted. To be left alone. It wasn't long, however, before he realized that his thinly disguised sulking had backfired. When he was sitting this close to Cat, his thoughts made for dangerous company. Especially when she was dressed the way she was.

Today, he decided, was the best outfit yet. Or the worst, depending on how you looked at it. He found it very hard not to look at her, a major risk for a man driving at a high speed on unfamiliar roads.

Had she worn that outfit deliberately to drive him crazy? he wondered, slanting yet another glance her way from behind his sunglasses. Thank God for dark glasses. He was certain his eyes must have about popped out when she sauntered to the parking lot and said good morning. Too bad they didn't make body glasses, so he could hide all of his body's revealing responses to her.

Some guys might not find what she was wearing all that alluring, and he supposed on anyone else it might not even strike him that way, either. But as far as he was concerned, with Cat inside it, it beat satin and sequins hands down. For starters, she was wearing a tank top again. It must be some sort of fetish of hers, he decided. This one was white. Over the tank top she was wearing short black denim overalls, and under it she was wearing nothing at all. From his vantage point by her side, he was in a position to know that for a fact, and it was confirmed each time she lifted her arm or they hit a bump in the road. The overalls were short and snug, doing more to emphasize than hide her full breasts and rounded backside.

Overalls, he thought disgustedly. How in the world could overalls be sexy? Kids wore overalls, for Pete's sake. But then, compared to him, she was a kid, he reminded himself. He had to keep reminding himself. It was one way to keep from thinking about pulling off the road and un-snapping her straps and peeling down the denim bib covering her breasts. He wanted to find out if he could see through her white shirt almost as much as he wanted to slide his hands up inside it and find out if her skin there was as soft as it was everywhere else. He wanted *her*, damn it.

"You're frowning."

"What did you say?" he snapped.

"My goodness, you don't have to take my head off," Cat retorted.

"I wasn't trying to take your shirt ... I mean, your head off." He felt his neck growing warm and muttered something impolite under his breath. "I simply asked what you had said."

"And I simply said that you were frowning."

"So?"

"So nothing. It was an observation, that's all."

"Fine." He nodded toward her bag. "As long as you're in the mood to observe things, maybe you could fish the map out of that grab bag and see if you can observe where the turnoff is for Route 81 south."

"No problem."

The map Cat had been given, as well as his own in-tended route, called for them to follow Route 95 south from Baltimore to Florida. However, they weren't going to Florida, at least not directly. First they were going to Charlottesville, Virginia, so that Cat could visit some horse-breeding ranch that had been in the same family since be-fore the Civil War. Evidently the great-great-granddaughter of the original owner was an avid book collector and she had agreed to let Cat photograph her library.

After that they were going to Charleston, South Caro-lina, and then Savannah Georgia, and on to some small town called Dixie Union. Bolt didn't even want to think about how long all that was going to take, how many hours and days of being cooped up in this car together, his hor-mones stuck in overdrive like some drooling adolescent. In his current mood, he could only handle one challenge at a time. Right now he was thinking about Charlottesville and how to get there without going through Washington, D.C., at rush hour.

Judging from his quick look at the map that morning, Route 81 was the best choice. Taking it would mean adding a hefty number of extra miles, but at the same time it would virtually eliminate the possibility that he might find himself stuck in traffic for hours, with only a head full of regrets and a woman he couldn't touch for company. He seemed to recall that the turnoff was coming up sometime soon and he was determined not to miss it. The way he was feeling, every minute counted.

Cat quickly located the turnoff on the map and told him that according to her estimation it was coming up in about three miles. She was right on the button. Yesterday, he would have smiled and told her she was a darn good navigator. Today he just grunted his thanks and kept his eyes on the road ahead.

"Can I ask you a question?" she said once they had safely made the route change.

He nodded without looking at her.

"Do you intend to drive the rest of the way to Florida without talking to me?"

"I talked to you," he replied. "I asked you to check the map."

"That's right, you did. Let me rephrase. Do you intend to drive the rest of the way without talking to me except to ask mc to chcck the map or pass the salt or hand you the money for the next toll? Or, to put it even more directly, do you intend to go on pretending that nothing happened last night?"

He glanced at her briefly. "Nothing did happen," he reminded her, tossing that hollow technicality at her in the hopes of short-circuiting a discussion he didn't want to have.

"It sure felt to me like something was happening," she said softly.

Bolt managed a grim chuckle, but his pulse leapt wildly. "Had a change of heart overnight, have we?"

"No," she said, her matter-of-factness one more blow to his ego. "My heart still feels the same. It's the rest of me that's having a problem dealing with this."

"Join the club," he muttered.

"I mean that I'm having a hard time understanding what's happening between us."

"Us?" he echoed, shooting her an incredulous look. "You can't understand what's happening between us?"

She looked both flustered and annoyed. "I mean I don't know why it's happening. Why I feel the way I do."

"Oh, that. Maybe I can help you figure it out. It's happening because I'm a man and you're a woman and that's the way nature wants it. Any of this ring a bell from Biology 101?"

"There's no need to be sarcastic. It's obvious that we—"

He broke in. "Back up. There is no 'we' around here. There's you over there and there's me over here and that's the way it's going to stay. Got it?"

She folded her arms, staring at him as if he was lint on her favorite sweater, and said nothing.

"Think of us as strangers," he continued, "which is actually pretty much what we are. Strangers thrown together on a tour bus or as sole survivors of a plane crash or—"

"Trapped together in an elevator?" she interjected.

He glanced at her sharply, then grinned. "Whatever turns you on . . . sweetheart," he drawled with distinct sarcasm. "The key thing is to remember that we're strangers. Strangers who got a little carried away one night and almost made a big mistake. That's not going to happen again, and one way for us to make sure of that is not to rehash our feelings about it ad nauseam. Got it?"

"Yes. And for the record, in the future you can skip asking me if I've got it every other minute. When I don't get something I'll let you know. Got it?"

"Perfectly."

It was going to be a long ride to Charlottesville, Cat decided as she opened her book and pretended to read. Long and silent. She wasn't sure she could ride for hours without talking. Especially not when the turmoil of her thoughts was making her crazy. Ever since last night she'd been plagued by regrets and second thoughts, half the time wishing she had never goaded Bolt into kissing her in the elevator and the other half wishing she had never made him stop.

All her life she'd wanted one thing above all else, to meet and fall in love with the man who was destined to be her soul mate, the one man she would love forever. Now she found herself wanting something totally at odds with that dream. As shocking as it was, she had to acknowledge the fact that she wanted to make love to Bolt, a man who, when you came right down to it, was more nemesis than soul mate. As inner conflict went, it wasn't a simple one to reconcile.

It might be a little easier, she seethed to herself, if she could talk over the matter with someone. Unfortunately the only someone available for the foreseeable future made it clear he had no intention of discussing the subject of their thwarted dalliance, or anything else, for that matter.

Her hunch proved right. The drive to Charlottesville seemed endless. The roundabout route Bolt insisted on taking made it longer still, but she thought it wise not to point that out to him. At least he proved to be gentleman enough to stop periodically without being prompted. Although, given a choice, Cat might have preferred a chance to remind him. At least then she'd have an excuse to speak and would know for sure that her vocal cords hadn't atrophied during the day.

They arrived in Charlottesville in the early evening, and though Cat wouldn't have thought it possible, the night that followed was even longer and more miserable than the ride there. Bolt pulled into a motel in the historic district without asking her opinion. They registered and he handed her one of the room keys. He didn't follow his usual pattern of suggesting dinner plans, and Cat was reluctant to risk asking and being told to her face that he preferred not to break bread with strangers.

Strangers, she fumed, as she stood by and waited for him to pronounce her room safe. In spite of the fact that he had nothing to say to her, he still insisted on checking it out before leaving her alone. All part of the macho-butthead syndrome common to the military species, she told herself with acrid amusement. The male counterpart to PMS. This time as she waited for him to run through his paces she found herself wishing something scary would jump out from behind the shower curtain and grab him. It was actually the latest in a string of nasty things she'd wished on him throughout the day and, she told herself, only a fraction of what the man deserved.

Naturally no monster appeared to grab him and he started to leave.

As he reached the door she suddenly ran out of self-control. "So what do you plan to do now?" she asked, trying to sound nonchalant rather than desperate.

He turned to her. "What do I plan to do? Let's see, I think I'll order something from room service, eat, then try to convince myself that I really can be trusted alone with you before I have to call your uncle and give him a progress report on that subject."

Surprise flickered in Cat's eyes. "I didn't know you called to check in with Uncle Hank."

He shrugged. "He worries about you."

"I know. He shouldn't."

Bolt's smirk revealed his opinion on that issue, but he said nothing. "Anything you want me to tell him for you?"

"Yes," she replied. "Tell him I'm still furious with him for butting in and I'm not talking to him...at least not until I get home."

That was pure bravado. Actually, at that moment she was ready to talk to the wallpaper just to hear the sound of her own voice.

"I think I'll just tell him you send your love and let him figure the rest out on his own," he said dryly, turning to leave.

"Bolt, wait," she called after him.

He paused, his hand on the doorknob.

"For what it's worth," she told him, "I trust you."

He gave her a pained look. "Thanks, that's just what I wanted to hear. Stay put, all right?"

He slammed the door behind him.

Cat tossed her bags in the corner of her room and collapsed on the bed.

Well, she'd tried to make amends. It wasn't her fault he was as approachable as a porcupine. What a stiff, she thought irritably. An automaton, just as she surmised from the very start. If not for his gorgeous smile and intriguing golden eyes and incredibly sexy body, the man would have absolutely nothing going for him. Except, perhaps, she amended silently, the way he had of making her feel warm all over with just a look. And his way of listening when she talked, as if what she had to say was the most important thing going on in his life at that moment.

So he was a good listener. What good did it do her if he refused to let her talk to him?

Sighing, she rolled to her side and reached for the room service menu. She stared at it disdainfully without even opening it to look inside. And exactly where did he get off telling her to stay put, anyway? Just because he wanted to hole up in his room for the night was no reason she had to follow suit. Sure she was tired, and longing for nothing more than a hot shower and a soft bed, but she wasn't his clone any more than she was his responsibility. No matter what delusions he held to the contrary.

She could look after herself, and if she wanted to go out for the evening, she would. She had no qualms about dining alone. If she had made the trip by herself as she'd intended, she wouldn't have had anyone along to keep her company over dinner. She wouldn't have hesitated to go to a restaurant by herself then and she wouldn't now. If she felt like it. Afterward she might even go shopping or to a movie if she was in the mood for one.

But she wasn't making the trip alone, she conceded, her spirits sinking a little lower. Through no choice of her own, she was making the trip with Bolt, and much to her chagrin, she'd grown accustomed to having the big oaf around.

After years of struggling for her independence and the freedom to do what she wanted to do when she wanted to do it, she suddenly had absolutely no desire to see a movie by herself. Resigned to the inevitable, she turned on the lamp and flipped open the menu.

Everything looked a little brighter in the morning, for her at least. A good night's sleep left her feeling invigorated and ready to make a fresh start. One look at Bolt, however, convinced her that he didn't come close to sharing her improved mood. He met her in the lobby at noon as planned, looking like an escapee from a film noir, a man in desperate need of a friend and a shave, not necessarily in that order.

"Growing a beard, I see?" she observed brightly.

He scowled and rubbed his jaw as if to find out what the heck had given her that crazy idea.

"No," he replied. "I just never shave on the road." His smile bordered on being a sneer. "I figure it's my reward for being here."

Cat deemed it best not to give him an opening to tell her why he felt he deserved a reward for it. Instead she smiled sweetly and handed him the directions to the DelMar Horse Ranch, which Barbara Delmartin had told her was located a short distance west of the historic city. She had suggested that Cat come around one in the afternoon, and from talking with her beforehand, Cat expected to spend about three hours touring the ranch and getting the shots she needed. She explained all that to Bolt as they walked to the car.

"How about if I come back for you at four, then?" he asked as he opened the door for her.

"Come back for me?" Her startled gaze followed him as he circled to the driver's side. "Aren't you going to stay and help?"

"Not this time," he told her. "I have some things of my own to take care of." He glanced at her with a bland expression that didn't fool Cat for a second. "You keep reminding me that you can take care of yourself, so I'm sure you can handle this on your own.''

"You bet your..." She paused and gathered her composure. "Yes, of course I can."

She could handle it by herself, all right. After all, she'd been using a camera long before Mr. Bolton Hunter came barging into her life, unannounced and unwanted. If she'd sounded upset it was simply because, just as she'd grown accustomed to having him around all the time, she'd also gotten used to having him there while she was working. It wasn't so much the help switching cameras and moving things around she would miss, although she'd already come to count on it. It was more the luxury of having him there to bounce ideas off and to help entertain the subject while she went about getting the right shots. While technically she didn't need him there, she couldn't help wondering how she would she have fared with James Buchanan if she hadn't had Bolt by her side.

His decision not to come along caught her off guard. Cat was surprised and hurt by it. Her basic sense of fairness told her that she was probably no more surprised or hurt than Bolt had been when she called a sudden halt the other night in the elevator. She might have felt resentful, as well, if she had any sense that he was refusing to come along to the ranch simply out of retaliation. She was sure that wasn't his motive. Not that she bought for a second his excuse about having other things to take care of. What other things could he possibly have to do in Charlottesville? No, she understood that he was simply trying to avoid being around her as much as possible.

His retreat, both emotionally and physically, was best for both of them. She understood that, but as the day wore on she decided that she didn't like it much. The Delmartin clan was friendly and made her feel instantly at ease, but she still missed Bolt. She missed his smile. She missed his sometimes dumb, sometimes brilliant suggestions about lighting and placement and she missed his teasing comments.

From time to time during the long afternoon, she was struck by a sudden memory of lying in her bed the night before and the night before that and missing him even more ardently than she did now, in the bright light of day. Alone in her bed she had missed the way he smelled and the way his skin tasted when she touched him with the tip of her tongue and the way he made her feel when he touched her.

What did that mean? She wrestled with that question and the obvious answer to it even as she exclaimed over the Delmartins' new foal and scanned the library shelves to select books to pile on the coffee table in the foreground of a shot of Barbara. It meant that she wanted to make love with Bolt, of course. She wasn't so naive she didn't know that, no matter how he had chosen to misunderstand her confusion in the car yesterday.

It could be simply a case of lust. It had to be that, she told herself firmly, and nothing more. Unfortunately, the powers of reason kept throwing up arguments against that theory. She'd dated lots of appealing men, guys she liked and enjoyed being with. A few to whom she had been very, very attracted at the time. But she'd never felt this . . . this craving that seemed to build from within and crowd out everything she thought she knew and wanted and needed in life.

Lust. She swallowed hard and steadied her hands as she got the shot of Barbara with her books. The last shot of the afternoon, she thought gratefully. Lust. Maybe that's all it was. And maybe if she kept reminding herself of that she'd eventually believe it and snap out of it.

Lust. Meaningless, forgettable lust.

But why now? And why, of all the men on earth, did she have to feel it for this one?

Chapter Nine

"Next stop, Charleston," Bolt announced as they approached the entrance to the freeway the following morning.

He seemed to be in a slightly better mood today, Cat observed. It was really a shame she had to ruin it.

"Uh, not exactly," she said.

He shot her an impatient look. "What do you mean, not exactly? I have the list right here." He pulled it from his jeans pocket and recited from it without looking at it. "Baltimore, Charlottesville, Charleston. Then Dixie Union, wherever in Hades that is, and home. Isn't that the list you gave me?"

He pushed it at her. Cat gave it a perfunctory glance.

"Yes, it is. But there's been a slight change in plans. An addition, so to speak."

"Sorry," he retorted. "We had a deal. No changes, no additions."

"I'm sorry, too," Cat replied, feeling her back stiffen as if for battle. "But I really have to insist on making this particular stop. It's very important to me."

"And getting home as fast as possible is very important to me."

"It will only take one extra day."

"No."

"How can you say no without even knowing what it is?"

"Easy. No. In fact it's easier if I don't know what it is, so don't tell me."

"You're unbelievable. How could the same man be so reasonable back in Vermont and so pigheaded now?"

He shrugged. "Change in altitude?"

"If you ask me, a change in attitude is more like it. Your attitude, to be specific."

"Is there some hidden meaning in there? If so, you did such a good job of hiding it that I don't know what you're talking about."

"Then let me spell it out for you. I think you're being stubborn about this now for the same reason you've spent the past two days sulking . . . because I refused to go to bed with you."

He glanced at her, his lips a narrow line. "That was a cheap shot. And I haven't been sulking. Hell, I even told you I was sorry about what happened."

"You never did."

He looked surprised, then sheepish. "I didn't? I meant to. It's the truth—I am sorry."

"Sorry about what happened or what didn't?"

"Both, I guess," he admitted with a grudging twist of his lips that was as close to a smile as she hoped to get. "Mostly I'm sorry because I never should have put you in that position. Not that it really matters. Being sorry doesn't change the way I feel."

"How do you feel?" she asked quietly, knowing she shouldn't.

His grip tightened on the wheel as he shot her a sardonic look. "How do you think? I want you as much now as I did the other night. Maybe more. But I'm dealing with it, okay? And my way of dealing with it is to just pull back completely.''

"You don't have to do that. There's no reason we can't—''

He cut her off. "Be friends? Buddies? Trust me, that's not possible. This is my way of handling things, the only way I know, so leave it alone.'' He almost smiled at her again. "Okay?''

"Okay.'' She tucked her hair behind her ear nervously. "And I'm sorry I accused you of...you know, trying to get back at me for saying no.''

He nodded.

"But I was desperate.'' She wet her lips. "Bolt, this stop I want to make is really important to me.''

Bolt sighed.

"I know it will mean arriving in Florida a day later than we planned and going a little out of our way, but—''

"How little out of our way?'' he interrupted to ask.

"Just a couple of inches. I checked the map before we left.''

"In miles, Cat,'' he said, sounding as if he was exasperated, but weakening. "Tell me how far in miles. Better yet, just tell me where it is you want to go this time.''

"Virginia Beach,'' she said and held her breath waiting for his response.

It wasn't long in coming, or much of a surprise.

"Virginia Beach,'' he shouted. "Do you realize that's all the way back on the coast?''

"Most beaches are,'' she agreed, feeling a little less nervous now that he was shouting. Years of dealing with Uncle Hank told her that from this point it was simply a matter of holding on and riding out his temper, and she would be on her way to getting what she wanted. "Charleston is on the coast, too.''

"But at a different angle from where we are now.''

"It's the same coast,'' she reminded him, rolling her eyes.

"But miles apart. Literally. Take my word for it.'' He pushed air from between his lips in a disgruntled rush.

"Why couldn't you have told me you wanted to go to Virginia Beach while we were in Baltimore...which is also on the east coast, in case you've forgotten?"

"Because I only decided I wanted to go there after we got to Charlottesville. Besides, if I had told you in Baltimore we still would have had to drive inland to get to Charlottesville. If you look at the map you'll see it's like traveling in a big triangle."

"A triangle, huh? Then why do I feel like I'm going in circles all the time?" he demanded, his voice dripping sarcasm.

"I don't know," Cat retorted. "Maybe your equilibrium is off from lack of sleep."

"I'm sleeping just fine," he told her. "But thanks for your concern just the same." He shook his head. "Virginia Beach."

"Actually, it's a small town south of Norfolk just before you reach Virginia Beach. I wrote out the directions and route numbers for you."

She held out the paper she'd written them on.

Bolt slid his glance from the road to the paper, then to meet hers. Finally he took the paper from her hand. Cat sighed inwardly with relief. He was going to do it. She was on her way to Baxter, Virginia, a place she'd never thought she'd want to visit.

"So who's in...Baxter, is it?" he asked, darting a glance at the directions in his hand.

"Right. Baxter."

"Who's in Baxter that we have to go out of our way to see?"

Taking a deep breath, Cat replied, "My parents."

His head twisted in her direction, his expression one of astonishment. "But I thought—"

"I don't mean we're going to see my parents," she explained hurriedly, before he had to ask any awkward questions. "I'm sure my uncle told you that they were killed in an accident when I was five."

"The general told me they died when you were very young and that he raised you after that. That's about it."

He slanted her a self-effacing smile. "I guess he doesn't like to talk much about personal stuff any more than I do."

"Don't think it's escaped me that the two of you have a number of personality defects in common," Cat told him. "I wouldn't be surprised to find out he was your role model."

He shrugged. "I figured I could do worse."

"You figured right," Cat agreed, her tone softening as a small smile claimed her mouth. "We've had our ups and downs, but Uncle Hank is the best."

"Don't look now," he advised, his deep voice becoming conspiratorial, "but I think we may have found something we agree on."

"I won't tell anyone if you don't."

"Deal."

Their laughter blended and was carried away on the breeze that cooled their faces and whipped Cat's hair no matter how tightly she anchored it in a ponytail. The tangles were the price she paid for the joy of riding with the top down. All of a sudden the strain of the past couple of days seemed to be gone, and she was a bit jolted by how relieved and happy that made her.

"So tell me what connection your parents had to the town of Baxter," he said.

"The accident that killed them happened there," Cat replied, swallowing hard on the lump of painful emotions that just the mention of her parents' tragic death inevitably brought to her throat. "At a two-lane intersection outside of town. They were on their way to do a show in Virginia Beach when they evidently got lost on the back roads. It was late at night and raining and another car turned and hit them head-on. They both died instantly."

"I'm sorry. I shouldn't have forced you to go dredging up bad memories. I know how that feels."

"It's all right, really. If I'm going there to learn more about the accident, I have to expect to talk about it. And I can't go choking up every time I do."

"Sounds to me like you already know most of the crucial details. What more do you hope to learn by visiting Baxter?"

"I didn't mean learn in that way. I do know all the facts and details about the accident itself. Uncle Hank has always been very up front and direct with me about anything concerning my parents. If I had questions, he answered them." She smiled affectionately. "And boy, did I have questions."

"That's only natural. They were your parents. And you don't have any brothers or sisters, right?"

"No." An old familiar sadness touched her. "My mother was pregnant when she died, but I was their first and only up to that point. Uncle Hank is really all the family I have . . . and vice versa."

"Like I said a few minutes ago, both of you could do a lot worse."

"I suppose. When I was little, I would sometimes pretend that I had a sister somewhere who for some reason no one ever knew about, or else that the baby had miraculously survived the accident, but they could never get hold of Uncle Hank to tell him and that one day she would just show up on our doorstep." She smiled. "Of course, she never did."

"Funny," Bolt said, his tone an ironic counterpoint to her wistfulness, "I sometimes used to pretend that someone showed up at my door to tell us that all my brothers and sisters really didn't belong there and take them all away. Then I would get to have my own room, a bike that wasn't second or third hand, my own dog, not to mention my folks' undivided attention once in a while."

"I had my own room and dog and bike and much too much of my uncle's undivided attention for my taste." She grinned, one eyebrow arched mischievously. "Is it too late to trade childhoods?"

"Much too late for one of us, Tiger," he replied, a rueful note in his voice. "Hell, it's been a long time since I thought about those days."

"You may not have thought so at the time, but you were very lucky to be part of a big family that loved you."

"I guess it's the old 'the grass is always greener' scenario, huh?"

"Except that the grass really was greener at your house," she insisted. "It's always better to have two parents and brothers and sisters, people who care about you and share your memories. And your dreams."

"I know. I joke about it, but I know you're right. I remember going home every Christmas and how good it felt to be back in that narrow bed in my old room, with my brother snoring away in the next bed, his radio tuned to a station I hated." He paused thoughtfully. "I spent a lot of time in a lot of ugly places, wondering if I was ever going to see that room again."

"You said you remembered going back home for Christmas as if you don't go any longer," she remarked, curious.

"I don't. I couldn't make it home one Christmas a couple of years back. I was stuck in a hospital with a broken back, and since then I . . . I just don't go, that's all."

"A broken back . . ." Cat winced. "That hurts just to think about. How—"

"An explosion," he said before she finished the question. "I didn't move quickly enough. That's the whole story."

She doubted that, but she'd learned enough about him not to press.

"So your back healed and you haven't been home for Christmas since," she said, taking an only a slightly less nosy approach to finding out more about him. "Is there some sort of trouble between you and your family?"

"Nope. The trouble's all with me."

He flashed a grin that said he knew he'd piqued her curiosity and had no intention of satisfying it. Cat resisted the impulse to stick her tongue out at him. She had a suspicion he considered her too young to be taken very seriously, and she refused to add to that impression. She wasn't a child and she didn't want Bolt to think of her as one.

"Now tell me what it was like growing up with old Lucifer in charge," he urged.

"Like perpetual boot camp," she retorted.

He laughed. "No surprises there."

"Actually, he was wonderful to me. He still is...in spite of a tendency to be overprotective."

"Just one of those little faults that add to his charm," he suggested wryly.

"Yeah, right. At least I can laugh at it now. Let me tell you, at sixteen I found him a whole lot less charming. But then," she continued with a philosophical shrug, "I suspect that's true of all sixteen-year-old girls and their fathers. I may call him Uncle Hank, but for all practical purposes, he's been my father for seventeen years."

"It couldn't have been easy for the general, either," Bolt remarked. "Having to step into the role of father with no experience and no warning."

"I know. And I can't imagine anyone doing a better job. He took care of all my physical needs, of course, a home and schooling, but he also took care of the hundreds and hundreds of other little things that it usually takes a mother and father to handle. Things that someone else who had a bratty niece dumped on them might have ignored." Her smile was rueful. "He may not have handled all of those little things the way I wished he would at the time, but then, I'm sure my parents wouldn't have, either. Uncle Hank always made me feel loved and protected and wanted, and that's what counts."

The traffic was light and Bolt was able to take his eyes off the road long enough to give her a reassuring smile. "I don't know how bratty you were to start with, but the finished product is a credit to you both. I think he deserves to be named father of the year."

"Thanks," she murmured.

She was blushing. Cat couldn't believe it. Of all the dumb things to blush about, she thought, searching for something to say to ease the silence that followed his unexpected compliment.

"He wasn't merely a great father," she said. "He was a great substitute father, and I think sometimes that's much tougher. He was great at it because he never forgot that he was a substitute and he never let me forget it either.

"Uncle Hank is the one who's kept my parents' memory alive for me all these years," she continued. "He talked to me about them when everyone else was afraid to bring up the subject around me. He answered all my questions about the accident and he would tell me stories about my mother when she was a little girl. I liked his stories better than all the fairy tales in my books. He told me about how she always wanted to be a dancer and about how she met my father and joined his act, instead."

"What sort of act?"

"Magic," she said, the word alone capturing all the wonder and excitement of her memories. "He called himself the Inexplicable Bandini."

"Catchy," Bolt said without much enthusiasm.

Cat laughed. "What can I say? He was a child of the sixties and you know how that was."

"Please, I'm not that old."

"How old are you?"

"Thirty-five," he said.

"Thirteen years older than me," she countered after rapidly doing the calculation. "My father was twelve years older than my mother."

"No kidding?" he said without expression.

"Anyway, my mother was a dancer at the time they met, an aspiring dancer, that is. They met at an audition in New York and fell in love. She wanted to join his act and her parents put their foot down." She pursed her lips, her head tipped to one side. "Feet down? Whatever. They were both teachers and, according to Uncle Hank, they thought having a dancer for a daughter was bad enough, they weren't about to have one who earned her living by getting sawed in half nightly."

"I can't say as I blame them for that."

"I can. When you're as much in love as my parents were, nothing else matters."

"So did your mother go ahead and join the act in spite of their opposition?"

"Of course," she replied, puzzled that he even had to ask. "I told you, they were in love. They ran away and got married and the rest, as they say, is history." Her exhilarated expression clouded.

"At least it should have been history," she amended. "It would have been except for the accident. The job in Virginia Beach was their last road appearance before they started a big run in New York City. My father had told Uncle Hank just a few weeks before he died that their agent had almost closed a deal for them to appear at Radio City Music Hall. Can you imagine? My father, the Inexplicable Bandini, at Radio City Music Hall?"

She smiled, staring without seeing at the road ahead. "Uncle Hank says he was as good as Copperfield. Maybe better. If he had lived . . ." She faltered, blinking back the tears that were stinging her eyes. "You know what I wish most?" she asked softly.

"What?" Bolt countered, his voice low, almost rough.

"I wish they had used camcorders back then the way they do today. I wish I had a tape of them, of their act." She grinned suddenly. "I've always had a hunch that Uncle Hank got it wrong, that any parents of mine would be closer to Penn and Teller than Copperfield."

"That would help explain the inexplicable," he said.

"Ooh," she groaned. "Bad joke."

"What can I say? Driving does that to me."

"How about letting me take a turn?"

He shook his head. "Thanks, but I'm okay for now. I'll tell you when I need a break."

"The problem is you don't tell me often enough. You keep going until you're exhausted and have no choice but to take a break. It would be much fairer if we did as I suggested and worked out a schedule to drive in shifts."

"Are you finished?" he asked, acting as if he'd heard it all before, several times, which of course he had.

"Yes."

"Good. Because you still haven't explained to me why you want to go to Baxter all of a sudden."

"It's not easy to explain. It's sort of a...feeling that I've been getting." She paused while she searched for the right words. "I never thought about going there before now. I never thought I would want to see the place where they died, but all of a sudden, I do." She shrugged self-consciously. "Like I said, it's a feeling I have. Maybe it's because it's nearby."

She caught his sardonic glance and smiled ruefully as she added, "Relatively speaking, that is. All I know is that something inside is telling me I should at least see it once. I want to stand at the spot where it happened, maybe bring some flowers. Sort of a tribute. Is that dumb?"

Bolt shook his head. She saw the cords in his throat flex as he swallowed hard, and she was touched by that small sign that he understood how she was feeling and what this side trip meant to her.

"No, it's not dumb at all," he told her. "The opposite, in fact. I think it takes wisdom, and a lot of courage, to face up to the painful moments in your past. So do you know exactly where the accident happened?"

She shook her head. "No. I could always call and ask Uncle Hank, but he'll only worry more about me if I tell him what I'm planning to do. I've thought about it, and it seems to me that the local newspaper office might be able to help. That is, if they still keep copies of the paper back that far. I'm sure something must have been written about the accident at the time."

"I would think so, too. If not, the police should still have the accident report on file somewhere. Seventy-eight, was it? They might have it on microfilm."

"I hadn't thought of that. I'll start with the newspaper and if that doesn't work out, I'll check with the police. Thanks for the suggestion."

"No problem."

"And thanks for agreeing to take me to Baxter. I mean it, Bolt. I know I'm not in any position to go asking you for favors and expecting you to say yes and—"

"Quiet." He reached over and placed his finger against her lips to enforce the command. It worked. As soon as he touched her, Cat's throat went dry and she couldn't have continued even if she had been able to remember what she wanted to say. "Like I said, it's no problem."

Not for him, maybe, but she'd never before in her life grown weak when a man touched her. Neither had she craved and dreaded a man's touch at the same time. It was a big problem as far as Cat was concerned, and she had no idea what to do about it.

Baxter, Virginia, was not at all what she had expected. At the risk of being macabre, if she'd had to envision a proper place for her parents' exciting, glamorous lives to come to their premature end, it would have been somewhere in New York City, Times Square or Rockefeller Center when it was awash in bright lights for the holidays, somewhere as inspiring and unique as they were. Certainly not the parched, run-down outskirts of a hole-in-the-wall town like Baxter.

Even if it did have to happen in a small town, she would have preferred someplace worthy of a Norman Rockwell depiction. Someplace with a town square bordered by flowers and where the houses were painted white with shiny black shutters. Baxter was more of a rusted-out-pickup-parked-in-the-driveway, pile-of-old-tires-in-the-side-yard kind of place. Cat found the sight disheartening.

It made her even sadder, and more unsettled, to drive through what passed for the downtown area, a string of about six run-down shops and several boarded-up storefronts. It disturbed her to think that this might have been the last sight her mother and father saw. Seventeen years was a long time, of course, but something told her Baxter was the sort of place where nothing ever changed much.

She kept her fingers crossed that this held true for the newspaper staff, as well. Maybe she would get lucky and find someone who remembered the accident and could give her directions to the site. She and Bolt located the newspaper office without too much trouble. It was actually a branch office of the county paper, housed in a two-story brick building about a block from the shopping area.

Bolt stopped in front and shifted the car into park. "Are you going to be all right?" he asked her.

"Yes." Something in his manner gave her a sudden sinking sensation in her tummy. "Aren't you going to come with me?"

He shook his head. "I don't think so, Tiger. This is pretty personal and if you don't mind, I don't want to get any more personally involved than I already am."

Cat chewed her lip. She could hardly argue with his reasoning when she was the one who had made it clear she didn't want to get involved with him in the first place.

"I understand," she said reluctantly. "So are you just going to sit out here and wait?"

"This could take you a while. I thought I'd get some gas, maybe try and find a car wash and scout out a place to stay tonight. How about if I meet you back here in an hour?"

They agreed that he would be waiting outside in an hour and if she wasn't through, she would come out and let him know how much longer she needed. Cat got out of the car and climbed the concrete steps to the door of the newspaper office. At the top she paused, swept by an unexplainable premonition that made her shiver in spite of the late afternoon sun. She was a strong believer in premonitions.

She quickly turned to the street, suddenly more than willing to swallow her pride and ask Bolt to come with her after all, but it was too late. She watched as he took the corner at the end of the block and drove out of sight. As usual he forgot to turn off his signal light after the turn and the Chevy's old-fashioned blinker kept flashing as he drove off. As if, Cat thought, the old car was winking at her.

An omen, she told herself, taking a deep breath as she opened the door to the building. Obviously she was meant to handle this one alone.

The receptionist, a sweet lady wearing a pink ruffled blouse, listened to Cat's inquiry about back issues and directed her to the newspaper's morgue in the basement. Trying not to dwell on the official name for her destination, Cat hurried down the stairs and followed the signs through a maze of corridors. It was much cooler down there, with its old cement block foundation that was a capable forerunner of modern air-conditioning.

The morgue was located at the far end of the building. She gave a perfunctory tap on the windowed door and pushed it open. The door creaked, announcing her arrival, and a man who could have been anywhere from sixty to eighty glanced up from the index cards that covered every square inch of his desk. He was slightly built, his wispy gray hair circling his head like an open-topped cap, a pair of Ben Franklin spectacles perched on his nose.

"Well, hello there," he greeted her. "What brings a pretty little lady like you down here on such a beautiful day?"

Cat returned his broad smile. "Hello. The receptionist told me this is where I might find back issues of the paper."

"Depends," he said, scratching his forehead as he slowly got to his feet and approached the chest-high counter that separated them. "How far back are we talking?"

"Nineteen seventy-eight."

He grinned. "You're in luck. Nineteen seventy-eight was a very good year. No basement flooding, no mold, even had the humidifiers working full steam by then, pardon the pun. Yes, sir, this is your lucky day. Now if you had asked for seventy-five, or worse even, eighty-three, I would have had to send you down to the big morgue at the main office and let you squint up your eyes and try and read off their fancy microfilm machine."

Curbing her impatience, which was strong now that she was actually standing there, about to confront the events of that long-ago night for herself, Cat smiled at him. "Great. So how do I go about finding the papers I want to see?"

He chuckled. "You don't. Only one person goes messing in those stacks," he told her, inclining his head toward the rows of towering metal shelves across the room that stretched out of sight in the dimly lit recesses of the basement. The windows were tightly covered in the area, and Cat could hear the steady drone of the humidifiers he'd referred to.

"When it comes to the archives here, I designed 'em, I stacked 'em, and I take care of them. Now you just tell me what you want and I'll go find it. Do you have a particular date you're interested in seeing? Or just a general subject?" He rubbed his chin thoughtfully. "Seems to me seventy-eight was a big year for protesting the nuclear power plant they talked about building over by the lake. Had that scuffle with the police where that college girl ended up in the hospital. That what you're looking for?"

Cat shook her head, her smile bemused. "No, but your memory is absolutely amazing. I'm interested in the paper from July 12, 1978. In particular a story about a car accident that took place somewhere around here. It happened late at night, at a crossroads. It was raining hard and—"

"And that young couple from up north was killed," he broke in urgently. "I remember it, all right. He was a musician, I think..."

"Magician," Cat corrected.

"That's it. Magician. They were headed over to Virginia Beach, to one of the big hotels there, to do a show."

"That's right." She nodded excitedly. "Do you remember exactly where the accident happened?"

He squared his shoulders indignantly. "Of course I do. It happened right out there where Route 10 splits into Ashland Road. It's a bad turn even on a clear night." He shook his head. "Damn shame, it was. Those two being so young and all. I said it back then and I say it now, too often lately it seems, only a tool mixes drinking with driving."

She stared at him, startled. "The man who caused the accident was drinking?"

"As I recall. There was something else about that particular..." He rubbed his chin again, squinting his eyes as if that would help focus his memory. With a sudden frown, he said, "But then, there have been a lot of accidents out there over the years. Best for you to read the facts for yourself, seeing as that's what you came here for in the first place."

"Yes, of course," she replied, wondering why Uncle Hank had never mentioned that the other driver, the man who had hit her parents' car practically head-on, had been drinking.

"If you like, I can bring you the papers for the week or so following the accident, too," the man behind the counter offered. "Sometimes there are follow-up stories."

"Yes, thank you, I'd really appreciate that."

"Won't be a minute," he said as he disappeared into the stacks.

He returned shortly with a pile of about ten newspapers, the paper yellowed.

"Be gentle," he said as he laid them on the counter before her. "They're old and fragile, sort of like yours truly."

Cat managed a smile.

"There's a desk in there that you're welcome to use," he told her, nodding at a small room behind her. "Make yourself at home. Of course, there's no clipping coupons or anything of that sort allowed."

"I understand."

"Good luck," he said in an oddly gentle tone. "And take as long as you need. Just make sure and bring them back to me when you're through."

"I will," she promised, picking up the papers, her tense smile slipping as soon as she turned away. It surprised her a little that he hadn't asked why she was so interested in an accident that had happened almost two decades ago. She knew she would have asked if she'd been on the other side of the counter. But then, she reasoned, he probably met lots of people looking for information about lots of strange things from the past. Maybe he'd simply lost his curiosity after a while. Or maybe, she thought, he'd discovered that sometimes it was better not to know.

The small room contained a single desk and straight-backed wooden chair designed with utility, not comfort, in mind. It didn't matter. Cat was so anxious she wouldn't have been able to get comfortable in a feather bed. Besides, she didn't plan to be there long.

The news accounts would just reiterate what she already knew. She was mostly interested in visiting the scene itself Thanks to Uncle Hank, she'd always felt close to her parents, but for the past several days, ever since it occurred to her to make this side trip, she had had the unmistakable feeling that coming here would make that mystical bond even stronger.

Her palms were damp and her fingers shaking as she unfolded the paper dated July 12, which was actually the day after the accident. She didn't have to look far. From the bottom of the front page the headline jumped out at her.

Two Killed in Late Night Crash

She closed her eyes briefly, whispering a short, familiar prayer. Then she focused her gaze on the story below the painfully blunt headline, which began like hundreds that appeared in newspapers every day, promising to be formal and to the point, an orderly presentation of facts.

"An accident at Route 10 and Ashland Road last night claimed the lives of two out-of-staters." Cat took a deep breath and read on. "The one-car accident occurred just before midnight as the victims' vehicle, a late-model van, approached a difficult turn in the road where numerous accidents have prompted nearby residents to call for reduced speeds and a traffic light."

Cat forced herself to finish reading the sentence all the way to the end, in spite of the fact that the first few words had turned her bones to ice.

One-car accident? That had to be a mistake, she told herself, wondering what kind of shoddy reporting had been done on this story. There had been two cars involved, the van her parents used to transport props to shows and the car that had smashed into them. She ought to know, she'd heard the story often enough. Uncle Hank had told it to her the day after the accident and then again and again afterward, whenever she asked why her mommy and daddy couldn't be with her anymore.

Gripping the edge of the wooden desk with stiff fingers, she hurriedly read the rest of the article, finding it riddled with even more ridiculous errors. According to the reporter who wrote the piece, her mother was actually outside the van when the accident occurred, walking at the edge of the road. The van supposedly hit her from behind and then swerved into a tree, resulting in the instantaneous deaths of both "victims," as the reporter repeatedly referred to them.

Her parents weren't victims, she thought, resentment like an icicle at her core. Unlucky, yes, whimsical and perhaps a bit too reckless, but not victims.

Her breath was coming in short, rapid pants. How could anyone have gotten it so wrong? These weren't just typos or minor mistakes, these were…discrepancies, she thought, biting her bottom lip. She tasted blood without feeling any pain. Absently she dabbed with her fingertip at the marks her teeth had left in her soft flesh.

Discrepancies. No, worse than that. A difference in the time of the accident between the news account and her uncle's would be a discrepancy, or the use of a different route number, something factual that it was possible to mix up. This… She glared at the paper in horror. This was no mix-up. This was an entirely different story from the one she'd been told by her uncle.

The paper was wrong, she thought defiantly, straightening in the chair. It had to be, it was that simple. Because if the paper was right, then Uncle Hank was wrong, and that she knew with every fiber of her being was impossible. Uncle Hank might be rigid and overbearing at times, but in her entire life she'd never known him to be flat-out wrong about anything that mattered.

Why, the man was an absolute stickler for facts and details, for heaven's sake. How many times, she asked herself, her throat so dry it hurt to swallow, had she arrived home from a date to find him waiting at the door to remind her that twenty-three hundred hours meant exactly that, twenty-three hundred hours, not one minute past twenty-three hundred hours. He didn't overlook details and he didn't make mistakes.

Especially not about something like this. Hank Hollister had adored his baby sister. He had flown to Virginia early the morning after the accident and had accompanied the bodies of her and his brother-in-law home. If it happened the way the paper said it did, he would have known.

He would have known, she told herself again. He would have known the truth about what happened out on that dark, slippery road that awful night.

He would have known.

Cat clung desperately to that thought, but still she couldn't keep others from seeping into her head.

He would have known, but would he have told the truth to a little girl who had gone to bed secure in the love of two parents who doted on her and woke up an orphan?

Or would he have told her something that would make the loss easier to deal with? A less ugly, less painful version that, once told, could never be corrected or taken back.

Trembling violently, Cat reached for the paper dated two days following the accident and hurriedly read the follow-up story, which included statements from witnesses who had seen her parents in a local restaurant about an hour before the crash. According to the eyewitnesses, they had stopped for coffee and directions and had argued loudly in the parking lot afterward.

There were other witnesses who had seen the van slam to a stop on route ten and a woman jump out. The article also included remarks from police officers who had been at the scene, who theorized that the argument in the parking lot had continued in the van and that the woman had either gotten out in a huff or been pushed out and left alone on the roadside. The van had then been seen speeding away, only to make a U-turn several minutes later. It was as the van traveled in the opposite direction on Route 10, toward the town of Baxter, that she was struck from behind.

The police report stated that the poor visibility that night, the angle at which the woman was struck and the open bottle of vodka found inside the van were all taken into consideration in determining that both deaths were accidental.

The papers for the next several days contained progressively smaller stories about the tragedy, mention of the bodies being identified and claimed by the woman's older brother, General Henry L. Hollister, and reference to the autopsy finding that she had been seven weeks pregnant when she died.

The woman, Cat thought forlornly, wrapping her arms around herself tightly in the silent room. The victim. Her mother. Not the princess in a fairy tale, after all. Just a woman, a woman who was left alone on a dark country road and then run over by her own husband. My father, she thought, confused about what she should feel. A drunk? Maybe. An accident? She bit down on her bottom lip, once again drawing blood. Maybe. That didn't make her feel any better. Or change the weight in the pit of her stomach that promised that in a while, when the truth with all its implications had time to fully sink in, she was going to feel a whole lot worse.

Searching for some way to hold that impending nightmare at bay, she methodically folded and piled the newspapers. She double-checked the dates to make sure they were in chronological order and then lined up the edges with the military precision she knew so well and placed them at the far side of the desk, where they would be safe. Only then did she put her head down on the table and cry.

Chapter Ten

The Chevy's brakes squealed and pulled the front end hard to the left as Bolt slammed to a halt in front of the Baxter *Times*. That was why they invented anti-lock brakes, he reflected disgustedly, not to mention tubeless tires.

He'd been blithely cruising the back roads of Baxter, killing some time before he returned to meet Cat, when a blowout had almost sent him into a gully. No problem, he'd thought as he hopped out to take a look at the flat front right tire. After all, he was an old hand at changing tires in a hurry and under adverse conditions. Truck tires, jeep tires, once even a tire on the landing gear of a small two-man propeller plane. He could have changed this one without a hitch, too, if he—or anyone else in the general vicinity—had happened to have an inner tube handy.

An inner tube. His lips curled distastefully as he hopped out and crossed the sidewalk to the steps in three long strides. Who would pay good money for a car that still required inner tubes? If you asked him, nostalgia was nice from a distance, but a major pain in the butt in practice.

He'd turned the trunk inside out in hopes that whoever had polished the car's chrome so faithfully had also tucked away a spare inner tube, but no luck.

As he'd repacked it, he'd cursed, thinking that big old road yachts like the convertible were supposed to have trunks roomy enough to hold luggage for an army. Just not an army of pack rats like Cat, who seemed dedicated to arriving home with double the amount of stuff she started with.

He glanced at his watch as he yanked open the door to the newspaper office, once again muttering under his breath. He was over two hours late. And he was worried. All the way there he'd been praying Cat would be outside waiting for him, furious about the long wait, but safe.

When he'd realized he was going to be late getting back, he'd called and tried to reach her at the paper, but she wasn't there. He'd speculated that she might have run into a dead end at the paper and followed his suggestion about checking out the police report on the accident. He considered calling the police station to see if she was there and then, if necessary, calling every place in Baxter until he found her. Unfortunately that would have tied up the one-line phone at the one-horse service station that was trying to track down an inner tube on his behalf.

So he had been forced to just sit there and wait and worry. And pray. Something he didn't do well or often and never on his own behalf.

Obviously his prayers hadn't been answered this time. Cat wasn't outside waiting, and the woman at the front desk had no idea where she might have gone or when, only that she had directed her to the basement in search of back issues of the paper hours ago.

It was nearly six, closing time, so he hurried down there, still praying. Maybe he would find her there after all, too engrossed in her search to hear herself being paged. Maybe it had taken longer than either of them expected to ferret out a news story nearly twenty years old. Maybe she'd left for some reason and returned without the receptionist seeing her.

Maybe, maybe, maybe. There were other maybes he'd rather not think about. He was right back where he'd been that day at the rest stop, scared and worried and cursing himself for mistakes and oversights he was too late in recognizing.

For the past two days he'd been so immersed in his own problems and so busy feeling sorry for himself, he'd dropped his guard like some rookie put in charge of the candy store and getting sick on chocolate. Had the Mustang been anywhere around in the past forty-eight hours? He had no idea. He hadn't been watching very intently. Maybe it had been there and he'd missed it and now he was going to find out how high a price he would have to pay for his mistake this time. Maybe, maybe, maybe.

Cat wasn't in the newspaper's morgue, either. The old man in charge greeted Bolt with a smile and sauntered over to the counter to ask if he could help him.

Bolt told him who he was and what he wanted in a rush. The old man listened, nodding emphatically.

"She was here, all right," he said when Bolt finished. "But it was, oh, at least a couple hours ago that she left. And yes, she was asking about an accident that happened out on Route 10 back in '78. Even wanted me to write out the directions for her to get out there."

Of course. The pressure in Bolt's chest eased slightly. Once she had found out what she needed to know, Cat would never have sat around waiting for him before she did what she had come here to do. Especially not after he'd told her he didn't want to be part of it, he thought, feeling like a heel.

"Did you give her directions?" he asked the older man.

"Of course. Couldn't see why I shouldn't."

"Of course not. Could you please tell me how to get there?"

He shrugged. "Don't see any reason why I shouldn't now, either."

Bolt listened to the simple directions. "Thanks. Just one more thing. Did she ask to use the phone to call a taxi? Or mention anything about how she intended to get there?"

''No,'' the man replied thoughtfully. ''But I sort of got the feeling she planned to walk. I told her it wasn't more than a couple of miles.''

He pursed his lips, his bushy steel brows lowering into a troubled frown.

''What is it?'' Bolt asked him.

''Nothing, maybe, and none of my business to be sure. But... Ah, what the heck? You said you're a friend of hers, right?''

''Yes. A good friend.''

''Then maybe you ought to know that I did notice how reading those old news stories really upset her. I looked in there at her once and she was crying her heart out, poor thing. I just let her be. When she left, she had dark glasses on. To hide her eyes, I suspected, but I didn't ask.''

Bolt nodded, his heart twisting in his chest. Damn, he should have been here with her. He wished he had been, instead of off nursing his stupid wounded pride.

''The couple killed in that accident were her parents,'' he explained.

The other man winced and gave a small nod. ''I wondered if that was it. That explains it, then. A tragedy like that... it's hard to face at any age. We all like to think our parents never made any stupid mistakes.''

Bolt was only half listening as he thanked him for his help and left. He'd driven the old car hard on the way back to town from the service station, but he pushed it even harder now. When he caught the red light at the corner, he drummed his fingers on the wheel impatiently and took the opportunity to double-check the simple map the old man had insisted on drawing for him.

Two miles, he'd said. If he was right about her walking, that should have taken Cat about a half hour, forty-five minutes, tops. That still left a lot of time unaccounted for. He suddenly recalled that she'd said something about bringing some flowers with her. Finding a bouquet of flowers in Baxter could have taken her a while, he reasoned. Or else maybe he was overreacting entirely and he would any minute run into her as she made her way back to meet him.

The trouble was, he didn't like maybes any better than he liked messing up. The light finally turned green and he took off, flooring it as he followed the sign for Route 10. As he drove, his gaze darted ahead in hopes of catching a glimpse of Cat walking along the roadside. Fragmented thoughts and worries bombarded him. Amidst all that inner turmoil, he suddenly recalled one of the last things the old man at the *Times* had said, something about no one wanting to think their parents made stupid mistakes.

Now that he thought about it, Bolt was relieved that the old goat hadn't had a chance to discuss his warped view of the matter with Cat. He happened to be something of an authority on stupid mistakes, and in his opinion, getting killed in an accident that wasn't your fault didn't come close to qualifying. Working in that basement must have gotten to the old guy.

At least his directions were accurate. He had described to Bolt the place where Route 10 intersected with Ashland Road, forming a crooked X, and the flashing yellow light that cautioned drivers in all directions to reduce speed. When Bolt saw the flashing light in the distance and still no sign of Cat, his heart sank. He'd been so sure he would find her out there somewhere.

What now? he was asking himself even as he caught sight of a flash of white on his left. There was an old stone wall set about ten feet from the road. Sitting there with her back against the wall was Cat.

Bolt drank in the sight of her in jeans and a white T-shirt, her legs crossed in front of her, her long hair hanging loosely over her shoulders, the color of corn silk in the setting sun. Relief like he'd never felt before rippled through him, and for a few seconds he felt strangely weak. He found himself praying once again, almost unconsciously, thanking whoever was in charge of such things for keeping her safe for him and promising that he would never take chances with her again.

The grassy strip between the road and the wall provided ample room for him to pull over and park the car. He climbed out slowly, still savoring the knowledge that everything was okay, amazed at how powerful an emotion relief could be. He'd had many much closer calls than this in his life without feeling this way afterward. But then, usually before he had been the one at risk.

The relief he'd felt when he made it safely past the danger those other times was nothing like what he felt now as he slowly walked over and lowered himself to the ground by Cat's side. Either he was crazy or the entire world had suddenly gotten a lot prettier, the sky bluer, the grass greener. The sounds of the birds in the branches overhead and the rustling of small creatures in the woods behind the wall sounded like music to his ears.

Cat still hadn't looked up or acknowledged his presence. Bolt understood. No matter how good it felt to him to find her safe here, she had very different matters on her mind. Matters, he reminded himself, that were bound to leave her feeling sad.

He looked at her, seeing the tearstains on her cheeks where they fanned from beneath her sunglasses and the bunch of wildflowers that lay near her feet, as if she'd tossed them aside.

He thought of explaining why he'd been late and telling her how worried about her he'd been, but no matter how he phrased it, it all seemed ridiculously inconsequential compared to what she must be thinking and going through as she sat there.

"How are you doing?" he asked finally.

She didn't speak, didn't even turn her head.

Bolt forced himself to remain quiet. If she wanted to just sit there, he'd sit. Hell, at that moment he'd have jumped though fiery hoops like some trained circus animal for her. Anything so long as she didn't tell him to go away. Sitting with her would be a pleasure. Actually, at that moment, he couldn't think of anything he'd rather do than sit beside her, just be there for her if she should need him to talk to her or hold her or even to simply chase away the mosquitoes that occasionally emerged from the tall grass tufts in the wall's crevices.

He loved her.

It hit him out of the blue. Just like that. No warning, no deep thinking and absolutely no possibility of misunderstanding. He was as certain of it as he was that night followed day. He was in love with her, Catrina Amelia Bandini, a woman who was too young, too vulnerable and much too closely related to the general.

None of that mattered. He was in love with her, that's what mattered, that's all that mattered, and along with that knowledge came the realization that from that moment on his love for her would affect every aspect of his life.

He felt breathless and exhilarated at the same time. Following quickly came an overwhelming urge to tell her. He stopped himself. He'd never before actually told a woman that he loved her. He knew now that he'd never really loved another woman before Cat. But as inexperienced as he was, he knew this wasn't the right moment to announce it.

He tucked the knowledge away, like a kid pocketing a shiny stone to wish on later, and took a couple of deep breaths.

When he looked at her again she seemed not to have moved, as if she was frozen at whatever level of pain she'd descended to. Bolt's heart ached for her. The urge to do something to help her was bridled by the frustrating fact that he had no idea where to begin. If she were to ask him to take a beating or risk his life for her, he would be prepared and more than willing. But what she needed to help her through this was something else, something he didn't understand.

Unable to resist any longer, he reached out and stroked her arm. At last she moved, turning her head just a fraction in his direction. Bolt had no idea how familiar he'd become with every line and pore on her face until he instantly noticed the marks on her bottom lip.

He cupped her chin and turned her face toward him fully, frowning. "What happened to your lip?"

"Nothing." Her voice was soft and laced with raw emotion.

"It doesn't look like nothing to me," he observed, running his thumb over her soft flesh and feeling a totally inappropriate response all the way to his toes. "Does it hurt?"

Cat shrugged and shook her head. "I can't even feel it."

Oh, Cat. He sat with his jaw tightly clenched, aching to do something for her, damning himself for not knowing what.

"You were right, you know," she said as he sat there feeling useless.

Bolt snatched at the meager overture. "I was? About what?"

Again she shrugged, so feeble a version of the haughty gesture he'd grown accustomed to seeing that it tore at his heart. "Everything," she said. "Life. Destiny."

"What about destiny?"

"It's not what it's cracked up to be."

"Ah, Cat." This time the ragged groan was out before he could stop himself. He moved his hand to the back of her neck, kneading gently. "I know how hard this is for you. Coming here must bring back all kinds of memories, making you think about things that would be tough for anyone to handle."

"The only thing I keep thinking is what an idiot I've been."

"You mean for wanting to come here? Don't think that. It's natural to—"

She didn't let him finish.

"What I mean is that I was an idiot for believing such a line of bull for so long. It was all a big lie," she continued, faltering, revealing a tearful undercurrent to her words. "All of it, and I believed it, hook, line and sinker."

Bolt recalled thinking something very similar about her gullibility, but he didn't like hearing it come from her. No more than he liked the edge of bitterness that had crept into her tone.

"What are you talking about, sweetheart?" he asked, knowing that if she challenged his use of the word now, he could tell her honestly that he'd never meant anything so much. "What lies?"

"Everything Uncle Hank told me about my mother and father. It was all a lie. About the accident—about how it happened, that is. There was no other car," she told him, the words coming in a sharp, hurried torrent that told Bolt how painful they were for her to say. He listened without interrupting, wanting her to get it all out.

He listened as she told him how she had found out that there was no other driver at fault for the accident, no other driver at all. He listened, horrified for her, to the reports and rumors about how her parents had argued just before the accident, about the liquor in the van and finally about how her father had been the one who had struck and killed her mother, dying an instant later himself, maybe without ever knowing what he had done.

"That might be the worst of all," she said, sniffling. Bolt handed her a clean handkerchief. "All these years I've had this picture in my head of them dying holding hands or something. Maybe grabbing for each other in the last second as they saw the other car coming at them. Soul mates to the end."

She gave a broken laugh, and Bolt's heart constricted painfully. He ached for her. He wished there was some way his sympathy could ease her suffering.

"What a joke, huh?" she continued. "Now I know there was no other car. And no such thing as soul mates, either, no magical fairy-tale love affair. Definitely no happy ending."

Bolt reeled from the sense of powerlessness that gripped him. He was no damn good at this, he thought, frantically wishing for some words to say that might comfort her. If she could be comforted. He understood now where her starry-eyed view of life and love had come from... from a little girl's memory of her parents, fueled and encouraged by her uncle. If the man had been anyone other than Hollister, he could easily have hated him for the lack of judgment that had brought Cat to this moment. But knowing that the general probably felt as ill-equipped to deal with the pain of a five-year-old as Bolt was feeling right this moment, he could only empathize with him and wish to hell it hadn't happened.

But it had. He slid his arm around Cat's shoulders and gently pulled her closer so that she was leaning on him. It had happened and it had understandably shaken the roots of everything she believed in. She wasn't grieving just the death of her parents, but the death of a dream. Everything she had been taught to trust and believe in had been shattered. It was one thing for him not to believe in fairy tales. It was entirely different for Cat to have that belief ripped away from her without warning.

What the hell was he going to do?

He rubbed her shoulder, tilting his head so his cheek rested against the top of hers.

"Bolt, I feel so... empty," she whispered.

"Oh, baby." He pressed his lips to her head, feeling her hair slide like warm silk against his mouth. "I wish I could turn back the clock and make it so you'd never come here, never found out any of this."

"I'm glad I did," she said. "It certainly makes things simpler."

"The toughest lessons usually are the simplest. I just wish there was some way I could make this easier for you."

"There is," she said simply, startling him. "Make love to me, please, Bolt."

He went from being startled to shocked. As he struggled in silence to make some sense in the abrupt turn the conversation had taken, she twisted around in his arms to gaze at him. Her sunglasses had fallen aside and her eyes were a deep, clear violet full of urgency.

"You don't want that," he said, feeling his body tense at the mere thought of making love with her.

"Yes, I do," she said in a sure, quiet voice. "That's exactly what I want. I wanted it the other night and I want it more now. For years I've watched my friends and roommates fall in love and share the closeness and intimacy that comes along with loving someone. But I always held back, refusing to let myself get that close to anyone, telling myself it was worth the sacrifice—or would be someday—because I was waiting for something really special...for something and someone that doesn't even exist. I know that now, and I'm not willing to wait any longer."

"Slow down," he urged patiently, as her hand moved on his chest, an innocently yearning gesture that he found much too stimulating. Hell, everything about her was like that, innocent and erotic at the same time. He struggled for control.

"Cat, listen to me," he said. "Just because your parents didn't have as perfect a relationship as you believed they did doesn't mean that you won't someday meet the right man for you and have a good life together with him."

Me, something inside him cried so insistently he had to pause and bank down on the urge to speak out. *A man like me,* he wanted to say. *Let me love you and take care of you.* He longed to say all that and more, but he didn't want to take any chance that she might later think what he said and what he was feeling at this moment were somehow prompted by her situation. He wasn't taking any chances this time at all.

"Their relationship wasn't simply not quite perfect," she said. "He ran her down, for pity's sake."

"Shh, shh." He pulled her head against his chest as her voice cracked. "It's okay."

"It can be," she whispered. "I know now that there is no Mr. Right waiting out there, looking for me the same dumb way I've been looking for him."

Want to bet? The words burned on his tongue.

"I know now that you have to make things right for yourself, and you have to reach out and take what you want when you have the chance. Because...because you never know when it might all end." She tipped her head to meet his gaze. "Will you make love to me, Bolt?"

"I would. In an instant," he murmured. "But I don't think this is the right time for you to be deciding how you feel about something so important."

"It's already been decided," she replied placidly. "I've been sitting here a long time, thinking and making decisions about the future."

"How did you come to the decision that losing your virginity will make you feel better?"

"I'm not sure it will. I only know that I need to feel something."

"You don't need that. Not tonight," he insisted, his insides drawn as tight as a bowstring, ready to snap.

"You wanted me the other night," she reminded him.

"I still want you, damn it. More than you'll ever know."

She rolled to her knees and reached for his hands, tugging gently. "Then take me. Please, Bolt. Let's go someplace where we can be alone."

It was an impossible situation. Cat and every fiber of his being were urging him on. Every part of him, that is, except for a very fragile thread of scruples.

She was damn lucky he was a man with a conscience, he thought roughly. If he wasn't, and she looked at him the way she was looking at him now, she would be on her back in that car and wouldn't have to worry about being a virgin any longer.

Following hard on that thought was one about how in only a few days she would be home and surrounded by men who might have considerably fewer conscience pangs when it came to taking up the offer of a beautiful and vulnerable woman looking to prove something to herself. Men without his understanding of what had happened here today to change and confuse her. Men without his willpower.

Men who didn't love her.

Resistance roared up inside him until a single thought filled his head. No. He couldn't let that happen.

He couldn't risk having her go running to another man in this mood, couldn't let another man make love to her when he loved her more than he'd known it was possible to love someone.

If anyone was going to make love to her, it was going to be someone who understood and cared about her. Someone who loved her.

Forget all that, he thought feeling a fiercely proprietary surge of emotion. If anyone made love to her it was going to be him.

And it was going to be real, he decided. Not some frantic coupling, or a quick surrender to his desire and whatever Cat might be interpreting as passion.

It was inevitable that what she had found out today would change her and play a major part in anything she was feeling now. He knew as well as anyone that painful losses and adjustments were part of life, and there wasn't anything he could do to stop them. But he could at least see to it that the fairy tale she'd once believed in came true. If only for one night. Even he ought to be able to play the part of Prince Charming for one night.

His mind whirling with plans, he got to his feet and drew her up to stand beside him. He lowered his mouth, taking hers in a quick kiss tinged with passion and promise.

"All right, Tiger, let's go find someplace where we can be alone."

Cat was willing to stop at the first motel they passed. Now that she'd made up her mind, she was eager to get on with it. She didn't consider that she was about to lose her virginity so much as escape from it...and along with it, all the illusions of the past. She wanted to start fresh, with her eyes open, and she wanted to make that fresh start with Bolt.

She hadn't entirely lost her mind and suddenly decided he was right for her. While she might no longer believe in magic, she wasn't dumb enough to discount the importance of things such as compatibility and shared interests. But while he might not be the right man, he was decent and kind, and she was more attracted to him than she'd ever been to anyone else. Maybe, she told herself, that was the best you could hope for in life, a little kindness and a little passion. For sure her situation tonight was better than some she could think of...better than being pregnant and stranded alone in the rain on a dark highway.

Closing her eyes, she willed away that painful thought and all others that centered on her parents and the past. She had the rest of her life to think about all that and decide how it would change things for her, her hopes and plans, even her relationship with Uncle Hank. She didn't have to think about it tonight. She wasn't ready.

It was growing dark, and up ahead a flashing red vacancy sign came into view.

"How about that place?" she asked.

Bolt shook his head. "Too seedy."

They were on a road she didn't recognize. "You're not trying to get us lost, are you? Or else planning to stall all the way to Florida just to get out of this?"

He looked at her with more tenderness than she had once believed him capable of.

"I have no desire to get out of anything. Trust me. I have someplace in mind."

The place he had in mind, she soon discovered, was set far back from the road at the end of a narrow, winding drive lined with flickering gaslights. As they pulled closer, she realized that the gaslights weren't the only thing about the place reminiscent of another era.

Carlysle House wasn't a motel, or even a bed and breakfast as the small, discreet sign purported. It was a castle. Built of stone that shimmered like silver in the moonlight, it had turrets at the corners of its three-story frame, mullioned windows and a portico out front where they parked the car.

Cat stared in amazed silence for a minute, then turned excitedly to find Bolt watching her, his expression cautious. "Bolt, how on earth did you know about this place?"

"I found it earlier when I was driving around. I thought you'd like it."

"I do. It's wonderful." She eyed him quizzically. "You mean you planned to come here all along?"

"No," he admitted, his tone rueful. "My plan was to leave you alone."

"And now?" She held her breath, feeling a strange yearning down low inside.

He reached for her hand and brought it to his mouth, kissing first the back, then the palm before pressing it to his heart. "Now my plan is to see to it that you never regret this night."

"I won't," she whispered. "I promise you, I won't."

The castle's heavy wooden plank door was shaped like a battle shield, and instead of a doorbell there was an elaborate wrought-iron knocker mounted there. As they waited for someone to answer, Cat studied the crest imbedded in the stone beside the door. Love, Truth, Honor was engraved beneath it. She turned away with a sigh. It made a pretty slogan, but if truth and honor had anything to do with love, she would eat the little stone stool by her feet.

The heavy door was swung open by a short, plump, middle-aged women with a friendly smile. Joan Carlysle greeted them and explained that she and her husband, Allen, ran Carlysle House. To the accompaniment of an obviously oft-practiced welcome speech, she ushered them inside and gave them a quick tour of the public rooms on the first floor. Fascinating tidbits about the castle's design and the furnishings, which were a striking mix of antiques and reproductions, peppered her brief remarks.

"So," she said when she'd finished and brought them back to the front entrance where a wide stone staircase with a massive banister carved from black oak curved upward and out of sight. "Would you like to be our guests for the night?"

"We'd like that very much," Bolt told the woman as Cat stared at the darkness at the top of the stairs in fascination.

That was all it took to set in motion a very well-oiled operation. A short ring of the bell on a nearby table quickly summoned Allen Carlysle to whisk their bags upstairs. At Bolt's request they were given the suite on the third floor. A younger woman appeared with a card listing the dinner prepared for that evening, and after handing it to Cat was dispatched to ready their suite.

The card carried a description, written in flawless calligraphy, of a feast of roast Cornish hen with a host of accompaniments. Cat's mouth watered as she read it, reminding her that she hadn't eaten since early that morning. Joan Carlysle agreed so readily to Bolt's inquiry about having dinner brought to their room that it was clear she'd dealt with the same request from romantic-minded young couples many times before.

"I'm sure you'll be comfortable," she said as she led them to the bottom of the stairs, clearly sensing their eagerness to be alone. "It's very quiet and private up there. Just follow the stairs all the way to the top. You can't go wrong."

Can't go wrong, Cat echoed silently as Bolt took her hand and led her up the stairs. Yes, she agreed with that. If she hadn't been sure before he'd brought her to Carlysle House, she was convinced now that whatever truths she might have to face in the morning, for tonight she would be safe with Bolt.

The suite was comprised of a large, sumptuous sitting room and an even more spacious bedroom. A king-size four-poster bed, swathed in burgundy silk and satin, held center stage in the room. On either side were positioned small sets of wooden steps. For good reason, Cat mused, marveling at the height of the mattress. She ran her hand over it, smiling as she felt the unmistakable softness of a feather bed. A small fire smoldered in the fireplace, pleasantly offsetting the coolness preserved by the stone walls.

Cat turned in slow circles, trying to take it all in, and ended up slightly dizzy and feeling, ridiculously she knew, as if she'd been transported into the pages of one of her favorite novels.

That, she surmised, had been precisely Bolt's intention in bringing her here. As he approached, she reached for him to steady herself.

"You okay?" he asked, supporting her effortlessly.

"I am now," she replied, leaning against him. "Twirling makes me woozy."

He laughed softly. "You look beautiful woozy."

"I'm also starving."

Another laugh. "Want me to run down and get you some pretzels from the car?"

"No, I can wait for dinner."

"Joan said it might be an hour before it's ready."

She smiled and slid her hands down his chest. "Well, then..."

"Don't tempt me," he murmured, sweeping her hair from her face, his eyes molten in the firelight. "What I have in mind for you will take a lot longer than an hour."

"It's a start," she offered.

"I also need some time to take care of a few things first."

"Such as?"

"A shower, for starters."

"I thought only women primped beforehand," she teased, "and that men were always ready, able and willing."

"I plead guilty to being able and willing," he countered, proving it by brushing his hips against hers provocatively. "As to the rest, you've got a lot to learn."

Her expression sobered. "Teach me, Bolt."

"I intend to, sweetheart. With great pleasure." He kissed her lightly and pulled away with a tantalizing smile. "Be patient, wench. I'll be back."

Cat arched her brows. "Wench?"

"Blame it on the atmosphere," he told her as he left.

He was gone less than an hour, time enough for Cat to explore all the nooks and crannies of the suite, try out the bed and all the overstuffed chairs and draw a hot bath in the oversize claw-footed tub she was delighted to discover in the bathroom.

The bath was actually three adjoining rooms, one with the basic facilities, another with a double sink and shower stall and the third, the size of the living room in her apartment, which contained the tub set beneath stained-glass windows that were backlit for use at night. All three rooms were decorated in the same regal shades of crimson and gold, and no expense had been spared on the plush satin-edged towels and array of scented soaps and oils arranged on a gilded tray.

She felt like a princess as she soaked in rose-scented bubbles to her shoulders, the soft background music she'd chosen filtering through the suite's speaker system. She was going to need a new goal to replace all the ones she was going to have to abandon, she decided, and she knew exactly what it was going to be. Somehow she was going to make enough money to build her own castle. Bandini House, she thought, first giggling, then weeping, which seemed to be the full spectrum of her emotions at the moment.

She had composed herself but was still lingering in the tub when Bolt returned. She heard him open the door to the suite and call out her name. As she answered she had to fight the urge to jump up and grab a towel. If she was going to share a bed with the man, she told herself, she'd better get over feeling self-conscious around him.

She lay back against the bath pillow provided, listening to the sounds of him moving about in the other room. She heard the tinkle of ice against glass and a rustling, like a plastic bag being crumpled. Her puzzled frown quickly gave way to a knowing smile. Of course, he must have gone to the store to buy protection. She felt a rush of affection that he would go to the trouble to do so even without being asked. Something that in her nervousness she probably wouldn't have remembered to do. She was even more pleased that he wasn't prepared to the point where he carried them in his wallet at all times.

As she listened, waiting for him to come looking for her, she heard the shower running and then the water in the sink outside the door, interspersed with the low pitch of his humming. Water, humming, more water, more humming. It seemed to go on and on. What on earth was he doing? she wondered.

As soon as the door opened, she had her answer.

"You shaved," she said, her stomach fluttering at the sight of the sexy near-stranger standing in the doorway. He looked different. Younger. Even more appealing.

He nodded. "I remembered that I left marks on you when I kissed you the last time."

"I didn't mind."

"I did."

"I've never seen you completely clean-shaven before," she told him. "You're pretty sexy sans stubble."

"Sans stubble?" he countered, chuckling and coming away from the door. He was barefoot, and the white shirt he'd pulled on hung open, baring his chest above the low-slung waistband of his jeans. Cat's gaze dropped to his belt buckle and she shivered in spite of the still warm temperature of the water. "Is that French for no beard?"

"Something like that," she murmured.

"And you think I'm sexy this way?"

He stepped closer.

Cat gripped the rounded edges of the tub. "I know you are. Very sexy. I think you know it, too."

He shook his head, his eyes reflecting honest surprise. "No. I do okay with women, I suppose, but sexy...I never thought of myself that way."

"Trust me," she returned dryly, "the women you've done okay with, to use your terminology, thought of you exactly that way." She nonchalantly swatted at the bubbles near her hand. "So, were there lots of them? Women, I mean."

His mouth twisted ruefully. "Is this the obligatory precoital exchange of sexual histories?"

"If it is, we both know how brief mine will be."

"Mine isn't all that lengthy," he retorted. "There have been a handful of women in my life. None serious."

Cat studied his expression, noting the way his mouth pulled tightly at the corner. "Are you sure about that?"

"I'm sure." He hesitated. "There was one I thought was serious at the time, but...it didn't work out." There was another pause as he briefly shifted his gaze away from hers. When he turned back to her he offered a resigned smile that seemed to pain him. "You want details, right?"

"Not if you don't want to tell me."

He sighed. "There's nothing I don't want to tell you, Cat. It's just...not something I usually talk about. I'm not sure I can."

She waited, not pressing him.

"It was while I was still on active duty," he said at last. "I was sent to South America, Colombia to be specific, to watch over the sister of a drug dealer who had made a deal with the government to testify against her brother. Her name was Angelina. She was young and..."

"Beautiful," Cat supplied when he hesitated.

"Yeah, she was beautiful, but something else, too...contagious, if that makes sense. She made you want to be around her, she made you want to do what she wanted to do. At least," he concluded with a self-derisive sneer, "that's how she made me feel."

"What happened?"

"There were three weeks remaining until the trial when I arrived, and my job was to make sure her brother's men didn't get close enough to make good on their threats to do whatever necessary to stop her from testifying. The plan was to keep her on the run, moving through a series of safe houses in the mountains, a new stop every night."

"I see. If you spent three weeks alone with her, it's easy to see how things might have become serious."

"I only spent a little over a week with her, but sometimes that's all it takes," he said. The look he slanted her made Cat blush and look away. "Like I said," he continued, "I thought it was serious, one of those at-first-sight deals you were talking about the other day."

"Please." She groaned. "Don't remind me of all that."

"All I know is that the way I was feeling, I was more than willing to go along when she asked if we could stay one more night at the cabin where we first..." He glanced at her awkwardly.

"I understand," she said.

"So I agreed." He dragged his fingers over his short hair, sagging into the chair next to the tub. "It turned out to be the biggest mistake I ever made."

"Why, Bolt? What went wrong?"

"Everything. We found out later that she was in contact with her brother the whole time and never intended to make good on the testimony she promised to give. She wanted to stay at the cabin another night because she knew his men had followed us there. And I played right into her hands," he continued bitterly. "The second night we were there, they tossed an explosive into the cabin."

"Bolt, that's awful. Was anyone hurt?"

"I got out in time, but ended up with a broken back from crashing through a window. Angelina got away clean... We figured they must have signaled her to get out right before it happened. And my partner..." He exhaled deeply and shut his eyes. "He'd been scouting ahead and he circled back to find out why I hadn't made the move as scheduled. He was outside and got caught right in the middle when it went up and—"

She placed her wet hand on top of his where it gripped the arm of the chair. "Bolt, you don't—"

"He was killed," he said, breaking in to finish in a rush. He looked at her, and at that moment Cat would have given anything to wipe away the pain etched in his golden eyes. "I didn't even know he was there. He shouldn't have been. He wouldn't have if I hadn't ignored orders and messed up."

"You had no way of knowing—"

"I had every way of knowing the right thing to do," he snapped without allowing her to finish. "I was trained, experienced, the best... or so I thought until that night." He pursed his lips to exhale, and the breath seemed to carry with it a lot of the anger she had sensed building, as if he just couldn't hold it all.

He hunched forward, his elbows on his knees, as he said, "Ben Johnson wasn't just my partner. He was the best friend I ever had."

"Bolt, I'm so sorry." She placed her hand on his arm, shaking her head in dismay. "I'm sorry about what happened to your friend... and to you. I'm sorry for making you talk about it. This certainly seems to be my night for dredging up bad memories."

"That's all right," he told her, the corner of his mouth lifting in a not very convincing smile. Cat longed to touch his smooth cheeks and pull him closer. "Maybe that's where I've been going wrong all this time. Maybe you have to dredge up all the bad memories and look them right in the face before you can leave them behind."

Chapter Eleven

Bolt stood, held out his hand to her and waited.

The connection between his comment about leaving old memories behind and the night that lay ahead of them was nonetheless clear for being unspoken. His silence was both invitation and promise. And perhaps something else that left Cat wondering. A warning?

He waited, his hand outstretched, without speaking a word or displaying a trace of impatience. It was as dramatic a moment as Cat had ever lived through. That is, if she did live through it. The fierce hammering of her heart gave her a moment's pause.

Finally she put her hand in his and let him help her from the deep tub. Pearlescent bubbles clung to her breasts and tummy and thighs, but hid nothing. Bolt made no secret of his interest, or his delight as his gaze roamed slowly over her body. Her skin, flushed from the warm water, grew even pinker beneath the heat in his eyes. Not even when he reached for a towel with his free hand did he look away.

It was the first time any man had seen her completely naked. She'd always imagined that this particular milestone in her life would take place in the dark, perhaps even under the covers. She expected to feel embarrassed by such a well-lit perusal, especially since he was still half-dressed. As comfortable as she was with her body when clothed, there were a number of curves she'd prefer a bit less curvy if given a choice in the matter.

She wasn't thinking of those imperfections now, however, and she wasn't embarrassed. It felt amazingly right and good to have Bolt looking at her, his slight smile unabashedly approving. She relaxed even more as he turned her around and draped the bath towel over her, caressing her through the soft velvety cloth as he dried her shoulders and back, working his way down the back of her legs to her feet before turning her so that she was facing him again. Pulling the damp towel away from her, he reached for another to dry the rest of her. His eyes glittered like hammered brass as he rubbed her breasts for much longer than necessary to dry them, the sensation so exciting and unexpected that Cat had to bite her lip to keep from making a sound.

Leaning slightly to one side, he dried her tummy with leisurely strokes and pats. She sucked in a sharp breath as his hand moved steadily lower. His gaze caught hers, watching her eyes go wide and liquid as his towel-sheathed hand slipped between her thighs, imparting a gentle pressure that made her knees weak and her hands land against his chest for support.

He smiled with satisfaction and held her for a minute before kneeling to dry her legs. Tossing the second towel aside, he wrapped her in the thick terry robe hanging nearby.

He led her by the hand to the bedroom. If there were any lingering ghosts or bad memories still with them, they were left at the door as they entered the room lit by what seemed to be hundreds of white candles. The flames flickered and danced all around them, casting a luminous glow that made the whole room shimmer like a scene from a dream.

Cat gasped with pleasure at the sight.

"My goodness, Bolt, I've never seen so many candles all lit at once."

"A night like this only comes around once," he told her quietly. "Something extraordinary seemed in order."

"This is certainly that . . . extraordinary."

Turning slowly, she gazed around the entire room, at the all narrow candles gathered in clusters of five or six around the bed, and the shorter, thicker pillar-shaped ones that lined the dressers and mantel. Her gaze stopped at a silver pedestal bucket filled with ice and an open bottle of champagne. Beside it, a small table draped in white linen held what she guessed was their dinner under silver warming domes.

"It was waiting at the door when I got back," Bolt explained.

"Even the champagne?"

"That I requested specially." He reached for the bottle and poured two glasses.

"Aren't you afraid I'll start singing?" she joked, a little taken aback by all the trouble he had gone to while she'd been killing time in the bathtub.

"Not at all." He glanced up from his pouring. "I know how to stop you, remember?"

Cat laughed, remembering all too well how he had silenced her in the elevator, as well as what had followed. Tonight wouldn't end that way, she thought with satisfaction. It wouldn't end with angry words and her lying awake in her bed, alone with her regrets.

She took the fluted glass of champagne Bolt handed her, eyeing him awkwardly. "I feel as if we should make a toast or something."

"Go ahead," he urged, his small smile indulgent. He watched with interest as she sought the right words. "To tonight," she said finally, lifting her glass.

He touched his to it lightly. "To tonight."

They both took a sip.

"Would you like to have dinner?" he asked.

She shook her head, tugging on the tie of the oversize robe. "I really don't think I could eat. Now."

He smiled. "Me, either." He reached behind him and picked something up from the bed. "For you," he said quietly, holding out a sheer nightgown of white silk and lace.

"It's beautiful," she exclaimed, taking it from him and holding it up, exclaiming all over again when she saw the intricate detail on the bands of lace and felt the suppleness of the silk. "It's the most gorgeous thing I've ever seen."

"I guess I should have handed it in to you while you were in the bathroom and waited for you to put it on." The rueful note in his voice did nothing to disguise the obvious pleasure he took in her reaction. "But I couldn't wait that long to see you."

"I'll put it on now," she said, eager to see herself in it and feel the sheer fabric against her skin.

"Even knowing that I'm going to take it right off you again?" he asked, his eyes gleaming fiercely.

"Even so," she whispered, shivering. "Turn around please."

He chuckled and obeyed.

It took her only a few seconds to shrug out of the bulky robe and pull the floor-length nightgown over her head. It drifted over her body as if it had been made for her alone, hugging her narrow waist and the full curve of her hips, the fine silk feeling like a feather boa against skin made sensitive by his touch.

"All right," she told him. "You can look."

Bolt turned and stared at her without smiling or saying word. He didn't need to. The dark glitter in his eyes and the way his throat muscles flexed as he swallowed hard told Ca he liked what he saw very much.

"I was right," he said at last. "The saleswoman told m that most women prefer wider lace straps." As he spoke h slipped one long finger beneath one very narrow strap "But I told her that I wanted as much as possible of you beautiful shoulders left uncovered."

He bent his head and kissed her left shoulder, dragging his tongue along her collarbone to the base of her throat. Cat arched her neck in response.

"She insisted," he continued in that same deep, lazy voice, "that most women found the wider straps more comfortable." He kissed her right shoulder and slid his hand beneath her hair, winding it over and through the long strands still damp from her bath. "I didn't think it polite to tell her that I wasn't interested in making you comfortable... only in making you mine."

Using his hold on her hair, he tipped her face up to his and stared deeply into her eyes as he lowered his mouth to hers, moving with excruciating slowness, angling his head and parting his lips in a way that sent a rush of anticipation through her.

His kiss was long and hard, and Cat had to breathe in deeply for a minute afterward before she could talk.

"Bolt," she began, vaguely troubled, "why did you buy this nightgown for me? And order the champagne and light all these candles?"

"I told you. I wanted this night to be special."

"Is that all you want?"

He cocked his head to the side, his expression darkly amused.

"I mean," she added hurriedly. "I hope you don't expect... too much from me."

"I don't expect anything at all," he said, rubbing her back, making her want to curl against him like a satisfied cat in spite of her sudden reservations. "If you want to call a halt right now, or any other time, just say the word."

"I don't," she whispered. "I just don't want to... let you down. Now or... afterward."

"You won't. You couldn't," he assured her, his voice husky as he cupped her face in his hands, kissing her lightly on the mouth and the tip of her nose. His smile was sultry. "Did it occur to you that maybe I did all this as much for me as for you? I meant it when I told you I never believed in fairy tales. Please let me believe in tonight."

Cat hadn't the power to resist such a heartfelt plea even
if she had wanted to. He followed it by pulling her against
him and kissing her until she was beyond reason. Using his
teeth and mouth, he peeled first one strap from her shoulder, then the other. He smoothed his hands over their
rounded curves and down her back, his thumbs dragging
the bodice of the nightgown to her waist.

"I did warn you," he whispered, leaning back slightly to
gaze at her breasts.

Cat trembled as he bent his head and touched his tongue
to her nipple. It puckered in response, earning a more
lengthy caress as he painted warm, wet circles around it
before shifting to her other breast and doing the same.

His hands fell to her hips, and once again his thumbs
caught in the folds of silk and dragged it down, down, until it was a moonlight-colored puddle at her feet. He helped
her step free of it and with a gentle tug pulled her with him
down onto the bed. They laughed breathlessly as their
combined weight sent them sinking deep into the soft
feather mattress.

"Better hold on tight," Bolt whispered as he rolled on
top of her, carefully taking his weight on his knees and his
hands, "I could lose you in here."

Obediently she wound her arms around his neck. "I have
no intention of getting lost tonight."

She smiled at him, her expression expectant, her face
bathed in the soft light from all those candles. They had
been a very wise investment, Bolt assured himself as her
hand moved to his face and caressed his cheek. So had the
time he'd spent with the razor.

Her caress was much too mild a touch to suit his suddenly urgent mood, and he had to remind himself of how
slow and gentle he had vowed to be with her tonight. It was
the very least she deserved. All of it, the candles and
champagne and silk nightgown, was less than she deserved. He wanted to give her everything and this was the
only way he knew to start.

It wasn't easy to remember to take his time when her
body, a soft, pliant invitation to heaven, was spread so

sweetly and so close. It wasn't a simple task to hold back and scatter kisses along her throat, as he was doing now, when he was already burning to be inside her.

He wanted to soothe and protect and possess her all at the same time. He wanted to bury himself in her so deeply he felt nothing but her all around him. He wanted to drown in her body and fill her with himself, the only proof he could offer of all the things he was afraid to say.

Straightening his arms, he peered at her with a tenuous half-smile.

"Help me with my shirt," he whispered, wondering why he'd put the damn thing on in the first place. Because, he remembered, he hadn't wanted to go barging in on her bath stark naked and offend her virgin sensibilities.

Virgin. The word alone was an effective reminder and he unconsciously lightened his touch on her breasts as she struggled to work his shirt off one arm.

"You're not a big help," she grumbled.

"You just need more practice," he murmured, lowering his mouth to hers briefly. "Try the other arm."

She was no more efficient with that sleeve, mostly because of the distraction of his persistent mouth and hands. When she'd finally succeeded in tugging it off, she tossed the shirt aside and reached for his belt without being prompted. Excitement filled his chest, locking his breath inside as she unfastened the buckle and snap and lowered the zipper on his jeans.

With his steady hands compensating for her shaky awkwardness, he helped her work them down along with his briefs, relishing the light brush of her fingers and hands on his belly and thighs, hungering for so much more. Kicking the jeans aside, he covered her with his body once again, skin to skin, bone to bone, his strength pressed against her softness.

Sweet heaven, he thought, *let me make this right for her.*

Cat felt the heat and strength in every inch of him as he pressed his body against hers. So much more strength even than she had imagined, his muscles hard and unyielding under her exploring fingers. And the heat... She drew a deep, shuddering breath. He was hot all over, but especially the rigid part of him that lay heavy against her thigh. It seemed to scorch her flesh with each rocking movement of his hips.

She shifted with the sudden movement of the soft bed, her thighs parting just enough to let him slip between.

She froze.

He groaned.

He opened his eyes. A slow smile curved his lips. "Better roll over."

"What?" She blinked rapidly, confused.

"Just do it," he whispered, his hands helping her along so that she rolled over away from him. He eased to his side behind her, his chest to her back, and reached around to cup her breast.

"You're not any less tempting this way," he murmured against the side of her neck, "but with my control hanging by a thread, it's best not to leave things to chance...and this damn bed."

He lifted her arm to nibble the delicate skin along her side, making her quiver with delight.

"Oh, I like that," she said softly.

"So do I."

With one hand he tugged at her breast while his other slid down over her tummy, lower, tangling in the soft curls there. He was pressed to her from shoulder to buttocks. One muscled thigh rode between hers as he pulled her ever more firmly into the cradle of his body. A single finger was trailing up and down the inside of her thigh, a feather stroke that dazzled her senses and clouded her thoughts. Then his hand moved again and his finger slipped deep inside her.

He gave a heavy sigh of satisfaction as Cat went rigid at the sudden possession, limited though it was.

"Easy," he murmured against her hair. "I won't hurt you."

She believed him. She wasn't afraid and she thought of telling him so, but the pleasure spiraling through her from where his finger was moving in slow, rhythmic strokes made it impossible to speak.

He pulled her shoulder back, leaning over her so that his mouth could take her breast. He suckled her, the warm, tugging pull of his mouth in time to the penetrating thrust of his finger. It was too much for Cat to absorb, and wave after wave of feelings she'd never even dreamed of came crashing over her.

She was trembling, her forehead and the hollow between her breasts damp with perspiration as she pressed against him, wanting to get closer, wanting to feel more, wanting to feel everything she had forbidden herself to feel before now.

She opened her eyes and glanced down, awed by the sight of his dark head bent to her breast and the sinuous movement of the muscles beneath his bronzed forearm as he touched her intimately. That was the most arousing sight of all, to watch him bestow the pleasure that was steadily carrying her away.

The candles flickered around her, with Bolt the brightest light of all. His sure, gentle touch was illuminating the way for her, leading her into a world she knew nothing of, a world that instinct alone told her he had mastered long ago. She arched against him as he pressed his hand to her tightly. Bolt murmured and pulled her closer, his hand kneading, moving, the pressure exquisite.

She heard herself, heard the small helpless gasps that started somewhere deep within. His hands and mouth seemed to be everywhere at once. He surrounded her with himself, layering sensation upon sensation too quickly for her analyze and isolate what was making her feel so good from one heartbeat to the next.

She sensed his growing urgency, as well, and it made her mindless with need. She wanted him inside her, as proof of something, that she was still alive, perhaps, or that life went on. Cat didn't have a very good grasp on the intricacies of her feelings just then. She felt and wanted and yearned until primal instinct and his sure hands rolled her onto her back beneath him once again.

This time when his hardness pressed against her, she reached for him, pulling him toward her with all the fierceness of the desire his touch had awakened in her.

He made a low, masculine sound as he stretched, poised above her.

"Look at me," he whispered, his tone as urgent as the passion that seemed to crackle in the air around them.

Cat met his gaze.

"I love you," he groaned as pushed inside her for the first time. "I love you. I love you."

As gentle as he was, the unprecedented invasion was a shock to her senses, driving out all sound and thought. His thrusts were patient and measured, intended to give her time to adjust and accommodate his body, but they were also relentless.

Slowly, slowly, he moved against her, and slowly her body softened and relaxed. Surprise gave way to excitement. Pain became pleasure. When his lips nuzzled her throat, she arched her neck and whimpered. Her legs lifted and curled around his hips and she felt the gradual quickening of his pace.

His breath came hard against her neck. He sucked the sensitive skin there. His weight drove her down into the mattress. Cat was lifting to meet him now, wanting more and more with each thrust, all without knowing fully what it was she wanted. Wanting just the same, with an intensity that left her straining against him.

As his thrusts grew quicker still, they also became harder, their power pushing her forward toward that unknown destination. He was driving straight into her center, straight to the heart of her, and she was lifting, lifting, meeting him on each stroke until passion broke over her and she was there...crying and throbbing and clinging to Bolt as he collapsed against her with a fierce groan that was the sweetest sound she'd ever heard.

She fell asleep in his arms, beyond speaking, the candle still glowing brightly. She woke hours later in darkness, cramp in her neck where it rested on his broad bicep. She carefully freed herself from his embrace. Bolt murmured a sleepy protest, rolled to his other side and continued to breath in the heavy rhythm of deep sleep.

Only then did the words he'd spoken earlier sink in. *I love you,* he'd said. *I love you.*

Cat went cold, inside and out. That couldn't be. He couldn't possibly have said that. If he had, she assured herself, it was simply something he would say to any woman in the heat of passion. As she lay there, fully awake, she came up with a half dozen other explanations, none of which she could make herself believe.

Oh, damn, she thought, *so much for tonight not ending with regrets.*

She rolled to her side and stared at his broad back. What was she going to do now? Run? Pretend she'd never heard the words and hope he came to his senses by morning and didn't repeat them? Laugh if he did and trust he'd get the message?

She decided her approach would depend on Bolt. She would just have to wait and see what happened next. In the meantime, she leaned forward and, purely as an experiment in futility, pressed her lips to his back and whispered against his skin, "I love you, too."

Bolt awoke feeling like Sir Lancelot, ready to don armor and slay dragons or whatever else his fair damsel might want done before breakfast. Even tossing off a quick sonnet or two didn't seem outside the realm of possibility this morning. Did knights write sonnets? he wondered groggily. Didn't matter. If his damsel wanted a sonnet, so be it.

Speaking of damsels... Bolt opened one eye and saw her across the room. She was already dressed, he noted with only mild disappointment. What went on could come off.

"Bring me my trusty dagger," he muttered, enjoying an erotic vision of slicing off her cutoff denims and pale pink T-shirt.

Cat turned, stunning him all over again with her beauty. She appeared more spectacular to him than the most perfect sunrise, and he wanted to see her just this way every morning for the rest of his life.

"What did you say?" she asked.

"Forget it. What are you doing up so early?"

"Cleaning up."

He sat leaning against the solid headboard and observed that she had indeed cleaned up all traces of the night before. The candles were lined up neatly on the largest dresser, like soldiers given an early discharge, he thought dryly. The ice bucket and table with their untouched dinner were nowhere in sight, likewise the nightgown, which he had a sudden hankering to see on her again.

"Come here," he said, lifting one arm in invitation.

"No."

He cocked his head to the side, his eyes narrowed, something inside him pulling tight, like a whipcord around his heart. "No?"

She shook her head. "No."

"Have I missed something here? Like a twist in the plot between last night and this morning?"

"For heaven's sake, Bolt," she said, snatching the robe from where it lay on the floor and heading for the bathroom with it. "Just because this place looks like something straight out of a fairy tale doesn't make us characters in one. Plot twist." She disappeared, shaking her head.

Oh, yeah, he thought. He'd missed something all right. He folded his arms behind his head and waited for her to reappear. It would have been nice if Cat had woken this morning as aware as he was of the truth, that they belonged to each other. Call it what you like—chemistry, fate, destiny—she was meant to be his.

It would have been nice if she had accepted that fact as readily as he had, but he really hadn't expected it. She'd suffered quite a shock yesterday. Learning the truth about her parents' deaths had shaken her most cherished beliefs to the core, and whether or not she would admit it, that had a whole lot to do with all that had followed. He wasn't sorry he had made love to her. He understood that it had been inevitable. He just wished it could have happened under different circumstances.

This way, whatever Cat felt for him was bound to get all mixed up with her renewed grief for her parents and with the natural aftershocks of finding out that a good part of what she had taken for gospel in her life was really just a pretty fabrication intended to shield her from the truth. It was going to take time for her to work through all her feelings, and he was going to give it to her. Just as long as she understood that he was there for her when she needed him.

She emerged from the bathroom carrying the small flowered case that held her cosmetics and tossed it into her open suitcase.

"Don't you think you should get out of bed?" she asked without looking at him.

"Actually what I was thinking was that you should get back in bed with me."

"Forget it."

"I don't think I can do that," he said, quiet amusement in his voice.

"Well, you have to." She faced him at last, the color high in her cheeks, her violet eyes flashing, with what Bolt wasn't quite sure. Anger? At him? Herself? Both, most likely. "I mean it, Bolt," she said. "It's only going to make the rest of the trip harder for both of us if you go trying to make last night into something it wasn't."

He unfolded his arms from behind his head and dropped them to his lap, clasping them together lightly on top of the sheet. "Why don't you tell me what you think last night was and we'll go from there?"

"Sex," she said without hesitation. "Great sex."

"You being qualified to discern great sex from say, bad sex, or mediocre sex?"

"I know what I felt," she snapped, shoving her hair behind her ear. A dead giveaway that she was nervous, Bolt noted with satisfaction.

"Thank you for that, at least, acknowledging that you felt something."

Her eyes darkened. "You know I did."

"I wouldn't know from the way you've been acting this morning."

"I just think we should get moving," she said, turning away to rearrange the already neatly folded items in her suitcase.

"Are you in a hurry all of a sudden?"

"Yes." She glanced at him. "To tell you the truth I am. I've decided I want to get back home as soon as possible. I need to talk to Uncle Hank about...about things," she concluded grimly.

"I see. Can't wait to let him have it with both barrels, hmm?"

"No." She looked horrified. "I would never do that. He did what he did to protect me, just as he always has. I don't always agree with his methods, but I can't hate him for it...or for making mistakes." She heaved a weary sigh. "Truthfully, if I was facing the task of having to explain a nightmare to a five-year-old, I'm not sure what kind of story I would have resorted to. No, I could never blame him for any of this, but there are things I'm ready to know about my parents that only he can tell me."

Bolt nodded, loving her even more at that moment than he had at the height of his passion the night before. He should have known she wouldn't be interested in recriminations or assigning blame for the mistakes of the past, but rather in moving on. Perhaps a woman to whom it came so naturally to forgive and forget could even teach the likes of him to do the same.

"I think that's real smart of you," he told her. "Staying angry is the best way I know to eat yourself up inside. And I can understand that you want to get back there to see the general, but stealing a few hours this morning isn't going to make a whole lot of difference. I was even thinking we might stay here another night and—"

"No." She looked horrified and the shake of her head was even more emphatic than her tone. Which was saying something, Bolt thought. "Bolt, I don't know how to say this except to just say it. Last night was...wonderful. I'll never forget your...kindness."

"Kindness ?" he echoed, his eyes narrowing dubiously. "Is that what you thought I was being? Kind?"

"I mean in going out of your way to make it special for me... and it was special, believe me. The champagne and candles. I can't imagine a more perfect night."

"But."

She wet her lips, so totally unaware of the effect such a gesture had on him that he wanted to drag her onto the bed and crush her mouth under his to clue her in.

"But," she said, "I'm not going to sleep with you again."

Something unbearably sharp sliced him right down the middle. It was a bloody miracle he could speak, much less sound cavalier. "Just like that?"

"Not exactly just like that, as if it's a whim or something, but that's the way it has to be."

"Mind if I ask why?"

"Because I don't want you to get the wrong idea," she replied, sticking her hands first in her front pockets, then the back, then linking them awkwardly in front of her.

"Is that something like asking if I'll still respect you in the morning? Because if it is, the answer is yes."

"I didn't mean that you might get the wrong idea about my morals or something, but about the future."

"Our future?"

"Yes. You see, the point is..." She shoved her hands in her front pockets once more. "We don't have one."

"We could," he countered softly when what he actually felt like doing was shouting and beating his chest like some Neanderthal. The fact that he was suddenly seeing and forced to deal with an all new side of himself made this conversation even more difficult.

"No. You see," she said, running her fingers through her hair, leaving it in disarray so that it reminded him of how it had looked spread across his pillow last night, "this is exactly what I was afraid was going to happen. That you would build last night up in your mind to be more than just—"

"Just what?" he challenged. "A roll in the hay? No? An experiment? I've got it, a lapse in judgment?"

"Maybe a little of each of those things. And now you're trying to make it something more."

"It was more," he insisted.

"Even if it was...you're expecting more than I can give."

The plaintive note in her voice got to him. "Come on, Tiger," he said, climbing from the bed with no thought of his nakedness. "I don't want to fight with you...especially not about this." He took her in his arms, easily overriding her resistance. "I know this is a real bad time for you. I know how it must seem you don't have anything left to give right now—"

"Or ever," she interjected firmly. "I'm not just saying this for now, I'm saying it forever."

Bolt jerked back to look at her face. "I love you," he growled.

"No." She wrenched free. "Don't say that, please. And please, for Pete's sake, put something on."

She averted her gaze while he found his jeans and yanked them on, not bothering with the button at the waist.

"Why shouldn't I say it?" he demanded, coming up behind where she stood looking out the window, her arms folded stiffly across her chest. "It's the truth."

"Please . . . I'm not quite that naive."

He grabbed her shoulders and spun her around to face him. "I don't think you're naive at all. You're young, sure. I admit that at first I thought you were too young and too vulnerable to get messed up with someone as jaded and washed-up as me. But I don't think that any longer. I think now that you're the most beautiful, wisest, kindest, sexiest—"

"Stop, please, just stop. Why do you want to put both of us through this?"

"Because I love you," he said again, bewildered that she couldn't seem to understand the utter, unprecedented wonder of that. He was in love, and that changed everything he thought or wanted or needed. And in the end, it was going to change her mind about this, too. He had no doubt about that.

"Love." Her laugh was lancing. "What do you know about love?"

"What you taught me."

She looked startled.

"For instance, I know that you don't get to dictate where and when and with whom it happens. I know that you can be with a hundred wrong women and not feel it, then feel it like that." He snapped his fingers. "When the right woman comes along."

"There's no such thing as the right woman," she said wearily. "That was all nonsense, a dumb kid's fantasy."

"Last night was no fantasy."

"I told you, last night was sex."

"Uh-uh. It was destiny."

She shook her head, her eyes filled with pity and something else. The same thing he'd seen there earlier. Fear, he realized, and suddenly he understood. "You'll learn," she said.

Bolt bent and landed a quick kiss on her gorgeous mouth. "Or you will."

Chapter Twelve

By the time Bolt had finished showering and getting dressed, Cat was packed and ready to go. And more determined than ever that she was doing the right thing. For Bolt as well as herself.

He might truly believe he was in love with her, or, much more likely in her opinion, he was trying in the only way he knew to console her after what had happened to her yesterday. Noble, but not his problem. Then again, perhaps for the time being he needed to believe it in order to justify having made love to her in the first place. She imagined that even a former soldier would have a few qualms about messing with old Lucifer's niece.

Another time she would have giggled wildly over that archaic prospect. But not today.

Whatever his reasoning, the indisputable fact remained that there was no future for them together. It seemed ridiculous to say she knew he wasn't the right man for her when she was no longer at all sure that such a thing even existed.

She could say with certainty, however, that he was the wrong man.

Last night had been wonderful and she wasn't sorry it had happened. She also wasn't naive enough to believe that a little good chemistry could compensate indefinitely for a total lack of compatibility outside the bedroom.

Perhaps if Bolt hadn't said that he loved her, she could have let things between them drift until they returned home and parted company. But as sure as she was that they would drive each other bonkers in no time, she was also sure that nothing resembling a casual affair would ever be possible with a man as intense as Bolt Hunter. He hadn't made his declaration of love lightly, and he wouldn't take her decision to end this thing before it really got started lightly, either. She was prepared to deal with that as best she could for the time remaining.

And she vowed to do everything in her power to make that remaining time as brief as possible.

With their bags waiting by the door, Bolt spread the map on the table in the sitting room to check the day's route one more time. It was something he did like clockwork every morning and the moment Cat had been waiting for.

She cleared her throat.

"I, uh, I'm not sure if it affects the route we'll be taking, but I wanted to mention that I won't have to stop in Charleston after all."

Still bent over the open map, his palms flat on the table, he turned his head to glance at her curiously. "Why not?"

She shrugged. "A change in plans. I decided the background of the writer I was going there to see was too similar to Madelaine Van der Court's, so I'm going to skip her. I've already called and made my excuses."

"All right. If that's the case, we'll still take Route 95 south, but push right on through to Savannah."

Cat clasped her hands, her damp palms sealed together. "Actually, I'm not going to make the stop in Savannah, either."

"Let me guess. A problem with that person's background, too?"

"Pretty much."

"Dixie Union?" he inquired, his eyebrows raised.

She shook her head.

Bolt tossed the pencil he was holding across the room. "Don't do this," he said quietly.

"I'm not doing anything. I just want to get home as soon as possible, and since these last few stops aren't crucial to my story, I decided to pass on them."

"And at the same time reduce the amount of time you have to spend with me. Right?"

"That's not my intention—"

"Bull."

"All right. It is my intention, but I'm not doing this to hurt you, Bolt. The opposite, in fact."

"I told you I'm in love with you. So exactly how is getting rid of me early supposed to keep from hurting me?" he demanded, straightening.

"All right, maybe it won't. But if I have to hurt you, I'd rather do it now than drag this whole thing out and do it later when it will only be worse."

"What formula is that bit of logic based on?" he inquired in a dry tone. "Pain times number of days equals intensity?"

"I don't need a formula," she shot back. "Some things you just know in your heart are true."

A triumphant smile spread slowly across his face, so devastating that Cat almost felt like giving in to the urge to climb into that big bed with him and pull the covers over their heads and stay there forever.

"That's what I've been trying to tell you, sweetheart," he said quietly. "What I know in my heart is true."

Lacking any more logical response to that, she tossed her head and looked him straight in the eye and said, "I still want to go home."

"Okay. Home it is." He folded the map as he continued speaking, sliding it into his bag and then hoisting the bag to his shoulder. "We'll play this out your way." Before she could duck out of reach, he took her chin between his thumb and forefinger and forced her to maintain eye con act. "Just as long as you understand that this doesn't change anything."

There were at least a hundred different times during the day when Bolt cursed himself for agreeing to drive straight through on what was to be the last leg of their trip. And a hundred times when he considered simply pulling into a motel over her objections and coming up with some reason they absolutely had to stop for the night. The trouble was, the only reason he could think of for stopping was so that he could make love to Cat again. His sudden dearth in creativity was understandable, since thoughts of making love to her had taken up permanent residence in each and every one of his active brain cells, crowding out previous tenants such as logic and restraint. He thought about loving her constantly, with each breath, each passing mile, each highway sign that reminded him in a bold numerical countdown how close they were getting to home and that moment when she would tell him goodbye.

With Cat having several times reiterated her willingness to shoulder part of the driving, he couldn't very well claim fatigue as a reason for stopping. He drove most of the day and into the night, moving through North and South Carolina and deep into Georgia. It grew hotter and more humid as they got farther south, but the mood in the car remained at a constant stilted coolness. It was difficult to make conversation when she refused to talk about the only thing that was on his mind.

He finally let Cat take the wheel late that night, when the traffic had thinned and she was rested from a long after-dinner nap, during which he'd divided his attention between the road and the art of committing to memory every line of her beautiful face. He'd meant it when he told her that returning home would not in any way change his feelings for her or his conviction that they were meant to be together.

He didn't yet know how he was going to bring her around to his way of thinking on the subject, but he was resigned to the fact that high-pressure tactics would never work on Cat. Even if they would have, she was in much too fragile

an emotional state at the moment for him to even consider
such measures. He had made up his mind that for Cat's
sake he was going to have to—at this late date—learn patience and the art of compromise. Even if it killed him. He
also accepted the fact that such a strategy of restraint might
temporarily result in his going days at a time without seeing her. That was his reason for memorizing her face so
diligently.

Just once during the day did he think he glimpsed the
elusive black Mustang. It temporarily roused all his cu-
mulative concerns about Cuba and the car he was driving
and the men who had hired Cat to bring it to them. The
longer he knew her, the more she seemed an unlikely choice
for the job. The black car turned out to be a Firebird, and
once again his daydreams about the woman he loved over-
whelmed him. They were stronger and more persistent than
any distraction, especially one that had proved to have little if any basis in fact. He even felt a little ridiculous for
some of the sinisterly suspicious thoughts he'd entertained
along the way.

Somewhere in southern Georgia, with Cat at the wheel,
he nodded off. When he awoke they were in Florida
headed south on Interstate 95, with his watch reading 1:45
a.m. He stretched lazily until he caught sight of a sign announcing they were twenty-eight miles from Tampa. Instantly all sense of ease drained from him like water being
poured into a hole dug in beach sand. He frowned as he
gazed outside, not wanting to believe the sign, but sure
enough, he recognized enough familiar landmarks as they
streaked past to accept the fact that they were almost home.

"You're awake," Cat observed.

"Yeah." Bolt rotated his shoulders to loosen the muscles there. "I didn't mean to zonk out on you like that."

"No problem. It gave me time to think."

His quick glance was hopeful. "And?"

"And I decided it makes sense for me to drop you at your
place in Tampa and then go on to Sarasota myself."

"No," he said, thinking only how that would mean he
had even less time left with her.

"Trust me on this one, Hunter. It's the perfect plan."

He welcomed the note of humor that had returned to her voice even if he hated what she was saying. "Explain to me how your driving another hour by yourself is any kind of plan?"

"Because it means we both get to sleep in our own beds tonight."

"Is that supposed to be an incentive for me to agree?" he couldn't resist inserting dryly.

She silenced him with a look. "That is, if I can even get to sleep after all the coffee I've drunk in the last few hours. It also means I'll be able to deliver the car first thing in the morning and be done with it."

"Where's the drop-off?"

"I have to call Gator and he'll let me know."

"That figures," he drawled. "I still can't help wondering what this guy is skimming off the top as his incentive. Maybe I ought to be with you when you see him."

"That really isn't necessary," she assured him, her overly sweet tone alerting him that a zinger was to follow. "But if I do decide I need a macho, overprotective, thickheaded ogre to come along, I'll be sure to go straight to the best... Uncle Hank."

Bolt scowled out the window. He was no expert at this game, but it would seem that being lumped so unflatteringly with her uncle wasn't to his advantage. Sure, she loved old Lucifer, but he had sort of protected status in her life. Bolt didn't. Not yet.

Compromise, he reminded himself, working up an agreeable smile. *When in doubt, compromise.*

"All right, I get the message," he said. "You can handle things yourself from here."

"Actually I could have—"

"Handled them yourself from the start," he finished for her. "I know that now. Thanks for letting me tag along."

She slanted him a look that said she wasn't sure if he was being sincere. When his smile assured her that he was, she gave him a rueful grin. "I hope it wasn't too bad for you."

"Not at all. I wouldn't have missed taking this trip for anything." It had changed his life for the better, and for-ever. In return, he was going to change hers the same way. But she wasn't ready to accept that yet.

"You'll have to give me directions to your place," she told him. "All you've said is that you don't live too far from the office."

She seemed surprised and relieved when he didn't argue any further about who was going home first. Bolt told her what exit to take and directed her the short way to the apartment complex where he'd lived for two years but had yet to hang a single picture or unpack his personal belong-ings except for those he needed to survive.

He already knew he was going to invite her to come in and he already knew that she was going to refuse. As much as he would prefer her to spend the night, there was a bright spot to her refusal. He wanted Cat's love, not her pity, and he knew that the latter was what would be stirred by the sight of the bleak way he'd chosen to exist since leaving the Army.

This way he would have time to hang a few things on the walls and stack the bookshelves before she saw the place. It was time, he decided. He smiled to himself as she fol-lowed his instructions to turn into the parking lot behind his building, thinking he would even buy a coffeepot and real coffee and some of those muffins Cat liked.

It was late and the parking spots closest to the building were all taken. Bolt could have had her pull up in front of the door and wait while he grabbed his bag from the trunk but he didn't.

"There's a spot over there on the end," he told her pointing at the last spot in the row across from the build-ing, where the bright glow from the streetlights didn't quite reach.

"Better turn it off," he warned when she shifted into park and let the engine idle. "You're getting low on gas."

She glanced at the fuel indicator, which was at three quarters full.

"I've been noticing that it sticks there and then shoots down all of a sudden," he lied. "Better to be safe than sorry."

She chuckled as she turned the key to off. "Boy, you really are like Uncle Hank."

Bolt bristled in silence.

"I guess this is it," he said.

Cat nodded, her hands dropping from the wheel to rest lightly clasped in her lap. "I guess. I want to thank you, Bolt, for everything. I really mean that, no matter how I might have felt about having you along at first."

"Hey, I understand. I wouldn't have liked having someone forced on me that way, either."

"But it turned out all right . . . for me, anyway—I mean, it was nice having someone with me. Especially . . ."

"I know," he said softly, longing to reach out and pull her into his arms and tell her that if she'd let him he would always be there with her, for the bad times and the good times and all the times in between.

"So, thanks."

Her tremulous smile pierced his heart. "Anytime, Tiger. Anytime."

"Fine. The next time I'm asked to drive a car here from Canada, I'll give you a call."

"You do that. But next time, do me a favor and make sure it's really coming from Canada, will you?"

"You got it," she agreed, wrinkling her nose above an impish grin. Bolt opened the door, knowing that each moment he sat there made it harder to leave her.

He pulled the keys from the ignition and opened the trunk to get his bag, slamming it afterward. Hitching the strap over one shoulder, he walked to the driver's side to return the keys to her.

"All set?" she asked, reaching for them.

Bolt held them just beyond her grasp. "Except for one last thing," he told her, chaining her suddenly wary gaze with his in the darkness.

"Bolt, please—"

"A goodbye kiss," he interjected. "That's it, I promise. I think I've earned that much."

She folded her arms, looked at the keys dangling from his finger, then tipped back her head and closed her eyes. "Go ahead," she grumbled.

"Nice try," he retorted, yanking the door open and her out of her seat. "I want a real kiss from you."

He got it...and along with it the answer he needed to take away with him. Cat's resistance to him had no more substance than cotton candy in the rain. It melted the instant his mouth claimed hers. She opened to him, letting him taste the heat and passion of the night before, urging him closer with her tongue and soft, breathless sounds even as her hands remained splayed against his chest.

It would take little effort or expertise to tip her into the backseat, he thought as he made love to her mouth the way he longed to make love to her right there in the car. Only slightly more finesse would carry her into his apartment and his bed. But he didn't want to seduce Cat or trick her. He wanted her to come to him with her eyes open, understanding what this was between them and wanting him in the same way he wanted her. To be his partner, his lover, his soul mate. Forever.

When he lifted his mouth from hers at last, he raked his teeth gently along the sweet hollow of her throat, a pleasure too tempting to resist.

Bracketing her face with his hands, he smiled at her tenderly.

"Cat, I've spent my whole life trying to figure out where I belong in the world, trying to find something I could do or have or be that was mine alone, that someone else hadn't done first and better. After not knowing what was right for so long," he declared, "I'm not likely to make a mistake when I find something that is. So don't try to tell me this isn't happening."

"Okay, I won't," she agreed between deep, telltale breaths. "Just so long as you understand that this doesn't change anything, either."

Cat had never felt so utterly alone as she did driving away. It was understandable, she told herself, trying to grip the wheel with sweaty palms and trying to ignore the still churning heaviness in her belly. She was alone, for one thing, in a big old car, without another set of headlights in sight anywhere. She was also still grappling with what she had learned about her parents, still plagued by dozens of painful questions that only her uncle could answer, still bowed under the weight of knowing that those answers were also probably going to be painful.

All of that was nothing, however, compared to the stark and frightening realization that the ice-cold loneliness at her core had to do only with the man who stood reflected in her rearview mirror, standing watch as she drove out of sight.

Bolt was right. She did feel something happening when he kissed her, just as she had felt something when he made love to her. Novice though she was, she had read articles and heard stories about first-time disasters, and she knew that her first time had been singularly perfect. She would always be grateful to Bolt for making it so.

That didn't mean she liked the way he was addicted to scheduling and routine or the way he barked orders or cut his hair, for that matter. Petty as those things sounded, she knew that once the glow of infatuation wore off, it was exactly that sort of petty concern that either made or broke a relationship.

She hadn't lived with Bolt long enough to discover all his annoying habits and stringent beliefs, but she'd lived with her uncle Hank, and the two men were indisputably cut from the same mold. Sparks would fly outside the bedroom when Bolt's predilection for neatness and order collided with the pack rat tendencies she had no intention of giving up.

She sighed, staying in the slow lane as she headed for Sarasota and home. In a way, they were both right. Bolt was right about the attraction between them, and she was right about its dim prospects for the long haul. Certain parts of her body, which were still warm and sensitive from his touch in the parking lot, clamored for her to forget about the long haul and go for the moment.

Impulse could have been her middle name if her mother hadn't been so partial to Amelia, and another time, she would have followed the urges of her newly awakened libido and done a quick U-turn right there and then.

But this wasn't just anytime. This was the day after she'd discovered secrets from the past that she'd never even dreamed existed. Uncle Hank had done a very thorough snow job, she reflected, torn as she had been much of the past day between resentment and appreciation. If she was having trouble handling this now, how would she ever have coped then? Or at thirteen or eighteen? Perhaps her uncle had planned to wait and tell her the truth at the right time, only to discover as the years passed that there was no right time for such a thing.

There was only now, and now that she knew the truth, she had to accept it and go on. She would, she mused, confident of her own resilience. She also knew, however, that it was going to take all the emotional strength and energy she possessed to get centered once again. If there was a safe time for her to have a fling with a man like Bolt, this surely wasn't it.

She arrived home a little over an hour after dropping off Bolt. She'd agreed to call him as soon as she got there to let him know she was safe. If she expected him to do more than thank her for calling, she was disappointed. The husky undercurrent of desire that had been in his voice earlier was gone and replaced by a familiar note of military crispness.

Automaton, she muttered as she dumped the receiver in the cradle and ambled off to bed.

She managed to sleep in spite of the coffee, her dreams filled with castles and white lace and Bolt. She woke up from one so vivid she opened her arms and reached for him, expecting to find him stretched out beside her, his hands moving over her naked body, his smile slow and seductive the way it had been in her dream. She sighed when she realized she was alone and rolled over to check the clock and see if it was time to call Gator.

She was eager to get rid of the car. Having such a gigantic reminder of Bolt parked right outside her front door wasn't what she needed right now.

She needed to put Bolt and men in general out of her mind entirely and concentrate on making peace with the past... starting with Uncle Hank, she thought. As soon as she'd dropped off the car, she would give him a call and ask if he wanted to come for dinner tonight.

Gator sounded immensely relieved to hear from her.

"What the heck took you so long?" he demanded.

"I'd hardly call this a long time," she retorted, irked. "Besides, you said there was no hurry."

"There wasn't really. But I sure didn't expect you to..." He paused. "Did you end up taking a friend along?"

"No," Cat replied, deciding that Bolt wasn't exactly a friend.

"No?"

"No. Look, it's a long story and I'm sort of in a hurry to get this over with."

"Oh, *now* you're in a hurry."

"For heaven's sake, Gator, give me a break, will you? I'm tired and ornery and I have a zillion things I need to take care of for myself today," she told him, staring at the bag of film from the trip and the grocery list she'd made. "Just tell me where to bring the car."

He told her about a service station a few miles out of town. Grant's, he said it was called.

"Wouldn't it be easier if I just... forget it," she added, deciding that perhaps LaCompte wanted a mechanic to take a look at it right away. In that case it would make more sense for her to bring it directly to the station than to his place. "What kind of station is it?" she asked. "Shell? Exxon? So I'll know what kind of sign to look for."

"Just Grant's," he replied, the edge of impatience still clear in his voice. Cat rolled her eyes, thinking old laid-back Gator was certainly taking his responsibility here seriously. You'd think he was the one driving the car. "I don't think there is a big sign or anything. Don't worry, follow that road and you can't miss it. I've still got your car here, so I'll drive that out and meet you."

"Fine, then I can give you a ride back to the shop."

"Yeah, well, don't worry about that."

Cat shrugged, as if she had the time and energy to take on any additional worries at the moment.

She showered and dressed and headed outside to the car. She found herself feeling surprisingly nostalgic as she drove, savoring the feel of the wind in her hair for the last time. In the short time she'd been around the Chevy, she'd developed a real fondness for it. If she had the money, she wouldn't mind owning it herself. It sure would bring back memories, she mused, both bad and good. Maybe that was the way it ought to be. Maybe life was never meant to be a fairy tale, and the bad times were a reminder to savor the good.

When she left the freeway and turned onto the road Gator had told her about, she was certain either he or she had made a mistake somewhere. She was in the middle of nowhere, with what looked like farmland and orchards all around and no one in sight to ask for directions.

She reached over and hauled her faithful tote bag onto the seat, fishing around in it for the notebook in which she'd written the directions as he gave them to her.

"Oh, no," she groaned, realizing she must have run out and left it by the telephone. Her unlucky streak continued, she thought.

Keeping watch for a phone booth, if such things existed that far from civilization, she drove on. At last, just as she was about to give up, she saw up ahead what she supposed could have passed for a service station in another era. Set back off the road, in a patch of weeds and dust, was a low building with a few old-fashioned, rusty-looking pumps out front. Cat frowned as she drew closer, thinking it had been a few years since those pumps had seen any action.

This was where LaCompte wanted his very expensive new toy dropped off? Must be, she decided, shrugging, since the sign out front—hanging from only one bolt so she had to turn her head sideways to read it—confirmed that this was

Grant's, just as Gator had told her. Of course, when she factored Gator into the equation, she really shouldn't be surprised by anything.

As she swung into the lot, she raised a cloud of dust that made her wish she hadn't put the top down that morning after all. She drove over to the side of the building, where her car was parked alongside a shiny new Cadillac. La-Compte's, she speculated, eager to get her first look at him. Coughing, she climbed out of the car and glanced around.

As she stood there, debating whether or not to lean on the horn, the door of one of the garage bays lifted and Gator appeared. His long blond hair was in its customary state of disarray, his hands thrust in his jeans pockets, sunlight glinting off the gold hoop in one ear.

"Good," he exclaimed. "You're here."

"In the flesh," Cat replied, her gaze moving past him as she struggled to see into the darkened garage.

"Great flesh it is, too," he drawled, whacking her playfully on the butt, which earned him a decidedly unplayful glare from Cat. He grinned sheepishly. "What can I say? I missed you, kid."

A slight exaggeration, she was certain, but Gator was one of those characters she liked in spite of herself.

"Looks good, looks good," he said, circling the Chevy. "Keys?"

She tossed them to him. He opened the trunk and quickly shut it again. "Great."

Cat failed to see what was so great about an empty trunk to make him grin idiotically, but she'd learned not to question whatever floated Gator's boat from moment to moment.

"Here are the keys to your chariot," he said, holding them out to her. "Uh, it needs gas."

"Gee, thanks." She looked around. "Isn't this supposed to be a gas station?"

"Not that kind of gas station."

"You mean the kind where you can buy gas?" she countered, deadpan.

"Right. Cheer up, though, at least you can afford to fill the tank...with high-test, yet," he added. "Here's a check for what's due you, plus a nice little bonus to cover expenses. This way you won't have to submit any receipts or anything like that." He grinned. "Receipts are so bourgeois."

"That reminds me," she said, recalling the close call involving receipts at the border, "how do I make sure the car registration is taken out of my name?"

"Relax. Tony will take care of all that. He's got connections."

She didn't doubt that for a minute. She'd been so excited to have the job that she hadn't thought too carefully about all the details beforehand. Now that she'd had time to reflect and, she was forced to admit, had the benefit of Bolt's take on matters, she shared his view that the whole deal was a little murky. She was glad it was over with, for more reasons than one.

Gator moved as if to return to the garage. "Thanks a mill, kiddo. You done real good."

"Gator, hold on." She sidled closer to him and angled her head toward the garage where she thought she could make out two men standing off to the side. "Is that La-Compte in there now?"

He looked surprised by the question. "Uh, yeah, actually, it is."

"Can I meet him?"

"I don't think that's such a good idea. He's kind of—"

"Shy?" she suggested sarcastically.

"Private. That's it. He's a real private guy."

"Well, seeing as I just drove his precious car all that way I think the least I can do is say hello to the man."

Gator caught her arm as she spun toward the garage. "Trust me on this one, kiddo. It's a bad idea. LaCompte can be downright rude when he wants to be."

He grinned. The man was impossible and irresponsible, but he had a grin that could chase clouds away and launch a thousand ships.

"Go home, relax and think about how you're going to spend all your money," he advised.

"Right. You mean think about which bill to pay first," she grumbled, reluctantly allowing him to escort her to her car.

He opened the door and waved her in with a flourish. "That sounds like fun too. Ciao, baby. I'll be in touch."

Cat started the engine and frowned as the fuel arrow barely moved above the warning line. Gator wasn't kidding about its needing gas. She rolled down the window to give him a little more flack about it, but he was already moving the Chevy into the garage. She felt a small pang at seeing it disappear inside and the heavy door roll down.

"So long, pal," she muttered under her breath. "It was fun while it lasted."

She pulled onto the road with her fingers crossed that she'd make it to a real gas station before the car hit empty. The little car's engine coughed and sputtered before achieving a measure of smoothness. She already missed the sweet purr of the old convertible, and the surge of power when she tapped the gas pedal, and the roomy comfort of those wide-open seats. And she missed looking over and seeing Bolt's long, strong fingers resting lightly on the wheel, making driving look as effortless as he did everything else. When you came right down to it, she missed Bolt.

To be expected, she assured herself, and altogether temporary.

She hoped.

She was all the way back to the highway when she remembered Soldier Bunny.

She'd tucked him down into the side well for the spare tire and forgotten all about him when she unpacked the trunk this morning. Without another thought she did a sharp U-turn and headed back to Grant's.

The Caddy was still there when she got back. So, she thought with satisfaction, she was going to get a glimpse of the elusive and difficult Mr. LaCompte after all.

As she approached the closed garage door, she heard loud noise from within, like the sound of a motor. They must be already working on the car, she mused, wondering what could have required such immediate attention.

She knocked on the door and then, when she got no response, pounded on it with her fist. Still no one came, and Cat reasoned that if the noise was that loud out here, it must be worse inside, surely loud enough to keep her from being heard.

She bent and grabbed the metal door handle, trying to lift it, but to no avail. It was either locked or rusted or just too heavy for her. Glancing around, she saw the door to what must have at least at one time been the office and went to try it. It opened easily and she walked inside.

Her timing was impeccable, although not necessarily fortuitous. Just as she stepped into the bay area of the garage, the noise ceased and a man wearing a protective mask of some sort and holding what looked like a fancy drill shouted, "Eureka."

Gator was standing at the other side of the trunk, armed with a similar mask and drill. "And then some," he added, whistling through his teeth. "Mother lode city, here we come. All right, grab that side and let's take a look."

Cat took a step closer and realized that what she took for drills were actually electric saws with long narrow blades, and that they had just sawed through the bottom of the trunk for some reason and were about to remove it.

"What on earth . . ."

She stopped and froze as together Gator and the other man lifted a sheet of metal the size of the trunk bottom, revealing neat piles of money packed beneath it. It wasn't merely the size of the trunk floor, she realized, it *was* the trunk floor, or at least a phony one intended to hide the money...money smuggled in from Cuba and then over the border into this country. By her, she realized in panic.

Gator had shoved off his mask and was staring at her in angry disbelief.

"What the hell are you doing back here?" he demanded.

"Funny, I was just about to ask you the same question. What are you doing? And where did all that money come from?"

Gator glanced anxiously at something over her shoulder.

"Is this the broad who drove the car?" asked a smooth, deep voice.

"Sure is," Gator replied. "The one and only Cat Bandini. Cat, meet Tony LaCompte."

LaCompte stepped out of the shadows, a tall, well-built man whom she could easily dislike. He had slick written all over him, from his well-cut hair to his shiny loafers. He looked like a man who liked getting what he wanted in life and didn't allow anyone to get in his way...especially not broads dumb enough to smuggle money and cars for him.

"Ms. Bandini," he said, nodding. "You should have taken your friend's advice and gone home when you had the chance."

When she had the chance? Meaning...what? Cat wondered frantically. She was too afraid to ask.

"I...I forgot...something."

"This something?"

LaCompte held up Soldier Bunny.

She nodded.

"Ah, Cat, over a stupid toy?" Gator said.

"It's a souvenir," she explained feebly.

"I would have brought it to you. You should have listened to me and gone home."

"Okay, then, I'll go now."

"Stop her," LaCompte ordered.

Ignoring him, she whirled around and ran smack into the human equivalent of a brick wall. She hadn't seen the third man move, yet there he was behind her without his drill or mask, blocking her escape.

"Hi, sugar," he drawled, smiling down at her. "Long time no see."

It was the man from the rest stop, the one who'd helped her when Bolt had loosened the wires on her car.

So Bolt had been right, she thought with a sick feeling that was quickly forming a knot in her stomach. None of it was merely a coincidence, after all.

Oh, Bolt, she thought as she felt Gator move in behind her, *why didn't I listen to you?*

Gator quickly jerked her arms around to the back, his grip hard and unyielding. As he wound a rope around and between her wrists, she tasted fear at the back of her tongue.

Oh, help me, help me, she prayed. *Please help me, Bolt.*

"I tried to warn you," Gator said in a sharp voice. "I told you that you coming in here would be a bad idea, a real bad idea."

Chapter Thirteen

General Hollister clapped Bolt on the shoulder.

"A job well done, Bolt. Yes, indeed, a job well done. Not that I expected anything less from you, of course. You're still the best."

Shrugging off what he considered undue praise, Bolt turned away and moved to perch on the corner of his desk. The general was comfortably ensconced in the comfortable leather chair in front of him. He had come directly to see Bolt when he arrived at the office and learned Bolt was back to work, demanding a full report on what he referred to as "that little assignment."

Several times since he'd finished telling him, Bolt had to tame a wry smile that was threatening to erupt any second. He wasn't convinced his former commanding officer would be so quite so pleased with the way things had turned out if he knew that Bolt's involvement with his niece had been considerably more than protective in nature, and that it was far from over.

He had no intention of keeping his feelings for Cat a secret from the older man indefinitely. He just felt it only fair that he should give her time to adjust to the idea that she was his before he sprang it on the only family she had.

"I owe you one for handling this, Bolt," Hollister said, "and I won't forget it."

"You took care of my files while I was away, General, that makes us square."

"Bah." Hollister dismissed that with a wave of his hand. "I just handed it all off to Robertson."

"Did I hear my name?"

Tom Robertson, who'd been with the firm about six months longer than Bolt, stepped into the office.

"I was on my way to the fax room and I heard someone mention my name. What's going on?"

"Nothing," General Hollister said brusquely.

Bolt reined in another smile. It was common knowledge that though the general relied heavily on Robertson's compulsive expertise in a number of areas, he had no patience for it.

"But I heard—"

"I was saying," Hollister said loudly enough to drown him out, "that you pitched in to handle Bolt's work while he was away."

"Yes, I did. I have all the files in my office . . . updated and diaried in chronological order," he added a bit reproachfully. Bolt just smiled. "I'll have my secretary bring them to you right away, Bolt. If I had known you'd be back today I would have been sure to—"

Bolt held up his hand. "That's all right, Robertson. didn't know for sure myself when I would be getting back."

Robertson's eyes widened behind his owlish glasses. "I it true you were off driving a fifty-seven Chevy?"

"It's true."

Robertson gave a shrill whistle. "What was it like?"

"She was a beauty," Bolt told him, thinking about mo than the car he'd just spent the week with. "All curves an spirit."

"Fast?" Robertson asked, eyes glittering.

"Fast enough for me," he said simply.

"Boy, oh, boy, would I love to get behind the wheel of one of those babies," Robertson said, sighing. "How about you, General?"

"Well, to tell you two youngsters the truth, I owned a fifty-seven Chevy back when it was the latest thing to roll off the assembly. The American Dream Machine, they called her. And with good reason," Hollister added with a chuckle. "Mine wasn't a convertible, of course. That would be a bit showy for my taste, but it was quite a car just the same." He shook his head, his eyes slightly glazed. "They don't make them like that anymore."

"You said it, sir," Robertson agreed. "Two-hundred-eighty-three-cubic-inch V-8 with optional Ramjet fuel injection. Golden grille, blade fins and all those miles of chrome, sweet chrome."

"And the trunk," the general continued as Bolt listened to the two of them with amusement. "You could fit everything you needed for a six-month trip in that trunk. Wide, deep, long..."

The trunk.

Bolt tuned out what they were saying, instead picturing the trunk of the Chevy with Cat's bags and camera cases in constant disarray from being shoved and squeezed and rearranged. Sure, he'd grumbled about her packing for an army, but Hollister was right, the trunk of a car that old and that size should have swallowed those bags like jelly beans and begged for more.

"The trunk," he muttered. "Damn it, the trunk."

He twisted around and grabbed his phone. "General, do you know Cat's number?"

"Of course," Hollister replied. "But why..."

"Please, General, the number."

He recited it for Bolt, who hurriedly punched it in and listened to it ring a dozen times before he gave up and slammed the receiver down.

"What's her address in Sarasota?" he asked, already starting for the door.

"It's 1522 Addison Way," the general replied, a worried frown deepening the creases in his forehead. "First floor left. But see here, Hunter, I want to know what's got you—"

"Later," Bolt interjected. "Don't worry, General, I'll explain it all to you later."

He made it to the car in record time and sped from the parking lot thinking he wasn't sure what he would have to explain to Hollister later. He purposely hadn't asked him along on what might well turn out to be another false alarm. It would be bad enough having to talk about that afterward, much less have the general witness the fruit of his paranoia.

All he knew right then was that the Chevy's trunk had been tampered with. Maybe there was an innocent explanation. Maybe the car had been in an accident or had rust damage and the trunk had been replaced with a smaller one from a different model. Spare parts were as scarce in Cuba as gasoline was, which accounted for why so many vintage cars in pristine condition could be found on the embargoed island. Maybe there was a simple explanation for the trunk, but he wouldn't bet on it.

He found Cat's apartment with little trouble, parked in a no-parking zone across the street and ran to the door. The convertible was nowhere in sight. Not a good sign.

He pounded on the door, waited and pounded some more. *Where are you, Cat? Where the hell are you?* The sure, strong sense that she was in trouble and needed him, which he'd been alternately trying to ignore and convince himself was simply the result of being overtired, was suddenly too strong and too certain to be denied.

His mind reeled with frustration and self-recriminations. Why hadn't he insisted on going along with her to drop off the car? Because he was too busy compromising, he thought with disgust, too busy being Mr. Patient and Agreeable. Well, no more. He loved her, damn it and there was no way he was going to let anything happen to her. If that meant being overbearing and bossy and impatient then that was what he was going to be. He also wasn't going to let her out of his sight again, he decided.

But first he had to find her, and this was getting him nowhere fast. There was only one thing to do. Something he'd done hundreds of times, but never expected to resort to again once his Special Services days were over.

He glanced around to see if any of her neighbors were watching. Not that it would have stopped him if they were. He was that desperate. He pulled his wallet from his pocket and removed a thin metal bar resembling a nail file. Forcing it into the space between the door and casing, he worked it in until he got precisely the right angle and leverage. Some things you never forgot, he noted with satisfaction. Then he landed his shoulder hard against the door and felt it give.

He was inside, surrounded by the colors and textures and scents of Cat, but he had no time to waste savoring any of it the way he had planned to the first time he was there. He hurriedly walked through the entire apartment, then looked for the telephone. She had an answering machine, but no new messages. He hit rewind and listened to the ones she'd received since yesterday.

There were several from friends whose names he didn't recognize, one from the magazine editor she'd mentioned and two from Gator, one returning her call and a second that she had obviously screened and picked up. Gator. That was a lot to go on. Why hadn't he thought to get that jerk's whole name from Cat? he thought furiously.

He was looking around for the phone book, wondering how many LaComptes there were in Sarasota, when he noticed the notebook shoved to the back of the cluttered countertop.

"Thank God," he muttered as he glanced at it and realized what he had found. The directions were written hastily, in a confusing sort of personal shorthand of letters and symbols that he recognized as Cat's. He could at least make out the route numbers, however, and the words "Grant's Ser Stat" with a box drawn around them.

Grant's Ser Stat had to mean Grant's Service Station, and if he was half as good at cracking codes as he used to be, it was located just outside of town on Route 17. That had to be where Cat had gone to drop off the car.

He tore the page out of the notebook and was out of there. With every mile he got closer to Route 17, the more convinced he was that something was wrong, and the faster he drove. This was just too far out of the way to be legit.

When he saw the drooping sign for Grant's up ahead, his heart clenched with fear. In the dirt out front was parked an old Volvo that had seen better days. Might be the old bomber Cat had referred to, he thought. Along the side of the building was parked a Caddy. Nothing sinister about that, to be sure, but his stomach started churning just the same. Always a bad sign.

He braked sharply, pulling off the road before reaching the run-down station, and approached on foot. Except for the cars outside, the whole place had an eerie, abandoned look, with the doors closed and the windows in the garage area covered with boards on the inside. An ancient advertisement for engine lubricant flapped against the office door, the sound it made a lazy counterpoint to his hammering pulse.

Moving cautiously, he circled to the back of the building, hoping for a way to get a look inside. He didn't find a window there, but he did find all the proof he needed that he wasn't paranoid after all. The black Mustang. He didn't need to take a closer look to make sure it wasn't a different car from the one that had shadowed them on the trip. That would have been too much of a coincidence, and while he'd changed his mind about a lot of things during the past week, that wasn't one of them.

He turned to make his way to the front and froze where he stood.

"How you doing?" drawled the man standing behind him. The small automatic in his hand was aimed at Bolt's gut.

It was his friend from the rest-stop men's room. The gun was a new touch, but Bolt recognized the shaggy blond hair and the earring. A faded rock-concert T-shirt had replaced the red plaid shirt he remembered.

"You sure do get around, don't you?" Bolt responded, his composure as ingrained as his methodical survey of his surroundings and his options.

"Me?" The man grinned. "I could say the same for you, pal."

"We do seem to be traveling in the same circles these days," he countered dryly.

"Don't let it get you down, the trip's almost over." He motioned with the gun. "Let's go inside."

"I think I like it better out here."

Another man rounded the corner of the building. Bolt recognized him as the man who had helped Cat with the loose wires on the Chevy.

"Gator, what the hell is taking you so long? Tony wants..."

He stopped abruptly at the sight of Bolt.

"Look what I found," the man with the gun said.

Bolt glared at him contemptuously. "You're Gator?" he asked. "Cat's friend? Or should I say her supposed friend?"

Gator's look was between a scowl and a pout. "Hey, don't try and dump this all on me. If you hadn't butted in to start with, everything would have gone just the way we planned."

"Meaning you could have used Cat without her ever knowing about it." Bolt breathed deeply, not wanting to sound as desperate as he felt as he asked the one thing he wanted to know above all else. "Where is she, Gator?"

"Come on inside and see for yourself."

Suddenly there was nothing he wanted to do more than go inside. He started walking, cognizant every step of the way of two important facts. There was a gun at his back, and he had nothing with which to defend himself or save Cat except his bare hands and his wits. From what he'd seen of old Gator, if he acted fast, that shouldn't be a problem.

He saw Cat the instant he walked in. Even before his eyes fully adjusted to the dim lighting in the windowless garage, there was no mistaking her as she sat huddled in the corner, her hands obviously tied behind her back. In that grimy, stinking hole, she was a beacon of everything good and light in his life. A single step closer and he was able to feel as well as see the panic in her eyes, and he was filled with a rage so powerful it had no focus or target, only a raw, burning drive to set her free.

"Bolt, you're here," she exclaimed, amazement lifting some of the fear from her face.

He smiled and winked at her. "Sure am, Tiger." He kept walking toward her, leaning down as if to help her up. "Now it's time to go."

All the while his attention was riveted on the tire iron laying on the floor about two feet to her left. If he could just grab it in time, he was convinced the odds would swing in his favor and they would be out of there in a—

"Bolt, look out," Cat screamed.

He straightened, but before he was able to turn he felt something as hard and heavy as a steel bat connect with the back of his head and he crumbled.

He came to with the smell of oil filling his head and darkness all around.

"What the heck?" he muttered, shaking his head to clear it and wincing as he was accosted by waves of pain. His head hurt, his neck hurt and his right arm felt as if it was broken in half a dozen places. It felt as if Gator and his pal had continued to amuse themselves with him for a while after he'd left the party.

What had they done to Cat?

He struggled upright and reached out to touch the wall beside him, feeling it slick with oil. Glancing up he saw daylight, or at least a patch of something marginally brighter than where he was, which he realized must be the pit under one of the garage bays.

He heard Cat's voice calling his name and had a feeling she had been calling for a while before his head had cleared enough for him to hear it.

"Here," he shouted to her. "I'm down here, Cat."

"I know where you are, Bolt. We have to get out of here."

"We will," he replied, struggling to sound confident. "Let me think."

"There's no time to think," she snapped. "Bolt, I think they started a fire around here somewhere before they left. I know I smell smoke."

He struggled to his feet, inhaling deeply. All he could smell was oil, thick and rancid, about fifty years' worth from the stench.

"I don't smell anything, so just try to calm down," he said, running his hands over the ten-foot-high walls that surrounded him. He could see clearly enough now to see that they were smooth and oil-slicked, with no place to get a decent hand or toe hold.

He was going to have to pull himself out.

He jumped and managed to just barely curl his fingertips over the edge at the top.

Somehow he was going to have to pull himself out.

"Did they leave you tied up?" he asked.

"Yes, but I've almost got the rope around the post behind me undone. Then it will only be my hands that are tied."

"Good girl. Keep working at it." He jumped again and missed the edge entirely. "I'll be out of here in a flash."

"Is there a ladder or something?"

"Not exactly."

"Then how—"

"Just be quiet, okay?"

"Okay."

She sounded worried, and very, very scared.

He might be hallucinating, but he swore he could smell smoke now, too. He jumped a third time, lowering to a crouch first to get a little extra power, and hooked his fingers over the edge. The pain that seared in his right arm sent him plummeting back to the bottom.

He cursed loudly.

"Bolt? Bolt, what happened? Are you all right?"

"I'm . . . fine, damn it all. I just fell."

There was a long moment of silence while he rubbed his arm.

"You can't get out of there, can you?" she asked at last.

Bolt's heart turned over inside his chest. "Oh, baby, I'm going to get out, just give me a minute. Then I'll get us both out of here safe and sound. I promise."

Silence.

"Listen to me, Cat," he said, standing once again. "Nothing is going to happen to us. I swear to you." He waited. "Say you believe me, damn it."

"I believe you, damn it," she shot back.

He grinned. "That's more like it."

"I did it," she shouted. "I got the rope undone."

Three seconds later she was peering down at him over the edge of the pit.

"Now I can help you out," she exclaimed excitedly. She hung her hands into the pit. "Come on. We have to hurry, Bolt. I know I smell smoke now."

He thought about the gas tanks buried right outside. He didn't have to wonder what would happen if they went up. He'd already seen a gas explosion turn a house into a pile of Lincoln Logs.

"Grab my hand," she ordered.

"Don't be stupid. If I grab your hand I'll end up pulling you in here with me."

"I'll hold on to this bar behind me with my feet."

"Cat, it won't work. I must weigh—"

"We don't have any choice," she cut in. "Just do it."

"No. I can make it on my own." He rubbed his hands together to wipe off some of the oil.

"Your arm hurts, doesn't it?" she demanded.

"I'll survive."

"No, you won't," she said frantically. "Bolt, listen to me. This place is on fire and it's full of gas and old oil cans and—"

"Get out," he shouted. "Right now, Cat. Get the hell out of here and I'll be right behind you."

"No."

"Look, don't—"

"Will you shut up and stop wasting time? There's no way I'm leaving here without you."

He made a frantic jump, bracing himself ahead of time for the pain in his arm, and managed to hold on.

"You are the most stupid, pigheaded, stubborn . . ." He grunted between words before he ran out of breath to do either and just hung on for dear life.

"Maybe," Cat retorted, "but I love you, Hunter. Don't you dare mess this up on me now."

He dragged his head up until he met her gaze. In too much pain to speak, he just stared at her, seeing everything she felt burning in her violet eyes, and he managed to pull himself up another inch.

She loved him. There was no way he was going to get blown up in this stinking pit and lose out on a lifetime with Catrina Amelia Bandini.

His elbows shook and his forearms quivered.

Sweat dripped from his forehead and ran into his eyes. They stung and burned from salt and the fumes and watered until all he could see was the blurred image of Cat's face. It was enough.

Another inch.

He grappled wildly with his feet, as if a foothold might miraculously materialize down there.

Another inch, then another. His head was above the edge, but pain was blazing in his arm and he couldn't feel his fingers on that hand. He could hear Cat urging him on as if she was far away instead if close enough to touch, and he could hear the sound of his own whimpering, like a puppy left alone in the night.

He was almost there. All he had to do was get his elbows up and then switch from pulling to pushing his weight up and over, and he would be home free. He just didn't think he had the strength to do it.

He grunted and strained, his elbows trembling as they bore all the weight of his efforts.

He bore down once again, heady with the pain and only vaguely aware of Cat's movements, of her still bound hands thrusting downward and then the tug on his belt as she gripped it and pulled for all she was worth.

It gave him just the lift he needed to reposition his elbows, and then he was pushing himself onto the dirty cement floor of the garage and sucking in gulps of stale air. It hadn't been pretty or graceful, but, thanks to Cat, it had worked.

"Let's go." He struggled to his feet, pulling her with his good arm. There was definitely smoke in the air, thin tendrils of it just beginning to drift under the door from the office area.

Obviously they wouldn't be leaving that way.

He bent and grabbed the handle of the garage door, but it wouldn't budge.

"Is it locked?" Cat asked.

The fear in her voice made him determined to keep it from his own.

"Jammed from the outside is my guess."

He turned and the Chevy was right in front of him.

He quickly glanced inside for the keys that weren't there. So Gator wasn't as dumb as he looked.

He shoved Cat into the front seat and quickly opened the hood. His earlier work under there paid off now. It took him almost no time to locate the right wires and cross them to start the engine.

Slamming the hood down, he slid behind the wheel and revved the engine.

"Get down and stay down," he ordered Cat, twisting to look over his shoulder as he stepped on the clutch, shoved the shift into reverse and stepped on the gas.

The old car punched a giant hole in the solid wood door, leaving the metal framework twisted and bent.

It didn't matter, since thirty seconds later the whole sorry mess went up with an ear-shattering boom that sent Cat straight into his arms. Where she belonged.

Say what you want about the sleek design and fuel economy of fancy foreign imports, Bolt thought as he sat with his head thrown back on the seat, staring at the bluest sky he'd ever·seen. When his back was to the wall, he'd put his money on good old American-made steel every time.

Chapter Fourteen

The cast on his right arm prevented Bolt from holding the telephone receiver with that hand, so he anchored it under his chin instead. His left arm was occupied, curled around Cat's shoulders as she sat on his lap on the sofa in her apartment.

"You're sure the police have all three of these characters locked up?" the general asked him.

It had been less than ten hours since the close call at the service station, but already it was beginning to take on an air of unreality for Bolt. Probably the result of repeating the details so many times for so many different police officers and federal agents and now in this phone call to the general. Cat and he had agreed it was best to wait until the ordeal was over and they were finished at the emergency room and police station to call and fill him in about what had happened.

"Actually, sir," Bolt replied, trying unsuccessfully to ignore the seductive movement of Cat's hand on his thigh, "I believe the three of them are in federal custody. Since the money in the trunk was counterfeit and originated in Cuba, the Feds have jurisdiction."

"Good. Because if I have any influence there, and believe me I do, they'll be out of commission for a long time."

"I don't doubt that, General."

"Counterfeiting, smuggling, arson, assault, attempted murder..."

As he listened to the general tick off their offenses, he lifted Cat's subversive hand to his lips and sucked gently on the tip of one finger.

"I think we've got a bad connection," the general said. "I hear static."

"Could be," Bolt agreed dryly. "Maybe I should let you go."

"First put Cat back on," the general ordered. "And, Bolt?"

"Yes, sir?"

"Thanks. For everything."

"No thanks necessary, sir. I'd do it again in an instant."

"I know you would, boy," the older man responded warmly. "Why do you think I sent you out on this one in the first place? When it matters most, you send the best."

"Yes, sir. Thank you, General. Here's Cat."

Cat sighed resignedly as she took the receiver from Bolt. She had already spoken at length to her uncle, assuring him that she didn't have a scratch on her, thanks to Bolt, and that there was really no need for him to drive down tonight to make sure of that.

Instead she'd suggested he come for dinner the following night. It seemed as good a time as any to tell him that he would be seeing a lot more of Bolt outside the office in the future.

She might even get a chance to ask him some of the questions about her parents that no longer seemed quite so pressing or volatile. They had made their compromises in the name of love, and she would gladly make hers.

She rested her head on Bolt's strong chest and listened as Uncle Hank told her for the umpteenth time to call him if she needed anything, anything, during the night.

She smiled wryly. Uncle Hank had no way of knowing it yet, but if she needed anything during the night from now on, help would be very close indeed. And she would be there for Bolt, as well. Though something told her his bad dreams were behind him for good.

"Are you nervous about tomorrow night?" she asked Bolt when she had finally managed to tell her uncle good-night and hung up the phone.

"Not as nervous as I am about tonight," he replied, stroking her back through her robe.

"Tonight? Why?"

"I want it to be as perfect as the night at the castle. I want to make every night that perfect for you, and I'm not sure a lover with a broken arm, wrenched back and pocket full of pain pills is up to the task."

"Then maybe," she countered, turning and sliding her leg so she was straddling him, "you ought to just lay back tonight and give me a chance to make it perfect for you this time."

Her soft voice was itself a caress of his senses, and the sweet pressure of her hips against his was pure magic. Bolt already felt more assured of the night ahead.

"The last time was perfect for me," he told her, sliding his hand under her and pressing her closer. He swept her hair aside and nibbled her throat. "Every time with you will be perfect for me. I already know that."

"You seem to know an awful lot all of a sudden."

He grinned lazily. "I guess I do, at that. For instance, I know you're not wearing anything under this robe." He loosened the tie at her waist to prove it, and she smiled and let him. "I know that any minute now I'm going to carry you into that bedroom and—"

"Carry?" she interjected dubiously.

He slid his good hand inside the robe and fondled her breast. "On second thought, maybe we could just spend the night here, after all." She warmed and firmed to his touch and made a small sound of pleasure deep in her throat. "I also know that someday soon I'm going to ask you to marry me and you're going to say yes."

Cat could feel his heart pounding beneath her hand where it rested on his chest. In spite of his attitude of lazy self-assurance, she sensed the apprehension in him, and the need.

"Smart man," she murmured and watched a slow, sexy smile spread across his face.

"Thank you," he whispered, running his hand along her waist and up and down her back. "Oh, Cat, I never thought I'd find you. I'll never let you go."

"Promise?"

"With every part of me . . . forever." He bent his head, touching his tongue to her ear and blowing lightly. Shivers ran along her spine. "You're my fairy tale, Cat," he told her. "My happy ending. My soul mate."

"If such things exist," she said quietly.

"They exist," he said, his tone certain and unyielding. "How else do you explain my knowing you were in trouble and that you needed me?"

"Instinct," she replied. "Experience, training. All the things you thought you'd lost or had failed you."

He shook his head. "It wasn't instinct that caught me in a spell this morning in my office. It wasn't experience that made me burn up inside when I saw you in that garage, or training that gave you the strength to help me when I needed you."

"Then what was it?" Cat challenged, wanting and needing him to make her a believer once again.

And he did.

"Destiny," he said, and with that one word, his final word on the subject and for the night, he gave her back a dream she could believe in forever.

* * * * *

Silhouette

SPECIAL EDITION™

Congratulations!

In September, enjoy a special tribute to life's happiest moments, featuring some of your favorite authors!

KISSES AND KIDS by Andrea Edwards (SE #981)
Pat Stuart's company wanted to reward him for a job well done. But the surprise present they gave him would lead to lasting love!

JOYRIDE by Patricia Coughlin (SE #982)
Catrina "Cat" Bandini had just graduated from college and was off on the road trip of lifetime. But she was about to get some *very* unexpected company!

A DATE WITH DR. FRANKENSTEIN
by Leanne Banks (SE #983)
Andie Reynolds was getting a new neighbor next door. Eli Masters was handsome, smart—and, yes, single. Would he be her dream date, or...

Be the first to congratulate the happy couples when love comes calling in September—only from Silhouette Special Edition.

Congratulations! Because life can be a celebration, and love is its ultimate prize.

CONGRAT

MORGAN'S MERCENARIES:
Love and Danger
By
Lindsay McKenna

Four missions *save Morgan Trayhern and each
member of his family. Four men: each battling danger.
Would rescuing their comrade help them discover
the glory of love?*

Watch for these exciting titles in this new series
from Lindsay McKenna:

In October:
MORGAN'S WIFE
(SE #986)

In December:
MORGAN'S RESCUE
(SE #998)

In November:
MORGAN'S SON
(SE #992)

In January:
MORGAN'S MARRIAGE
(SE #1005)

Don't miss any of these upcoming titles from
Lindsay McKenna and Silhouette Special Edition!

It's our 1000th Special Edition and we're celebrating!

Join us these coming months for some wonderful stories in a special celebration of our 1000th book with some of your favorite authors!

Diana Palmer　　　　**Nora Roberts**
Debbie Macomber　　**Christine Flynn**
Phyllis Halldorson　　**Lisa Jackson**

mini-series by:

Lindsay McKenna, Marie Ferrarella, Sherryl Woods, Gina Ferris Wilkins.

And many more books by special writers.

And as a special bonus, all Silhouette Special Edition titles published during Celebration 1000! Will have **double** Pages & Privileges proofs of purchase!

Silhouette Special Edition...heartwarming stories packed with emotion, just for you! You'll fall in love with our next 1000 special stories!

1000BK

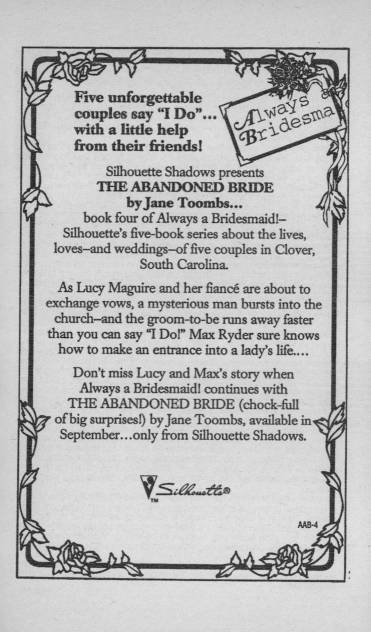

Five unforgettable couples say "I Do"... with a little help from their friends!

Always a Bridesma[id]

Silhouette Shadows presents
THE ABANDONED BRIDE
by Jane Toombs...
book four of Always a Bridesmaid!–
Silhouette's five-book series about the lives,
loves–and weddings–of five couples in Clover,
South Carolina.

As Lucy Maguire and her fiancé are about to
exchange vows, a mysterious man bursts into the
church–and the groom-to-be runs away faster
than you can say "I Do!" Max Ryder sure knows
how to make an entrance into a lady's life....

Don't miss Lucy and Max's story when
Always a Bridesmaid! continues with
THE ABANDONED BRIDE (chock-full
of big surprises!) by Jane Toombs, available in
September...only from Silhouette Shadows.

Silhouette®
™